A Wedding at the Comfort Food Café

Debbie Johnson is an award-winning author who lives and works in Liverpool, where she divides her time between writing, caring for a small tribe of children and animals, and not doing the housework. She writes romance, fantasy and crime, which is as confusing as it sounds!

Her bestselling books for HarperCollins include *The Birthday That Changed Everything*, *Summer at the Comfort Food Café*, *Christmas at the Comfort Food Café*, *Cold Feet at Christmas*, *Pippa's Cornish Dream* and *Never Kiss a Man in a Christmas Jumper*.

You can find her supernatural crime thriller, *Fear No Evil*, featuring Liverpool PI Jayne McCartney, on Amazon, published by Avon Books.

Debbie also writes urban fantasy, set in modern day Liverpool. *Dark Vision* and the follow-up *Dark Touch* are published by Del Rey UK, and earned her the title 'a Liverpudlian Charlaine Harris' from the *Guardian*.

🐦 @debbiemjohnson
f www.facebook.com/debbiejohnsonauthor
www.debbiejohnsonauthor.com

Also by Debbie Johnson

Cold Feet at Christmas
Pippa's Cornish Dream
Never Kiss a Man in a Christmas Jumper
The Birthday That Changed Everything
Summer at the Comfort Food Café
Christmas at the Comfort Food Café
The A-Z of Everything
Coming Home to the Comfort Food Café
Sunshine at the Comfort Food Café
A Gift from the Comfort Food Café

Debbie JOHNSON

A Wedding at the Comfort Food Café

A division of HarperCollins*Publishers*
www.harpercollins.co.uk

Harper*Impulse* an imprint of
HarperCollins*Publishers*
The News Building
1 London Bridge Street
London SE1 9GF

www.harpercollins.co.uk

First published by HarperCollins*Publishers* 2019
6

A catalogue record for this book is available from the British Library

ISBN: 9780008258887

Set in Birka by Palimpsest Book Production Limited, Falkirk, Stirlingshire

Printed and bound in the UK by CPI Group (UK) Ltd, Croydon CR0 4YY

MIX
Paper from
responsible sources
FSC™ C007454

For Charlotte Ledger, editor, friend, and honorary
Budbury resident – thank you for everything

Chapter 1

The latest meeting of the Budbury Ladies Coffee and Cake Club is in full swing. We are all present and correct in the café; it's a Monday and it's closed for business to actual paying customers.

The gingham-clothed tables are loosely arranged together in the middle of the large room, sunlight streaming in through the picture windows, the sea below shining and shimmering as it rolls into the bay. The various weird mobiles made of old seven-inch vinyl singles and shells and the wooden things you get inside spools of cotton are dangling in and out of the sun, striped in shade and light like golden tigers.

Beneath the dangling mobiles, we sit, gathered around the tables. We are fully equipped with all the necessary items: coffee in its rich variety of lattes and mochas and in some cases – by which I mean mine – espresso martinis. We have wine, and bubbly, and home-made cider. We have cake of every possible type, including tipsy meringue, black forest gateaux, strawberry pudding and a rich sherry trifle with way too much sherry in it. This is a stealth piss-up via the medium of pudding.

Most importantly, we have the Ladies. Or most of them at least. Me, my sister Willow, the café owner Cherie Moon (I always like to use her full name, because it's so awesome), Katie, Zoe, Edie, Becca and our guest of honour, Laura.

Off to one side is a long trestle table heaving with gifts, contributions from the village for Laura's baby shower-slash-hen-do. Everyone loves Laura – at least everyone who's met her. Normally that would be enough to guarantee that I'd at least try and hate her, out of sheer contrariness, but even I can't manage it. She's just too bloody lovely, with her crazy curly hair and warm smile and kindness oozing out of every pore.

I notice that she's staring at my espresso martini with something akin to lust in her eyes, and think that maybe I could learn to hate her – if she lays one fingertip on my glass she's dead. Or at the very least she'll get stabbed in the hand with my fork.

Becca, Laura's little sister, stands up and taps a spoon against the side of her own glass. She clears her throat in an exaggerated 'master of ceremonies' way, and gains our attention.

'Dearly beloved,' she says seriously, 'we are gathered here today to celebrate the single life of Laura. Laura who was once Fletcher, who became Walker, and who will shortly be Hunter. Assuming that Matt doesn't come to his senses and join the Foreign Legion. Pause for laughter.'

She looks up, and we are already obliging. She's funny, Becca – sharp and sarcastic and stinging. She's also teetotal, when most of us are at least on our way to being smashed. Being the sober person at a party always leads to some wicked observations. Often about me, as I'm usually the most drunk person at a party.

'Today, at this solemn occasion,' she continues, once we've stopped giggling, 'I would like to share with you something from Laura's past. Something she's probably forgotten exists. Something that our parents found when they were packing up their house, and thought I might be interested in. I was interested. In fact, I was so interested that I even got it . . . laminated!'

She waves a sheet of plastic-coated paper in the air dramatically, and we all react as though she's the villain in a pantomime, revealing the blueprints of a diabolical masterplan.

Everyone is in a good mood. Everyone is the most relaxed I've seen them, ever. Part of that is because all of our responsibilities, all the darling burdens we love dearly, have been taken off our hands for the afternoon.

Cal, Zoe's partner – think rugged Aussie cowboy, Thor on horseback – has taken all of the teenagers away to Oxford for the night to visit the college where his daughter, and Zoe's kind of step-daughter, will be studying later this year. With him are Lizzie and Nate, Laura's teenaged kids, freeing them up from worrying that anybody is roaming the village getting pregnant or skateboarding off cliffs.

Katie's four-year-old, Saul, is off on an adventure with Van, who is my brother and Katie's man toy. That always makes me a bit sick in my mouth, but they seem happy, so who am I to complain? He's also taken a mismatched set of two mums with him: Sandra – Katie's mum – who could create a crisis if she was alone on a desert island talking to a coconut head, and Lynnie – mine and Willow's mum.

Lynnie has Alzheimer's, and is recovering from bowel cancer. That sounds horrendously grim, but weirdly isn't – since we found out about the cancer and she had her op, she's actually been having an extended good spell. She still has no idea who we are half the time, but the aggressive episodes that had been getting more common have faded. Probably because she's not in pain any more. Pain will make anyone grumpy.

Me, Willow and Van care for Lynnie between us, and we all love her dearly – but I'd be lying if I said it was easy, and it's a relief to know she's off having fun with a responsible adult who isn't one of us. Plus she's with Saul, who has no idea what Alzheimer's is, doesn't remember Lynnie the way she was before, and simply reacts to everything she does with delight and love. Kids are great – as long they're someone else's.

Becca's baby, Little Edie, who's not long started toddling, is off with her dad, Sam. Even the dogs – Laura's Midgebo, an insane black lab, and our beguiling Border Terrier Bella Swan – are taken care of, enjoying the sunshine in the doggy crèche field outside.

This sense of being carefree is unusual for most of us, and adds to the sense of elation inside the café. Nobody is working. Nobody is looking after anybody. Nobody has responsibility for anybody but themselves. Wowzers.

That, plus the fact that we're half cut, makes us an easy audience for Becca's speech. She swoops the laminated sheet around for a while, like it's a magic wand, before putting her glasses on to read it.

They're not actually glasses with lenses. She's only in her thirties, and doesn't usually use specs. These glasses are plastic fancy dress ones complete with a honking great Groucho nose, moustache and eyebrows.

Again, we all find this unutterably hilarious, especially Edie, who laughs so hard that Katie and I share concerned glances in case she has a heart attack or chokes on her own merriment.

Edie is in her nineties, and suffered a nasty bout of pneumonia last year. I'm a pharmacist and Katie's a nurse, and I think we're the only ones who realised quite how close we were to losing our much-loved village elder.

She recovers, patting her tummy as she gulps in the air

she lost due to Becca's hilarity, and I give Katie a little thumbs-up sign as the speech continues.

'This,' announces Becca once the furore has died down, gazing at us from behind her plastic frames, 'comes to you directly from the mind of ten-year-old Laura. It starts with these priceless words: My Dream Wedding.'

Laura groans out loud, and we all laugh at her embarrassment. We're nice like that. Cherie, who is in her seventies but looks like an Amazonian Pocahontas with a fat silver and grey plait hanging over her solid shoulders, nudges her and grins.

'When I am older, my dream wedding will be all pink,' Becca reads, glancing at her sister over the Groucho specs to check that she's suitably mortified. 'I will have a pink carriage drawn by pink horses and all the guests will wear pink, even the men. My cake will be pink sponge with at least ten layers, and my dress will be pink silk. I will even have a pink dog, and pink ear-rings once Mum lets me get my ears pierced, and pink high heel shoes so big they make me look tall.

'I don't know how I'll get a pink dog or pink horses, but I will. Maybe some pink kittens as well. And I will wear pink lipstick and have pink rose petals thrown on the floor. It will be the pinkest day ever.'

The pinkness of Laura's Dream Wedding is making me feel a bit sick, and from the looks of it, her too.

I glance across to the other side of the table, and see

modern-day Laura. Modern-day Laura is almost forty, and the only thing pink about her is her cheeks. She's almost seven months pregnant with twins, and the size of a sumo wrestler. Her swollen ankles are propped up on a chair, and her arms are rested over the vast expanse of her baby-carrying belly. She still looks gorgeous – but not in a fantasy wedding kind of way. More of an earth-goddess-needing-a-nap kind of way.

'Okay, okay – so I liked pink!' she exclaims, grinning. 'Someone had to – Becca was already fantasising about her Satanic wedding!'

Becca nods at this, and the Groucho glasses bobble up and down.

'True that,' she confirms, in a mock ghetto accent. 'I was indeed a daughter of darkness. My fantasy wedding involved a vampire groom and cake with worms and goblets of blood. Now, I will pass along the sacred glasses of My Dream Wedding, and we will each share our own story, our hopes, our fantasies, our personal choices of veil and party food . . .'

I feel a slight twinge of panic at that particular announcement. Obviously, Becca intends this to be a round-robin of fun – but in my case, it accidentally touches a raw nerve, and makes my nostrils flare.

I love all the ladies here present, but discussing My Dream Wedding feels perilously close to facing up to something long hidden. It's a bit like I'm an archaeological site, and Becca is about to attack me with a trowel to unearth my secrets.

Looking around, and seeing how happy everyone else seems to be doing this, I wonder if perhaps my secrets are even worth keeping any more.

With great ceremony, Becca removes the plastic Grouchos, and walks to place them on Cherie's face. They're not big enough, and the arms stretch around Cherie's wide cheek-bones. Cherie stands up, and bows, majestic in a sequinned kaftan straight from the seventies, and begins.

'My dream wedding, when I was young, probably involved hallucinogenic mushrooms and Marc Bolan. My first wedding did involve hallucinogenic mushrooms, but not Marc Bolan. But my dream wedding . . . well, that was the one I had right here, a couple of Christmases ago, to my hero Frank.'

We all let out a communal 'aaaah' at that. I wasn't here for that wedding – I was busy perfecting my role as the black sheep of our family, travelling around and screwing up – but I've seen the photos.

Cherie and Frank – known universally as Farmer Frank due to his magnificent acreage – married late in life after being widowed. The ceremony was held here at the Comfort Food Café, same as Laura's will be – but unlike Laura and Matt's, which will hopefully be sun-drenched and balmy, theirs was a winter wonderland.

Cherie passes the now slightly bent-out-of-shape

Groucho specs to Katie, who looks borderline horrified at being thrust into the spotlight. Katie is in her late twenties, petite and blonde and pretty, and manages to combine both being one of the most blunt and honest people I know with being extremely shy. She also has rotten taste in men, clearly, or she wouldn't be hanging around with my brother. Uggh. Sick in mouth again.

'Ummm . . . okay . . . ' she says quietly, standing up and still barely matching Cherie while she's sitting down. 'I've never had a wedding. But I suppose when I was little, it maybe involved white dresses and Justin Timberlake. These days, I'd be happy with anything that involved a lie-in.'

She sits down very quickly, and Cherie pats her knee. I get where she's coming from. Saul is a whirlwind of a child with endless energy and endless questions. I'm pretty high energy myself, but on the few nights he's had a sleepover at our cottage, I've spent the rest of the day staggering around like a zombie. Last time, he jumped into bed with me at half five in the morning quizzing me about my favourite crustacean.

Katie passes the glasses along to Zoe, who inserts them into her masses of ginger curls, and stands up to her five foot nothing height. Us Longvilles are all tall and lean; we are giants amongst midgets.

'I have never had a dream wedding,' Zoe announces firmly. 'As a child I dreamt only of running off with gypsies

9

to travel the world in a brightly painted caravan, cursing unkind villagers and making friends with freaks. I found you lot eventually, so I suppose some of that came true. I still have no dream wedding, and don't intend on conjuring one up. Thank you very much.'

I realise, as the glasses are passed on to my sister Willow, that it will be my turn next. I feel a churn in my stomach at the prospect – not because I'm shy, or because of the many espresso martinis I've consumed, but because this is not a subject I want to discuss. I plan to make a sharp and timely exit to the ladies as soon as Willow nears the end of her talk, or possibly to pretend that I've fallen asleep, and sit snoring and drooling in my seat while the glasses of doom pass me by.

Or maybe I won't. Maybe this is the time. Maybe I should come clean. When I first moved back here, to help Willow with Lynnie, I had no idea how long I'd stay. It could have been days, or weeks, and now it looks like possibly forever. Things are different now – I have a small business, I have friends, I have a super-sexy man in my life. I'm probably not leaving Budbury any time soon.

I'm not sure what the right thing to do is, so I put off making any kind of decision until Willow has finished. I'm sure the right thing will come to me – a bit like when you're in a restaurant and can't choose from the menu, and can't come up with a decision until your waiter is standing right there with his notepad, and suddenly your instincts tell you: 'Yes! Spaghetti carbonara for me please!', and all feels well with the world.

Willow has neon pink hair, which would have looked great at Laura's wedding, and it dangles over the plastic glasses as she stands. It's been in a kind of bob for a while, but she let it grow over the winter so she could keep her ears warm. Makes perfect sense to me.

'Growing up as we did with Lynnie,' she says, nodding towards me, 'you can imagine that such traditional patriarchal nonsense as dream weddings was not encouraged. It was far more important to find love than to find a husband, and in all honesty I think that's probably fair. But I also think that if Tom and me were to plan a wedding, it would most likely be at Briarwood, and have a zombie theme.'

There are nods and giggles at this. Tom owns a big old Victorian mansion on a hill at the edge of the village, where he runs a kind of school for eccentric inventor genius types. He also has a dog called Rick Grimes, named after the hero of *The Walking Dead*, so it's a fair call. In fact it would be a great wedding. I'm pondering my costume when Willow continues.

'And now I'd like to pass the sacred Groucho glasses to my darling sister Auburn, who as far as I know is currently enjoying her longest relationship ever with the lovely Finn. Can't wait to hear about this dream wedding . . .'

Damn. I've been caught out – so busy planning my

milky-lens zombie outfit that I didn't duck out in time. Or maybe I subconsciously sabotaged my own escape plan. Gosh, I'm annoying.

There is a general buzz and shuffle and sounds of interest as she passes the specs along to me. She's right on one count – I am loved up at the moment. She's also right that Finn is lovely. I might even, in the dim dark recesses of my primeval girl brain, imagine being married to him one day – but that process would not be a simple one. Frankly, nothing ever is with me.

I scrape my chair back, gulp down the remainder of my espresso martini, and perch the glasses on my nose. I pause while they all refocus their attention. Might as well create a moment – show a bit of style. I've trapped myself in this moment, and this is the equivalent of the waiter hovering at my shoulder with his notepad – decision time.

I glance around at the smiling faces, the expressions of warm curiosity, and realise that I actually want to be honest with these people. Friends, family, community – none of it should be built on a lie. And none of this lot are going to judge me – it's not that kind of place. Deep breath, and in I plunge.

'Well, ladies and gentlewomen, Willow raises a good point,' I say. 'My dream wedding would be an elaborate cathedral of sound and light; a lightning storm in a haunted forest; a shipwreck off the coast of Zanzibar; a magical fairy glade inside a mystical stone circle. All of these things and more.'

I glance around at my audience – they're hooked, so I decide to hit them with the punchline.

'Sadly, none of these magnificent feasts for the senses are likely to take place. I won't be marrying Finn – because I'm already married! Booooom!'

I make a 'drop the mike' gesture, pass the glasses to a confused Edie, and give a low bow as they all stare at me – Willow, in particular, has eyes so wide they might break her face in half.

I grab a bottle of cider, and head outside. I really need a ciggie now.

Chapter 2

I find a perch on one of the tables and take a swig from my bottle. It's been brewed by our friend Scrumpy Joe, who lives up to his name by brewing cider professionally – his parents must have had amazing powers of premonition. Or maybe it's a nickname, who knows?

The garden of the café is higgledy-piggledy and laid out over uneven ground that makes balancing anything on the tabletops an interesting experience. I like sitting out here sometimes, waiting for people's milkshakes to start to slip sideways.

The café is on the top of a hill on the top of a cliff on top of the world. Or at least that's what it feels like, especially on a day like this, when the spring sky is a clear, vivid blue and the sea seems to stretch on for infinity.

The dogs let out a half-hearted woof when they see me, and I raise my bottle in acknowledgement as I count out loud. I'm counting because I'm curious to see how long it takes Willow to make it outside with her thumbscrews and eye-shining torch to interrogate me. I have a bet – with myself, so I'll definitely win – that it'll be less than thirty seconds.

Sadly, I'm all the way up to one hundred and eighty before she emerges from the café, pink hair blowing around in the breeze, striding towards me in her spray-painted silver Doc Marten boots. Her hands are on her hips, which tells me she means business.

'What took you so long?' I ask, tapping an imaginary watch on my wrist. 'What time to do you call this?'

'I had to listen to Edie's story,' she says, reaching out to punch me on the shoulder. For no good reason other than we're sisters. She's the baby of the family and, if I'm honest, was always the butt of our practical jokes and general twattery when we were growing up. Now she takes every opportunity to prove to herself that she's not the runt of the litter any more.

The rest of us – me, Van and our other brother Angel – all took off when we were young, and she ended up at home with an ever-declining Lynnie, looking after her on her own until she told us what the situation was. Then two of us came back – and I suspect there's part of Willow that thinks life was simpler without us.

'What was that like?' I ask, frowning up into the sunlight. Edie's fiancé died during World War II, and she never married. She simply convinced herself he's still alive, and talks about him in the present tense, and even takes food home for him from the café. I'm not one to judge

– we're all a bit barmy, if we strip away the layers, don't you think?

'It involved a swing band and the village hall and nylon stockings she'd been given by an American airman. But anyway . . . you're *married*?'

Her face is all screwed up, and I can tell she's both intrigued and a bit angry.

'Yeah. You want to say "WTF", don't you? Except you're too old to use abbreviations, so you want to say the whole thing. I can see the battle raging within you.'

'The battle raging within me isn't about saying "fuck", Auburn – I'm quite happy to say it! Fuck fuck fuck fuck fuck!'

I laugh out loud – because any word, when you say it repeatedly, starts to sound silly, doesn't it? Especially one that rhymes with duck and muck and yuck and other similarly amusing words.

I see her trying not to laugh, but that's not really in her nature, and she cracks eventually. She sighs, and sits next to me, and steals my bottle of cider. That would normally be a strong reason for me to wrestle her to the ground and dribble spit in her face, but I reckon she's had a shock, so I play nice.

'Why didn't you tell me?' she asks, her voice quiet and a tiny bit hurt. I glance at her, shielding my eyes from the sun, and see that she is in fact hurt. I'd never considered that. When we were young, we weren't close – in fact we were sworn enemies, forced to share a bedroom, where we re-enacted global conflicts every single day despite our lentil-loving mama urging us towards peace, love and understanding.

Now, though, as adults – bonded over Lynnie and the fact that we each have our own room these days – we're closer. Almost friends, in fact. The fact that I've kept this from her has dented her feelings, and I'm sad about that.

'I'm sorry,' I say, patting her knee. 'I didn't do it on purpose. I think I just kind of . . . decided to forget about it. I realise that sounds insane, and it probably is, but it was in a different time. A different life. A long time ago, in a galaxy . . . well, at least a few hundred miles away.'

'Well now you've remembered, tell me about it. I can't believe you're married! Does Van know? Does Finn know?'

'Nobody here knows. Like I said, I chose to bury it. I barely knew myself. If it wasn't for Becca and her Groucho glasses, I might have chosen to bury it forever. But . . . well. Here we are. Me, an old married woman, and you, my spinster sister. Sitting in the sunshine. Sharing a bottle of cider in a fair and equitable manner.'

I reach out to grab it back, but she's too fast, and holds it on the far side of her body so I can't get to it without falling off the table. I shrug, and pull my cigarettes out of my jeans pocket instead. She crinkles her nose up in advance, and I say: 'If you want to hear this story, you'll have to tolerate the second-hand nicotine, okay?'

I've been trying to stop smoking ever since I moved back to Budbury, our tiny corner of the Dorset coast. I've tried vaping, and patches, and exercise, but ultimately never seem quite able to shake off the habit. I'll manage for a while, but then as soon as something vaguely stressful happens – like stubbing my toe, or discovering my mother has cancer, or pretty much everything in between – I start again. I'm a little bit broken, and the ciggies are an external sign, I suppose.

I light up, and soothe myself with that first lovely inhale. I take two puffs, then stub it out on the tiny tin I carry around to use as a combined ashtray and butt collector. Nobody likes a litterbug.

'That was quick,' she says, blinking in surprise.

'It's my latest health kick,' I reply, stashing the tin. 'I only smoke a third of it. Expensive, admittedly – but you can't put a price on good health, can you?'

Willow rolls her eyes in a way that says she knows I'm stalling, and folds her arms across her chest. Very negative body language, that.

'Okay, okay . . . ' I say, realising that she's tucking her hands away to stop herself throttling me. 'Well, it was genuinely a long time ago. Eight years ago, in fact, when I was young and carefree and often off my head on various pharmaceutical products. It was when I was living in Barcelona, before I came to London to do my studies and became a productive member of society.'

'Is he Spanish?' she asks, not unreasonably.

'His mother is. His dad's English. He's called Seb — Sebastian, which in Spanish is almost the same, but kind of like "say-bass-ti-ann".'

'Okay. Say-bass-tian,' Willow replies, trying it out for size. 'So I know his name, and how to pronounce it. That's a start. What about the rest — how did you meet him? Why did you marry him? Why didn't it work?'

I spot movement from inside the café, and have the feeling that everyone is trying to lip-read our conversation without appearing nosy. The downside of our cosy and close-knit community is that everyone is supremely interested in everyone else's life. It's like an interactive soap opera, with a lot of cream teas.

'Erm . . . well, look, Willow, it's complicated. I was younger. I was . . . wilder, remember? I left home when I was young. I spent years in South America and Asia. I was the Queen of the Backpacking Tribe. And that had its consequences — this may come as a surprise, but I have something of an addictive personality you know . . .'

She snorts in amusement, and I shoot her a mock-angry look. Mock because I've just smoked a cigarette and have drunk approximately seventeen martinis and half a bottle of cider. The boat of normality has well and truly sailed.

'And?' she prompts, passing me the cider. Attagirl.

'And . . . I suppose I became addicted to Seb as well. I was living in a tiny apartment above a restaurant in the

Gothic quarter, working in a bar, and never seeing daylight. When I wasn't working, I was drinking. And when I wasn't drinking, I was clubbing. And when I wasn't clubbing, I was sitting on the roof of the building, smoking dope. And when I wasn't smoking dope, I was . . . well, you get the picture. I'd been on the road for so long, I think I'd forgotten how to live like a normal human being.'

'Those who knew you when you were younger,' Willow says gently, 'might say that you never learned in the first place.'

'You're right,' I reply, nodding. 'That's fair. I was always a little on the savage end of the spectrum. And for sure, spending so long living out of a rucksack and dossing down in hostels and only knowing people who were as transient as me didn't help. I only ended up in Barcelona because I could speak some Spanish, and because I was trying – in my own messed up way – to get home. I'd been in Ghana – don't ask – and someone offered me a lift all the way to Morocco. And from there I got a ferry to mainland Spain, and then Barcelona. Have you ever been?'

She gives me a sideways glance that tells me that's a silly question, and I nod.

'No. I suppose you've been busy,' I say. She's younger than me, and stayed at home, and became the One Who Looked After Her Mother. Not that the rest of us had any choice – we had no idea Lynnie was ill, and as soon as we did, Van and I returned to help out. All the same, I do feel slightly guilty about it.

'So. You're living the life of a twenty-four-hour party person in Spain,' she says, recapping the narrative. 'How does that end up with you being married? Were you drunk?'

'A lot of the time, yes – but not when we got married, no. There was a lot of paperwork, it was actually quite a long, drawn-out process to make it all legal. Kind of wish I'd skipped it now, but such is life – if you're going to make a hideous, life-altering mistake, you might as well do it properly . . .'

'Why was it such a mistake?' she asks, and Iknowthat her over-active imagination is working hard to fill in the gaps with all kinds of terrors.

'He didn't sell me into slavery or keep me chained up in a cellar, don't worry,' I reply quickly. 'Bad things happened, but nothing like that. I met Seb in the bar where I worked. He'd come in every night, and we'd flirt and chat and he'd buy me drinks. I'd drink the drinks. Then eventually he started staying after closing time, helping me clear up, and drink more drinks, and then we'd go dancing, and we'd take some pills, and then . . . well, I suppose it was a relationship based on lust and highs. The problem with highs is that there has to be a low at some point.'

'What happened, Auburn?'

'Shit happened, Willow,' I snap back. I hadn't been prepared for this when I woke up this morning, and I hadn't been lying when I said I'd buried it all. It's an episode of my life that was so crazy, so out of control, that I can't really cope with revisiting it.

'Okay,' she replies quickly, reaching out and slipping her hand into mine, squeezing my fingers as she senses my genuine anguish. 'It's all right. Is it why you came back? Why you went back to college?'

I gaze off at bay, and chew my lip, and squeeze her fingers in return.

'That's over-simplifying it, but in a way, yes. When things fell apart between us – pretty spectacularly, as you'd imagine – it made me think about my life. It made me think I'd made a mess of it. That I needed to change. That I needed less excitement and less highs and less lows. I needed a plateau. So I ran away, back to London, where I dossed around for a while before I decided to go and study. The rest, you know. And I think that's it for now . . . please don't nag me for more, and please don't feel hurt. I'm not talking about it because I can't, not because I want to keep secrets from you, okay?'

'Okay. I get it. That's fine. You can talk to me about it when you're ready. Just one more question . . .'

I nod, giving her permission to ask, and already knowing what the question is going to be.

'Why,' she says, calmly, 'if it's all over, and you haven't

seen him for years, and it's all in the past . . . why haven't you divorced him?'

I was indeed right. That was the question I'd been expecting. And to be fair it's one I've asked myself hundreds of times over the years. One I've never been able to answer. It's complicated, and many-layered, and fraught with emotional and practical potholes. I could explain all of this to her, but I can't bring myself to go there. Not yet. I need to keep it simple, for both our sakes.

'I think,' I say, eventually. 'it's because I'm a bit of a knob, sis.'

'Ah,' she replies, wisely. 'The bit of a knob defence. Well . . . I can't argue with you on that one . . .'

Chapter 3

Willow eventually rejoins the ladies inside the café, and I decide not to. I feel shaken and stirred, much like my martinis, and can't face the thought of them all looking at me in that concerned and curious way. I feel like enough of a freak as it is, without parading it in front of the cake collective.

None of them would judge, or push too hard, or be anything other than kind and understanding. They've all had complicated lives, with ex husbands and dead husbands and imaginary husbands and loss and pain and damage, and they've all managed to somehow rebuild. Here, in Budbury, where the rebuilding of shattered lives seems to be something of a regional speciality.

I know that if I fell, they'd spread their arms out and catch me like a big fluffy mattress. I care about them, and I like them, and I trust them. I'm just not 100 per cent sure I feel the same way about myself, at least not all the time. I'm trying to be a better person – staying rooted, staying with a family that needs me, doing a job that matters. Trying not to flake out and run. Trying to be my best self, as they might say on an American panel show.

But my best self is feeling somewhat battered right now, and wants to sneak away. In the Olden Days, I'd have snuck away to another continent – but my life is here. Lynnie is here. Willow is here. Finn is here.

I've been sitting on the table, enjoying the warmth of the sunshine on my face in that way you do when it first comes back after winter, wondering what to do next. The pharmacy is closed for the day in honour of Laura's party. Lynnie's away. I don't want to go back inside. I have a very rare free afternoon ahead of me, and until I think about Finn, have no idea what to fill it with.

As soon as I do think about Finn, I smile. This is a strange new feeling for me – the very thought of a man making me grin. Not just in a 'phwoar, he'd get it' kind of way – though that's there as well. But also because he's funny and kind and patient and strong in all manner of ways. Physically, yes – he's a bear of a man – but also in subtler ways. He's one of those people everyone pays attention to, even though he never raises his voice. A natural leader, I suppose, who might in an alternative reality have been some big cheese in the army, or elected as Boss of the Entire World.

In this reality, he runs Briarwood, Tom's school for grown-up brainiacs. It only opened last year, and initially he tried running it himself, but there were too many problems – like the fact that supremely clever people are sometimes also supremely stupid. There were fires, and meltdowns, and minor explosions, and crises involving re-enactments of famous Jedi battles using real glass light tubes.

Eventually, Tom – who is silly rich because he invents things I don't understand and have no interest in – decided to get someone in to manage the place. And the people who lived there.

I was involved in the interviewing process, mainly because I insisted, and Finn got the job. That was months ago, and we've been together for two of them. Two whole months, and so far, not a single crack has started to show – which is all the proof you need that Finn Jensen is indeed some kind of superior life form. If he's put up with me for this long, he's possibly eligible for sainthood.

I set off on what I know will be a long walk – Briarwood is outside the village, at the top of a hill, surrounded by the kind of wilderness Bear Grylls would find a challenge. I can't drive though, due to my alcohol intake, and anyway the trek will do me good.

I repeat this to myself over and over again during the next half an hour, as the warm sunshine gets warmer, and the booze wears off, and I start to yearn for a glass of cold water. By the time I finally arrive at Briarwood, I'm hot and bothered and also starting to realise something: I have to tell Finn about Seb.

I should have told him about Seb ages ago, but I didn't tell anyone about Seb. Now the cat is not only out of the bag but probably having kittens back at the café – it'll only be a matter of time before someone else casually mentions it to him, which would be unfair and crap and also embarrassing for both of us.

I bypass the main room of the building, which is vibrating with death metal music as I approach. Them crazy kids sure do like their death metal. I glance at the big bay windows, and see them at work: skinny jeans, bright hair, rock T-shirts, piercings, glasses, a life-size replica of ET. That's a new one, and it makes me smile as I walk through the entrance into the hallway.

The house itself is probably Victorian, and was once the home of local landed gentry who fell on hard times. It later became a children's home – a kind of posh private orphanage – where Tom himself spent a few key years after his parents died. That's where he first met Willow, when we were all kids – Lynnie, in her pre-Alzheimer days, used to work here, doing yoga and art workshops with the young people.

It fell into disrepair after that, until Tom came back and did CPR on it. Now it's lively and loud and full of energy and that makes me so happy. I walk down to Finn's office, where he also has living quarters, and where he will also have one of those lovely water coolers that make that nice glugging sound as it fills your glass. Bliss.

I pause outside his door, and quickly swipe some of my hair out of my face. My hair is long and straight and deep red, which is where I got my name. All of us siblings got given names that suited our appearance when we were born – Willow long and lean; Van with a funny ear; Angel a little cherub.

It's also, right now, a bit sticky and glued to my cheeks. Not a good look. Once I'm satisfied that I'm as tidy as I'm going to get, I knock on the door to warn him and go inside.

Finn is sitting behind his desk, looking god-like. He's tall and big and broad and thanks to his Danish grandfather, has silky blond hair that he keeps a bit long, crystal blue eyes, and today, like most days, golden stubble. His face is dominated by high, wide cheekbones, and a slightly crooked nose, and, the minute he sees me, a smile that immediately sends a tingle down my spine.

'*God dag, Mein Herr*,' I say, blending Danish and German on purpose because I know it exasperates him.

'*Guten morgen, mon petit chou-fleur*,' he replies quickly, leaning back in his chair.

'I love it when you call me a vegetable,' I say, perching myself on the corner of the desk and looking around the room. I spy some weird booty in the corner, with the word ACME scrawled on the side in marker pen, and ask: 'Is that a box full of dynamite?'

'Almost. It's a box full of fireworks. Confiscated from a particularly explosive member of the brains trust.'

This kind of thing happens a lot here. It's one of the reasons Finn was brought in in the first place. Fireworks. Huh. How stupid. How juvenile.

'What time does it get dark these days?' I ask, my mind filling with Catherine wheels and rockets.

'No,' he says simply, grinning at me. 'You can't have them. You're explosive enough without the fireworks. What are you doing here? Not that it isn't lovely to see you, but I thought you were at Laura's do?'

He pauses, looks me up and down, and says sadly: 'I can't believe you were at a party at the café and didn't bring me any cake.'

'I'm sorry,' I say, and I genuinely am. It's kind of a sin, that, coming back empty-handed from a visit to Comfort Food heaven. Cherie has done her usual trick of figuring out his particular favourite – some mad Danish rice pudding with almonds and cherry sauce – and serves it up to him so often he should be the size of a sumo wrestler.

He's not, though. He's just about perfect, especially today. He does a lot of rugged things like surfing and sailing and hiking, and it's not an enormous stretch to imagine him at the helm of a longboat planning a raid on the unsuspecting turnip farmers. As a result of all this outdoorsy-ness, he has one of those year-round touch-of-gold tans that makes his eyes pop and his stubble glow. Yowsers.

He's sitting there, wearing a white shirt with the top few

buttons open, which always gets me going. There's no dress code at Briarwood, but he wears these semi-formal shirts when he's working, saying it differentiates him from the others and makes them treat him more like a grown-up.

He definitely looks like a grown-up, and I'm already wondering if he has time for a quick trip into the adjoining boudoir for some adult time. I remind myself of why I'm here, and shake it off. Almost.

He's holding a letter which he's obviously been reading, and I stall for time by asking: 'What's that?'

'It's an invitation. To a conference.'

'Oooh! A conference! How exciting – can I come? Will there be a swanky hotel suite and rude movies? Will there be free pastries and name tags so I can pretend I'm someone else? What's it about? I love conferences!'

He quirks one eyebrow, amused, and replies very deliberately: 'It's about Institutional Financial Processes for Non-Accountancy Qualified Managers, and I'm staying in a Travelodge.'

'Oh . . . maybe not then. I think I'll leave you to it. When is it?'

'Few weeks away. Are you all right?

'Sort of. I've been better. Okay,' I say, rallying my thoughts. 'I kind of have something important to tell you. Not bad, but important. But I also kind of really fancy you right now, and am hoping that I can get you naked some time very soon. So the choice is yours – talk or sex?'

He taps his long fingers on the desk surface, and gives me a feralgrin that does nothing at all to help me calm my reckless libido.

'Well, that sounds intriguing,' he says, and I can tell from the readjustment of his sitting position that I've definitely piqued his interest in more ways than one.

'On the one hand,' he continues, 'I'm a man, so every instinct I have says sex first, talk later.'

I'm hoping he goes for that option, but something tells me he won't. He's too darned clever to fall into my evil trap like that.

'On the other . . . I might feel cheap if I let you have your wicked way with me, and then you tell me something unpleasant afterwards. So, reluctantly, I have to go for talk first. And, depending on what it is you want to talk about, maybe sex later.'

I nod my head, and bite my lip, and realise that there isn't a simple way to do this – other than to just do it.

'Right. Well. The thing is, I should have told you this earlier, I realise that, but the thing is . . .'

He sits, still and silent, his blue gaze steady and calm and irritatingly unyielding. I could probably crack that cool exterior if I whipped my bra off and jiggled my boobies in his face – that's always worked before –but I know I shouldn't. I know he's right.

'The thing is, I'm kind of married.'

I stare first at my knees, which are bopping up and

down nervously without me even giving them permission, and then up at him.

He still looks steady, but not quite as calm. He glances away from me, at the window, for a few seconds, before turning back in my direction.

'You're married?' he repeats, his voice low and an awfully lot less playful than it was a few minutes ago. Which I suppose is understandable.

'Yep!'

'But you're not with him?'

'No! God no!' I say, emphatically. I have the sudden realisation that he was perhaps thinking this is all a lot worse than it is. My fault, for not explaining myself properly.

'No,' I say again, grabbing hold of one of his hands and holding it in mine. 'It's not like that. It's not like one of those stories you read on the internet where I have a secret life, and a husband and triplets waiting for me on the Isle of Wight or whatever. Nothing like that, honestly. I got married, years ago, when I was much younger and much stupider and living in Spain, and we split up. I came back home, and I've not seen him or spoken to him in years. Years! He literally doesn't exist in my life at all, apart from on paper. It's completely over, and has been for so long, and I'm sorry I didn't tell you, and . . .'

I trail off at this point, because I can't think of anything else to add. He notices that I've stopped, and I see him churning it all over in his mind.

'So,' he says, slowly, 'to recap – you got married to a man I don't know. The relationship broke down years ago. You've not seen him since. I wasn't at all part of the reason for it not working?'

Finn, I should have twigged earlier, was bound to worry about that. He is the product of a supremely messy divorce – his dad had an affair, and it turned into one of those lovely scenarios where two grown-ups decide to use a child as a bargaining chip. As a result, he's fairly straightforward on the whole subject. He would never, ever forgive himself if he'd contributed to the collapse of a marriage.

'I absolutely 100 per cent promise you that you were not.'

'And I'm working on the assumption that now you've told me part of it, you'll tell me the rest at some point?'

'Of course I will,' I reply. I'm going to owe this story to a lot of people.

Finn nods once, firmly, and stands up.

'All right,' he announces, walking from behind his desk, grabbing my hands, and pulling me into his arms. 'Then I see no reason why we shouldn't proceed directly to the sex.'

Chapter 4

We do in fact proceed directly to the sex, passing 'go' several times. It's all pretty spectacular, which it usually is with Finn – but even more so this time. I suppose it's the hint of drama, making it all feel more real and more special.

We've never even had an argument, so this is the closest we've got to make-up sex, and I find myself feeling quite emotional when I'm lying in his arms afterwards. His little flat is getting dim, the spring sunshine fading to a dusky evening, the last rays filtering through the closed curtains as we hold each other close.

There had been a moment there – when I'd told him, and he was all strong and silent on me – that I'd felt such a rush of panic. Panic that I'd lost him. Panic that this would all be over before it even properly began. I hadn't even noticed how much I was starting to like this man until then – but I suppose I'm not the most self-aware of women, being the sort who can persuade herself to forget she's actually someone else's wife.

I run my hands over the silky fair hair on his chest – he's not one for manscaping, I'm glad to say – and sigh into his skin. He has me bundled up tight against him, and is grinning the grin of a chap who knows he's just shown a lady an especially good time.

'I really am sorry I didn't tell you,' I say, quietly, running the risk of ruining the moment. 'If it's any consolation I didn't tell anybody.'

'Not even Willow, or Katie?'

'Not even. And then today, at Laura's bash, it all kind of came tumbling out. It was a race against time to get here and tell you myself before one of them told one of the menfolk, and you found out by accident and ended up hating me.'

'I could never hate you, Auburn, you pillock,' he says, sounding as romantic as it's possible to sound with a sentence involving the word 'pillock'.

'You might say that now,' I reply, semi-serious, 'but you should give me some time on that front . . . Anyway, I am sorry. It was all so long ago, and feels a bit like a dream sequence or a flashback in a film. Like something that happened to a different person – my crazy alter-ego or my evil twin sister.'

He laughs, and twines his fingers into my hair, and I feel him holding strands of it up so the sun can fall through it. He's fascinated with my hair, the weirdo.

'I suppose it does perhaps lead us on to the bigger

conversation, though, doesn't it?' he says. I feel him tensing ever so slightly beneath my palms – so subtle I barely notice it, but in Finn world a major event. He's usually Mr Cucumber.

Of course, I get what he means, but I don't have to like it – even if he is right.

'Does it have to?' I ask, sounding like a teenaged girl whining about doing homework when she wants to watch *Love Island*. 'I like things just the way they are. You, me, naked, in bed on a work day. That's pretty perfect.'

'It is,' he agrees, turning my face up so we're looking into each other's eyes. 'Pretty perfect. And it's not like I'm going to go all demanding on you – I know this is new. I know we're both taking baby steps, that we both have our issues. But it's also not . . . casual, is it?'

I remember my panic earlier, when I thought I was losing him. I remember how I smile whenever I hear his name. I remember the fact that this man blows my mind in bed. No, this isn't casual – but I'm not quite sure what it is, either.

'No,' I reply, stroking his face, running my finger over the bump in his nose and kissing its tip. 'Not casual. I really like you, Finn. I'm happy when I'm with you – even when you have clothes on. But my life is . . . complicated. Actually, that's a cop-out – it's not my life, it's me that's complicated. I'm a work in progress, but I can't promise I'll ever be simple.'

'The fact that you've told me you're married to another man kind of tipped me off to that – as has knowing you for the last few months. What makes you think I want simple, anyway? Maybe I like complicated. Maybe I'd be bored if you were straightforward. Maybe I'm an emotional masochist who likes getting involved with savage redheads.'

I think about it, and shrug. Maybe he is. Or maybe he'll reach the point where I drive him mad enough for him to jump back into his longboat, and sail across the North Sea to escape my savagery.

'You're not simple either,' I say, prodding him in the ribs. Offence is the best form of defence. 'You do this whole cool, inscrutable Nordic thing, and you might fool everyone else – but I know there's more to you. You're not just saunas and A-Ha.'

'They were Norwegian, you philistine,' he replies in mock horror. Of course I knew that – but I enjoy winding him up a bit.

'All the same to me. Anyway . . . as for the bigger conversation, I suppose my half of it goes something like this: I like you. I don't want this to end. And if I think about it all too deeply, I'll do my usual thing of tying myself up in knots and convincing myself there's a disaster looming on the horizon. So, can we carry on getting to know each other, and feeling our way through this?'

He runs a hand down my side, over my hip, and onto my naked backside, which he squeezes.

'Like this?' he asks.

'Well, it's not quite what I meant, but I'm not complaining.'

He leaves his hand there, and kisses the top of my head.

'Yes,' he says, after a few moments. 'We can carry on doing that. I like getting to know you. It's fun. But I didn't like getting a shock like that one, so could we avoid that in future please? I don't mind you being complicated, Auburn – but I do mind being kept in the dark. As long as we're honest with each other, I think we'll be all right.'

I throw one leg over his hips in lieu of replying, because I found that last statement a bit scary. I mean, it's not like I go around lying all the time . . . no, actually, I do. I'm renowned for my tremendous fib-telling capacity. But that's just jokey stuff, like claiming I couldn't buy a round in because I'd left my wallet in the ladies' loos at Hogwarts – stuff nobody believes anyway.

That stuff doesn't matter. But the bigger stuff – like the fact that I'm secretly married, and why the marriage went horribly wrong, and big lost chunks of my life that I'm ashamed of and never talk about – matters. Not telling him might not technically be lying, but I can't imagine he'd see it that way.

I need to woman up, and make some changes.

Chapter 5

Laura is half-sitting, half-lying, all groaning, on the couch in the Budbury Pharmacy. The shop opened last year, and scarily I'm the person in charge. That fact never ceases to amaze me. I even have keys to a big cupboard full of some seriously heavy-duty drugs – not that we have much call for it in our village.

My average customer tends to need the odd asthma inhaler or some diabetes meds or antibiotics. Nobody's breaking bad, and most of my regulars are in fairly decent health. That might not be good for business, but it's definitely good for morale.

To make things work, we also sell a lot of extra stuff – toiletries and gifts and suncare and baby things and my personal favourite, the sugary whistle pops that you can both suck on and make music with. Multi-tasking at its finest.

Sometimes we're super busy – by Budbury standards – and sometimes we're not. Today is definitely a 'not' day. Katie is off at her son Saul's school for a parent–teacher thing, and I've been bored all day. That's never good for me, being bored – I tend to start planning world domination, or smoke sixty fags, or bite my nails down to my knuckles.

I was delighted when Laura wobbled her big round self into the store, as soon as I'd determined that she wasn't here because of any health problems. She's doing well, Laura, cooking two whole human beings in her tummy – but she is an older mum, and she was already a teensy bit overweight (in the way of all good cooks), and twins is always a shade more complicated.

She waved off my questions about her health, and slumped down onto the sofa, huffing and puffing and muttering something about how I should get a crane installed to help pregnant ladies get around.

The sofa is quite low, so I see her point. It's also bright red velvet, designed in the shape of a giant pair of lips – a gift from Cherie Moon when we opened up.

I get busy making Laura some tea – herbal – and some coffee – black and strong – for me, and join her, pulling up the stool so I can sit across from her rather than next to her, in case she spreads even further and squashes me.

'I had nowhere else to go,' she says dramatically. 'Becca's working. Zoe's working. The kids are in school and I get a bit worried about being all the way out in the cottages on my own. What a wuss.'

She's not a wuss. Laura, her partner Matt, and her two kids Lizzie and Nate live in a big house at The Rockery, Cherie's holiday-let complex a few miles out of the village. Laura's not keen on driving at the moment, which I can understand as she's already starting to struggle to fit her belly behind the steering column.

'That's not being a wuss,' I say, sipping my coffee. 'That's being sensible. Did Matt bring you in to work this morning?'

'He did – but they kicked me out, Auburn – can you believe it? Kicked out of the Comfort Food Café! That's got to be a first!'

'It might be – but I'm sure they had their reasons. Were you behaving yourself?'

She's been under strict instructions not to do too much, and to concentrate on the baby-growing business. I can only imagine how boring that must be, and she's not adapting well.

'Yes . . . no . . . a bit? But I'm allowed to be there in the mornings, we all agreed that! I'm allowed to bake the bread and make the cakes and get the sandwiches ready – it's not like it's hard!'

'Speak for yourself,' I reply, remembering the time I tried to microwave a ready meal in a tin foil container and blew the machine up. One of my more impressive culinary adventures.

'So why did they kick you out, then?' I ask. 'Aren't you

supposed to help with the kitchen work, get them set up for lunch, and then. . .chillax?'

She looks a little sheepish, and strokes the rounded mound of her tummy as she pulls an aggrieved face.

'Well. Yes. But there were a lot of people in because the weather's nice. And the tables needed clearing. And then the coffee machine broke again and needed fixing. And . . .'

'And you started waddling around like a very slow blue-arsed fly, waiting on, cleaning up, and carrying bin bags full of rubbish around?'

'Kind of,' she admits quietly. 'A bit.'

'Well, there you have it – mystery solved. You do realise they're only being like this because they care about you, don't you? There are worse crimes.'

'I do . . . yes, I realise that . . . but . . . God, I'm so bored, Auburn. And I feel so bloody useless all the time! Matt never says it, but I know he's always worried about me. The kids mainly laugh at me, which is fair enough as they're teenagers and their mum has turned into an airship. And now Willow and Cherie and even Edie are always keeping an eye on me, making sure I don't do anything too strenuous . . . I mean, Edie? She's a ninety-three-year-old woman for goodness' sake, and even she's more active than I am!'

I can't come up with an argument to counter that. I'd feel exactly the same, if Mother Nature was ever deluded enough to throw a pregnancy in my direction. I'd go crazy having to sit still and behave myself all the time. I pass her a Whistle Pop in consolation and sisterhood, and she's halfway through unwrapping it when she lobs it ferociously across the room. It's at that point that I remember – bad pharmacist alert – that she's also been told to keep an eye on her blood sugar level because of the risk of gestational diabetes.

'I can't even eat a bloody lollipop!' she yells, her eyes swimming with tears. She swipes them away angrily, frustrated with herself, with the pregnancy, and possibly with the whole wide world.

I stand up and head towards our simply stunning selection of diabetic treats. By stunning, I mean two varieties of boiled sweets. I choose a raspberry-flavoured one, and pass the bag to Laura.

'Sugar-free,' I say wisely. 'But don't have too many or it'll give you the trots.' It's that kind of gem that I went to college for.

She gratefully accepts the sweets, and pops one in her mouth. It might only be fake sugar, but it does seem to calm her down a bit. We sit in silence for a few moments, and then finally she laughs out loud.

'I'm sorry!' she says, chortling around the words. 'I shouldn't have taken it out on you – and I shouldn't moan. I'm really lucky and I'm really happy, most of the time. After David – Lizzie and Nate's dad – died, I never thought I'd be happy again. Then I moved here and the kids settled and I started working at the café, and met Matt and all the wonderful people here . . . and now I'm going to be a mum again. I'm so very, very lucky, and I shouldn't whinge about it . . .'

'That's okay,' I reply, opening a fake sweet for myself to keep her company. 'Speaking as a trained and qualified health-care professional, I'm confident in the diagnosis of the fact that you're human. Humans aren't perfect. You can come here and blow off steam any time you like. It'll be like Vegas – we'll never speak of it outside the sacred walls of the Budbury Pharmacy.'

She nods, and reaches out over her stomach to pat my knee in thanks.

'I'm grateful. Thank you, Auburn. I think I'm mainly just a bit sick of myself, to be honest. I have babies on the way, and the wedding, and so much is changing and happening around me, while I'm forced to sit still and be a good little pregnant girl. I'm thrilled I'm getting married, but I am starting to wonder what possessed us to do it before the twins arrived . . . anyway. Enough. I'm bored with it all. Please, please, please – talk to me about something that isn't related to my uterus or my wedding!'

I suck the sweet into one corner of my mouth, and ponder that one.

'World politics?' I suggest. 'The economic crisis in Asia?'

'Is there an economic crisis in Asia?'

'I have no idea. Probably. Football? Brexit? Prince Harry and Meghan Markle?'

She goes a little bit gooey-eyed at the last one, and I remember how much she'd cried during the wedding service. Cherie rigged up a big screen at the café, and we all drank Pimms and ate cucumber sandwiches and oohed and aahed at the stars and the frocks.

'Well, I do love to chat about those two,' she confesses, 'and of course I'm fascinated by global economics. But . . . no. Tell me about you. What's going on with you? How's Lynnie? How are things with Finn? He's delicious . . .'

She gazes off into the middle distance, and lapses into what I can only assume is some kind of trance-like state inspired by the sheer beauty of my boyfriend. Not that her Matt is any slouch – he's gorgeous in a young Harrison Ford kind of way, and I've seen them snogging up a storm on the dancefloor before now.

'Is it . . . you know, good? The private stuff?'

She blushes as she asks this, and the very fact that she calls it 'private stuff' but goes ahead and asks anyway is very typical Laura behaviour. Her nosiness overrides her better judgement, bless her. She's probably not feeling at her most agile or sexy or attractive right now, and a bit of vicarious pleasure never did any of us any harm.

I've noticed that Laura always appreciates a good-looking man. I mean, we all do – but with her it's only window shopping. From what I've gathered, there have only been two men in her whole life, and both were marriage material. She's the opposite of me – I've had lots of men in my life, and none of them have been marriage material. Even the one I married.

'It is good, yes,' I reply, before she can explode with embarrassment and make a mess all over the sofa. 'A bit wowzers in fact. But it's also good in the not private stuff. It's good just hanging out with him too. And he . . . well, he puts up with me. What more could I want?'

'Nothing!' she replies enthusiastically. 'Absolutely nothing! People take this for granted all the time – the way you can meet someone, and how exciting that is. Falling in love, and staying in love, growing together . . . they don't seem to realise that it's a kind of small miracle. So if that's what you've found, Auburn, then grab hold of it as hard as you can – because life has a way of sneaking up on and messing things up when you least expect it.'

I know that's what happened to Laura. David died after a fall off a ladder in their garden. A mundane death for the man who had been, until Matt, the love of her life. We've all seen my mum's former self and former life smashed to pieces by illness. Zoe moved to Budbury with Martha because Martha's mum, Zoe's best friend, passed away from breast cancer. Life can, indeed, be a bastard.

I also know this, and am aware of how smooth things are at the moment. I have a job I enjoy, friends I love, family, good physical health despite my best efforts, and a wonderful man.

Because of the way my brain seems to be hard-wired, though, a list like that doesn't make me count my blessings and do a little jig – it makes me anxious. The fact I have such a lot right now means there is a lot that can be taken away from me.

When I was younger, I used to keep diaries. I found them again when I moved home, hidden behind a piece of the skirting board I'd carved out of the bedroom wall. There was a pattern in those diaries, as well as a lot of Younger Self whinging. The pattern seemed to be that whenever I allowed myself to feel content, things went wrong.

Like, I was going out with Jason Llewellyn, after mooning over him for months. I was nervous and twitchy, convinced that he'd find some girl he liked better and break my heart. Then right after Valentine's Day, when he gave me one of those lockets with one part of a love heart on them, I started to relax and plan our wedding.

Two days after that, I found him behind the bike sheds with his tongue down Lynette McCreedy's throat. This was a pattern that repeated itself over and over again – about school, about friendships, about the bonkers state of my family. Every time I dared to let myself feel happy, something went wrong. I even had a name for it – 'Diary Irony'.

I know now, as an adult, that it's silly – but I can't quite shake it off. I have too much. I don't deserve it. Some disaster is looming on the horizon. And it's kind of exhausting, feeling that way.

I realise that Laura is staring at me as I gaze into space, and drag myself back into the present.

'I always feel like life is about to sneak up on me,' I say quietly. 'Which very often gets in the way of living it.'

She sucks her sweet, ponders this, and replies: 'I know what you mean. If you have some bad stuff happen to you, it can be crippling. It makes you so anxious you lose your ability to breathe. I was like that, the first summer I was here. I was halfway back to Manchester, willing to give it all up – Budbury, the café, Matt – because I was so scared of giving it a go.'

'What changed your mind?'

'My kids,' she says, shrugging. 'They were far more sensible than I was, and convinced me to turn the car around. Best decision I ever made, though I might not admit that when I'm on my way to the loo for the fiftieth time in a day. What are you worried about? Is it Finn?'

'Kind of,' I admit, nodding. 'All of it, really. Living here, feeling so settled. Being back with my family, even though the circumstances aren't ideal. And yes, Finn. You heard what I said in the café the other day, about being married . . .'

'I think I vaguely remember something along those lines,' she replies, smiling.

'Well, it's a complicated story, and not one I'm getting into now – but it's stuff like that. Things I need to talk to people about, even though I don't want to. For years I've lived alone, and none of it mattered. Now, I have people who matter to me – people who deserve some honesty.'

'Surely it's not that bad, though?' she asks, eyebrows raised. 'I mean, Finn doesn't strike me as the kind of man who would judge you, or walk away from this without good reason. He's too . . . what's the phrase? Emotionally intelligent! And if you switch roles with him, is there much he could tell you about his past that would upset you enough to finish things?'

Finn, of course, does have a past. A very messy relationship. Conflict with his parents. Screwing up his career aspirations because of all of that. It's not like he arrived at my doorstep fresh out of the box, free from hang-ups. The difference is that he always seems very self-aware about it– he's a much more evolved human being than me, I suppose.

'You're right,' I say, eventually. 'And none of this is his fault. I'm just a disaster area.'

'I suspect he knows that already, Auburn. So, whatever it is, you should talk to him about it. And if there's a problem, you should try and fix it. Show him that you're serious about making things work.'

I wonder how I could do that. Maybe I could get him

one of those love heart lockets. Or dress up like a French maid. Or write him a poem.

'You could always,' says Laura, interrupting my flow of thought, 'do something practical.'

'Like what?' I ask.

'Like get a divorce?'

Chapter 6

I'm not the best at being sensible, or doing paperwork, or generally behaving like a grown-up. Whatever elements of those things I do possess, I need to use for my work, and for my mum. For those two, I have to be good – I have to keep up to date on appointments, and qualifications, and news, and fill in forms, and respond to queries.

In my own life, though, there is something of a more relaxed attitude. Like I have no idea where my birth certificate is, and I don't have a lawyer, and I'm not registered with a dentist, and I keep all my important papers crammed into a plastic carrier bag so old it's starting to disintegrate. I've even let my passport expire – although I think that might be accidentally on purpose, to remove the temptation to ever do a runner.

None of this helps when attempting to navigate a tricky legal situation involving ending a marriage carried out in a foreign country. Luckily, what I do have is Tom – Willow's boy† and the owner of Briarwood.

Tom is a tech geek, and it was him who tracked me and Van down last year so Willow could tell us about Lynnie's situation. He's quiet and shy until you know him, super clever, and absolutely 100 per cent the shizz when it comes to stuff like this.

With his help, I take the first steps towards doing something I should have done years ago – getting out of a long-dead marriage. He helps me find out what I need to do, and he sets me up with a solicitor to help me do it, and he basically stands over me until I've started the first raft of paperwork.

When it's done – when those first tentative steps are taken – I feel really weird. I wasn't lying when I said I'd buried the whole thing. I'd trained myself not to give it much head space – because, given half a chance, Seb and my time with him would sneak right into that head space, and take it over, like some evil alien virus in a space station lab.

Don't get me wrong, I think about him every day. But I've developed the astonishing ability to derail that particular train of thought every single time it appears on the tracks. It's one of the reasons why I'm so twitchy all the time – I'm never still, and I know it drives people mad. I'm always biting my nails or tapping my toes or smoking or waving my hands or moving around in some way.

It's like I'm entirely made of nervous tics and mental self-defence mechanisms that allow me to function, and the way they show up to the outside world is through this constant jigging about.

After Tom has helped me, after I'm forced to re-engage with the whole thing, I feel some kind of strange meltdown going on inside me. It's like all my internal organs and my brain start to liquefy. I can barely move, or think, or do anything other than lie on my bed in the cottage I share with Lynnie and Willow and Van, and stare at the ceiling.

I don't suppose it helps that I'm staring at a ceiling I'm already familiar with, in the cottage where I spent most of my childhood. It's like I've come full circle, and everything in between leaving here in my late teens and being back in my early thirties never happened. Like there's this whole part of my life that I maybe dreamt, or imagined, or read in a book.

After almost an hour of tossing and turning and kicking the duvet and running a marathon while stationary, I glance at my phone, and see that it's just after 8p.m. Not late enough to go to sleep, even if I was capable of shutting down my brain long enough for that to happen.

I chew my lip for a minute to fill in time, and allow myself a moment to rethink, before calling Finn. When he answers, I can hear whooping and cheering in the background.

'What happened?' I ask, genuinely interested. The boffins at Briarwood are working on all kinds of interesting projects. 'Did they invent a new kind of jet engine? Cure for cancer? Phone that doesn't let you dial when drunk?'

'No,' he replies, sounding amused. 'They built a whack-a-mole where Star Wars characters pop up out of the holes. They're busy smashing Darth Vader up with mallets.'

'Oh,' I reply, slightly disappointed.

'Well, to be fair, the whack-a-mole heads are interchangeable – so you could have Marvel, or Disney, or whatever, depending on what licensing you could get. The marketing plan is to sell them as customised – so you could buy one with the faces of your enemies on, like your boss or your ex or your little brother.'

'That could definitely work,' I say. 'The possibilities are endless. It could be a very useful tool in anger-management classes, don't you think? They should pitch it to psychiatrists. And head teachers! I bet it'd be a great thing to have in a school for letting out some pent-up rage.'

'I'll pass on your very valid suggestions to the team. There's a long way to go yet, they need to check if they can patent it or if anyone else already has, that kind of thing. Anyway. What can I do for you, my tiny pickled herring?'

'Erm . . . I'm not sure. Some stuff's happened. Feel a bit weird. Feel a bit trapped in the cottage. Just wanted to talk to someone in the outside world to prove it still exists.'

'You do sound weird. Weirder than usual. Have you had anything to eat today?'

'Yes, of course!' I reply, outraged but also doing a silent recount of my calorific intake and finding it lacking.

'Anything other than a whistle pop?'

'Well . . . not much more, to be honest. Lynnie insisted on cooking tonight, and made a lentil pie with sugar instead of salt. We all had to pretend to like it and secretly throw it away afterwards. Except Van – I think he actually liked it, the freak.'

The background noise has died down, and I can tell he's walked outside. I picture him standing there, by the fountain outside the main house, in the rapidly fading light.

'I'll come and get you,' he says, 'in about an hour. I'll make sure the kids are all right, and I'll see you then. Wrap up warm.'

I agree, blow some kisses down the phone, and flop back down onto the bed. Obviously, being the very definition of contrary, my body decides that it's now very very tired, and would quite like to go to sleep.

I drag myself up, and into the shower, and into jeans and a T-shirt and a thick fluffy jumper with red and black horizontal stripes on it. It makes me look like a bumblebee that's gone over to the dark side.

When I wander through to the living room, Mum and Willow are both crashed out watching *Wizards of Waverley Place*. Mum's developed this strange taste for teen TV shows since she's been ill, and sadly she's sucked us all into her evil world of cute kids who live on boats and sweetly dysfunctional families and cheerleaders and nerds.

Lynnie looks up at me as I enter, and I see the quick momentary confusion flicker across her face. I reach up and touch my hair, pretending I'm tucking it behind my ears, and tonight at least, it's enough. She sees and registers the red hair. She smiles, her eyes lighting up as she recognises me. It's heartbreaking and lovely at the same time.

'You look like Dennis the Menace, Auburn,' she says, pointing at my sweater. 'If he was transgender.'

'Why thank you, Mother,' I reply, giving her a little twirl. 'That's exactly what I was aiming for. I'm popping out for a bit with Finn, is that okay with you two?'

Of course, what I actually mean is 'Is that okay with you, Willow', as she'll be the one left with Mum. Van's outside, in the VW camper van man-cave he calls home, so she'll have help if she needs it – but it's polite to ask. See how hard I'm working on being a good girl?

Willow grins at me and nods. She looks bushed after a long day at the café, her slender limbs sprawled over both arms of the floral-printed chair, her pink hair gusting around her face. Bella Swan, her Border terrier, is curled up in a small wiry ball on her lap.

'As long as you're home before midnight,' she says, stifling a yawn. 'In case you turn into a pumpkin.'

'Terrible story, that,' interjects Lynnie, frowning in contempt. 'Completely anti-feminist. What kind of a message does it send out to young girls, telling them they need a Prince Charming to rescue them, and that their sisters are ugly and evil? Patriarchal nonsense . . .'

Willow and I share an amused look, and nod. Every now and then, the old Lynnie pops up and gives us a rant, the kind we grew up listening to, and it's somehow very comforting. Our bedtime stories were never the bedtime stories that other little girls listened to.

There's a knock on the door, and I feel a quick surge in my heart rate. I'm like a giddy schoolgirl, which Lynnie wouldn't approve of.

She looks a bit surprised at the sound – visitors can be unnerving for her – and Willow quickly says: 'Auburn, that must be Finn. Your poor boyfriend. Off you go, have fun!'

We've got used to doing these subtle recaps for Lynnie's benefit, finding ways to gently remind of her what's happening around her so she doesn't get frightened, without making her feel stupid.

'Yes, have fun!'she adds, reassured that the knock on the door doesn't represent any kind of threat to her or her loved ones. 'Don't do anything I wouldn't do!'

As Lynnie has spent most of her life living on various artists' communes, having affairs with much younger men, and raising three kids on her own, she's something of a rule-breaker. I'm not sure there's much I could do that Lynnie hasn't done already.

I sprint to the front door and unlock it. We have to keep everything locked in case Lynnie goes walkabout, which she did last year and almost died. It's a pain, but not as much of a pain as searching the clifftops at four o'clock in the morning, looking for your mother.

Finn is standing in the porch, all tall and gorgeous, and I fight to keep down a little squeal. Mine, all mine. Just seeing him knocks some of the strangeness of the day out of me, and makes me feel more human again.

He's wearing jeans and a black chunky-knit sweater, and looks like he could throw me in his longboat and take me away for a good ravishing and a smorgasbord.

'Your carriage awaits,' he says, pointing at his four-wheel drive. Huh. Weird – it's almost as though he heard us earlier.

'Patriarchal nonsense . . . ' I mutter, leaning up to give him a quick kiss on the cheek.

'Nope,' he replies, evenly, 'a Toyota Land Cruiser.'

I climb in and buckle up as he sits beside me and starts the engine.

'Everything okay at home?' he asks, glancing at me through his mirrors. Lynnie, when she knows who he is, adores Finn. She calls him her Angel of Light, and clearly imbues him with all kinds of spiritual goodness. When she doesn't know him, though, it's a different matter entirely.

'Yes, fine,' I reply quickly to reassure him. 'I needed an escape route, that's all. Thank you, Star Lord.'

Star Lord was Tom's nickname for the person he was recruiting to manage Briarwood, and it's kind of stuck.

'You do know, don't you,' I say, as he pulls out onto the road and heads off to destination unknown, 'that you only got the job because of your name?'

'What? Being called Finn was part of the job description, was it?'

'No. I mean you got your job because your name has one syllable. Only men whose names have one syllable are allowed to live in Budbury.'

I see him running through the men he knows here – Joe, Matt, Cal, Sam, Tom – and realising that it's true.

'But some of their names are shortened versions,' he points out. 'Wasn't the other guy shortlisted called Simon? He could have been called Si.'

'Ah yes, but you're missing one very important point – I couldn't have given the job to someone I had to call Si.'

'Why's that?' he asks, his smile telling me he knows he has fallen into an evil trap but he doesn't mind.

'Because every time I was in a room with him, I'd have to dance around Gangam Style . . .'

He pauses, then replies: 'You do know that's spelled P-S-Y, don't you?'

Huh. I didn't, as a matter of fact. Bastard.

'Thank you, Admiral of the Pedantic Fleet,' I say, in a minor huff with myself for my lack of pop culture spelling knowledge. 'Where are we off to, anyway?'

'The cliffs near Durdle Door,' he says. 'For a picnic.'

'Did you bring whistle pops?'

'No. I brought salad.'

'Uggh. Why would you do that to me?'

'Because I'm me,' he says, grinning. 'And your body's a temple. If it's any consolation, I also brought Scotch eggs and blueberry muffins from the café.'

'That's all right then,' I answer, already figuring out ways to pretend to eat salad without actually eating it.

As it turns out, the salad was also from the çafé – Finn had been there earlier in the day and brought home some treats – and therefore it was delicious as well as healthy. Chunks of feta cheese and lots of olive oil and pine nuts make everything taste better.

He's spread out two zipped together sleeping bags on the ground, and laid various items of bodily sustenance across them. He's found a spot a mile or so away from the famous Durdle, and the view is amazing. It's properly dark now, the sky studded with stars, the only sound that of the sea rolling across the sand and the occasional rummaging of wildlife around us.

We eat, and chat, and all seems well with the world. I feel blessed to live in such a beautiful place, and to be with such a beautiful man, and to eat such beautiful muffins.

After we've had the picnic, he clears up, and we climb into the sleeping bags. It's been another warm day, but it's still spring and the night-time temperatures are not as friendly as they could be. I don't mind – I'm only human and, aware as I am of patriarchal nonsense, being crammed into a sleeping bag with Finn is not my idea of oppression.

He wraps me up in his arms, my head resting on his chest, and strokes my hair as we gaze up at the night sky.

'This is nice,' I say, burrowing into him even more. 'We're snuggling.'

He laughs, and replies: 'Snuggling. That's not a word I associate with you, Auburn.'

'Me neither! I don't think I've ever used it before in a non-ironic way. Maybe I've used it to incorrectly describe the illegal activities of those who import goods while also bypassing customs tax . . .'

'Would you call those trunks Daniel Craig wears in *Casino Royale* budgie snugglers then?'

'I'd call them heavenly. You should get some. We could role-play Bond together. I could be your Pussy Galore.'

He's silent for a moment, and I know he's thinking it through.

'Yes,' he says eventually. 'I'd definitely be up for that. I've got a tux. We could flirt and drink martinis. Could I persuade you to be a sexy secretary with your hair up and glasses on, and call you Miss Moneypenny?'

'Of course you could. I always thought she was very under-rated, Miss Moneypenny . . .'

'Good. Now we've planned that out, how about you tell

your very own 007 what's bothering you? You sounded really off on the phone.'

'Ah,' I say, taking a deep breath and preparing to bare all. 'That's because I asked Tom to help me start divorce proceedings. Hopefully, I'll soon be a single woman again. Well, not a married woman with a boyfriend, anyway. So, not single, but half as much more single again . . .'

He stays silent when I say this, possibly waiting until I run out of steam, and I try not to freak out and over-react. It's a big thing, and I know the way Finn works – he'll process it before he speaks. He's the anti-me.

I feel his arms tighten around me, and he says: 'That's good. I'm pleased. Not just for me, but . . . for you. It seems like something you should do. You can't leave the past behind if you're still legally married to it.'

'That's exactly right. Plus, then you can start shopping for diamonds for me . . . kidding!'

'I know you're kidding. I wouldn't get diamonds anyway. I'd get something unusual, like an emerald. If I was, in fact, planning on getting you anything at all.'

We're both feeling our way through this, keeping it light, both making the effort not to put a foot wrong. I kind of preferred it when we were snuggling and staring at the stars, but I had to tell him. It was stupid of me to hide the fact that I was married from him in the first place – and it'd be even stupider to hide the fact that I'm now in the process of becoming unmarried.

'I'm glad you told me,' he says, kissing the top of my head. 'Are you ready to tell me about him? About what happened? Because I'm not thick, Auburn – you go pale and shaky every time the subject comes up, so I can see it still affects you. Maybe it'd be good to talk about it.'

I'm not all together sure he's right. I've survived perfectly well without talking about it for years now. Or . . . okay, not well. Kind of unwell, in many ways. It's only this last year that I've started to feel okay again – thanks to Finn, and Willow, and the Budbury crew. Even though the reason for me coming home was a sad one, turns out it's had some pretty good side effects.

'I'll try,' I say, deciding that he is right after all. As usual. 'But I might get lost halfway through, okay?'

'Okay,' he replies firmly. 'Whatever you want. No pressure.'

'Okay,' I repeat, feeling him wrap one of his legs over me. 'Well . . . I met Seb in a bar, which is not an unusual thing, I suppose. I mean, lots of people meet their partners in a bar, don't they? But the difference with us was that we never left the bar. That bar, or other bars, or nightclubs, or parties. We were. . . wild. It felt like fun at the time – until it didn't. Until I realised that all we did was drink, or go mad, or sleep. Literally everything we did together involved some kind of booze or stimulant, or a hangover. There was no in between. No normal.'

'Right. I've had flings like that. Where once the adrenaline wears off, there's not much left.'

'You whack-a-moled the nail on the head there. Except this wasn't a fling – I was married to him, and living with him, and we were really, really bad for each other. I mean, I think living like that even on your own would be bad. But if you had an other half who saw that, and helped you rein it in, or occasionally suggested going to the cinema instead of a rave, maybe it would level out. But with us, there was no levelling out – we were living 100 per cent switched on, all the time.'

'So when did that start being a problem?' he asks, gently. 'Because I assume it did.'

My mind is time-travelling me back to a time and a place I don't want to go to: to Barcelona, all those years ago. To the time when I found out he was doing more than ecstasy and cocaine, and had started on heroin. To the time he locked me out of the flat for two days because he had friends around and forgot I existed. To the time his mother called me, saying he'd been taken to hospital with a suspected overdose. To the time – times, plural – he promised to clean up his act, always so convincing, but never managed.

To all the highs and lows and big losses and tiny paper cuts of disappointment, and the slow, dripping erosion of respect – for him, and for myself.

'Well, it was a lot of things,' I tell Finn. 'Lots and lots of things that happened. Bad things. He needed someone who wasn't me in his life – someone more mature, less insane. Someone who could have helped him with his problems. But I was a borderline basket case myself – I was never as into drugs as he was, but let's say I never went anywhere without an emergency hip flask of vodka, just in case.

'I don't blame him entirely. He was basically a nice guy with a lot of demons. He needed me to be his exorcist, and I was too busy trying to stop my own head from spinning around. So, things got worse and worse and worse . . . complete recklessness, punctuated by these cycles of attempts to live well. Except in our case, living well meant drinking our vodka with orange juice instead of straight. His parents hated me because they thought I was dragging him down. . . and maybe I was. Maybe he needed another mother, not a wife. He certainly didn't need me. I did him no good at all.'

I pause for a breather, and realise that I'm crying. Crying real tears of wetness, which is something I rarely do.

'I don't know why I'm crying!' I say, frustrated with myself. 'It was years ago, and it's all over now!'

Finn wipes away the tears, and replies: 'Because it's emotional. Because it still makes you feel sad, no matter how long ago it was. There's no sell-by date on sadness.'

It sounds so simple when he says it – and maybe it is. Maybe I should allow myself to be sad. For me, for Seb, for everything that happened.

'No, there isn't. And it does make me sad. It's why I pretended it never happened, I'm such a coward. So, anyway . . . we were trapped in this spiral for ages. Then, I don't know why, I started to notice that I wasn't happy. I wasn't happy with my life, with my husband, with the whole messy thing. I've always liked messy – but this was too much, even for me. So I started to try and control myself a bit. Now, this isn't a Hollywood movie, so it's not like I went along to AA and met some inspirational bloke who would've been played by Tom Hanks in the film or anything. I just . . . cut down on the drinking.

'Of course, the less drunk I was, the more messy things looked. It's like when you're the designated driver on a night out. By the end of it, it's quite funny watching all the drunk people repeating themselves and slurring their words and trying to pretend they're sober.'

'Oh yes. I know it well. And it is funny – every now and then.'

'Right. Every now and then. Except this was all the time. Twenty-four hours a day. And the less I joined in with our usual games, the more annoyed he got – I think maybe I wasn't as much fun, but also it was a bit like holding up a mirror to him. He didn't like what he saw, and it made him feel bad about himself, and feeling bad about himself made him drink more and do more drugs and look for even more ways to escape.'

'So you recovering made him worse?'

'Yep – really healthy relationship, wasn't it? And then . . .'

I pause, not wanting to carry on – but compelled to. Not only because he wants to know, but because I need to get some of this out of my system. Maybe it's been silently poisoning me for all these years, strangling me from the inside out.

So I breathe deep, and I tell him, in fits and starts and snuffles. Eventually, I get to the part where things crashed out of control. I tell him about the weekend that everything changed for good.

I'd managed to persuade Seb, with the help of his mother, to come away with me. To get out of the city, away from his so-called friends and his easy supplies and his barfly life. To come with me down to the coast, to spend some time together. Together, without the ever-present third parties.

It started well. He seemed to accept that what I was saying to him made sense – he seemed to mean it when he said he wanted to change. Then again, he always was convincing. His mum lent us her car, and we took off to a little village in the Costa Brava.

It was a beautiful place, all rocky coves and small sandy bays – not completely unlike home. We stayed in a small guesthouse, away from any tourists or commercial zones, and at the beginning I was hopeful. We ate good food. We took long walks. We talked and talked and talked.

I'd say it was like going back to the beginning of our courtship, but it wasn't – it was like two people meeting each other for the first time, because we were both sober. I was excited by that – by the potential to discover my husband all over again, to start afresh. We even talked about maybe starting a family one day, and although I knew there was a long way to go until we could consider doing something so reckless, I didn't rule it out. I even, in a fantasy future kind of way, liked the thought of it.

On the third night, though, things started to go wrong. We were out for dinner, and he seemed brighter than usual. More animated. He was talking too quickly, his hands were waving with every word, he was laughing at things that weren't funny, he was treating the waiting staff like they were long-lost friends.

I suppose part of me knew what was going on. Part of me spotted the signs, and understood that the previous days had been an illusion. We'd both been play-acting. None of it was real – we'd never live happily ever after. We'd never move to a new life by the sea. We'd never have a baby together.

But I ignored that part of me – I just wasn't ready to give up. I wasn't ready to abandon him, and us, and our future. I wanted to cling onto that hope for a few more hours, to give the seeds a chance to grow. He was so beautiful, Seb – dark like his mother, but with the vivid hazel eyes of his father. He was like a sculpture, all hard planes and angles. I wanted to hang on to the fiction for a while longer.

That's why I got into the car with him. That's why I let him drive. That's why we ended up crashing straight into the back of a parked van as we drove to the guest house.

Nobody was hurt, thank God – I'd never have forgiven myself if they had been. The van was empty, and we had our seat belts on, and all we suffered was a few bumps and scrapes and in his case a couple of broken ribs and a concussion.

His injuries didn't stop him jumping out of the car as soon as we regained our senses, though, yelling at me to get into the driver's seat before anybody came. We could see the lights coming on in the houses nearby, and the sounds of doors opening and people calling out to us, and he knew it was only a matter of time before the police were called.

And if the police were called, and he was caught driving, he'd be in a world of hurt. They'd find the cocaine in his system, and he'd be arrested.

Maybe I was an idiot, but I agreed – I pretended I'd been the one driving. My breath was clear, my blood was clean. Everything else about me, though, felt dirty – soiled and used and squalid. I sat beside him in the ambulance that had been called, holding his hand and telling him he'd be okay, but all the time I was on the edge of a melt-down.

I called his mum, and his parents drove straight down to meet us there. By the time they arrived, he was enjoying a morphine buzz, I'd been questioned by the police, and his mother and father were furious. With me.

From their perspective, I'd been my usual crazy self – crashed a car while carrying their precious son in the passenger seat. I suppose that was the last straw – getting blamed in his mother's rapid-fire Catalan, the words pinging towards me like bullets, his dad laying one hand on her shoulder to try and calm her down.

I can't blame them for thinking the worst. I'd not exactly been the model wife, and I'm guessing they were as disappointed as I was – like me, they'd seen this trip as some kind of fresh start. Now, in their eyes, I'd messed it all up, and almost killed Seb in the process.

I didn't have the energy to argue, or defend myself, or tell them what had really happened. My own self-esteem was in the toilet by that stage in my life anyway – I'd wasted years, made so many mistakes, let Seb reach this stage of self-destruction. I hated myself, and I was past caringwhether they hated me too. There was plenty of room in that lifeboat.

So I let them rant and rave and take out all their anxieties and fears on me – it seemed easier than stopping them. I also knew that it might be the last kind thing I could do for them – because there was no way I could stick around and carry on living this life. There was no way I could get straight if I was around him, and no way I could trust him any more.

I stayed for the rest of the night, to make sure he was definitely all right and there wouldn't be any complications, and then I left. I didn't tell any of them – I just went to the police station to make sure it was okay and then got the first train back to the city.

I packed my bags, such as they were, and decided to leave. It's not like a minor crash into the back of a van was going to result in Interpol being alerted, and I'd given the police my details – the insurance would cover the damage. To the van at least.

The damage to me was a bit more serious. I sat there in our flat, and saw it for what it was – nothing more than a squat. The cheap art posters tacked to the wall that I'd once thought were bohemian and charming now looked yellow and faded. The unmade bed we'd shared looked like a rat's nest. The empty bottles from Seb's last party with his pals were littering the room, making the whole place smell like tequila.

Everything I cared about fitted into my backpack – the same backpack I'd left England with all those years earlier. Over a decade of travelling and living; so many different countries, so many different friends and jobs and even a marriage – and I could still cram everything I needed into a backpack.

I left on the next flight to London, and that was the

beginning of what I like to think of as my new life. I barely spoke on that flight, and I desperately wanted to buy every single one of those little bottles of booze the ladies with the trolleys wheel around. But I didn't, which is maybe what saved me – I wasn't an alcoholic in the physical sense, but I was addicted to using it as a crutch. If I'd turned to it then, I might never have stopped.

'And what happened when you got back to the UK?' Finn asks, his voice a whisper, barely heard over the clamour of all these memories.

'I bummed around for a bit. Stayed on sofas, worked crappy jobs. Eventually got my shit together enough to decide to go back to college.'

'And you never saw him again, after that?'

'No,' I say firmly. 'Although I briefly spoke to his dad, a few months later, to make sure he was alive and all right. His dad was quite English about it all, didn't scream or shout or anything – I suspect he knew the truth, and didn't want to push me into telling him more than he wanted to know.

'Once I was studying, things changed – life calmed down. I had something to do, and a reason for doing it, and I started to live again. I knew I'd got enough balance to go on a night out, to go and see a band, to have a few glasses of wine – I started to trust myself again, I suppose.'

'What about now? Do you trust yourself now?'

'Up to a point,' I say, looking up to meet his eyes. 'If

we're doing this whole honesty thing, I trust myself up to a point. I'm happy here. I'm happy with you. I'm happy I can have a drink and a laugh and for it to enhance my life rather than rule it. But . . . well, I'm probably never going to be entirely normal, Finn.'

He leans down to kiss me softly, and replies: 'I think we've had this conversation before, Miss Moneypenny. I never signed on for normal. I signed on for you, in all your crazy glory.'

Chapter 7

I'm driving around Budbury and its beautiful surroundings in my little white van. It has a sign for the Budbury Pharmacy on the side, and I always feel a bit like Postman Pat when I do my rounds. I even asked Katie if I could borrow her cat Tinkerbell, but she put me off by reminding me that he was ginger, not black and white.

Despite the lack of a loyal and resourceful feline companion, I always enjoy doing this. It started small, dropping off a few prescriptions, but it's expanded a lot. I think it was the thing with Edie last year that made me step things up.

When Edie developed pneumonia, it was only the fact that Katie checked up on her and had an instinct that something was wrong that saved her. We ended up breaking into her house in the village, and managed to get her off to the hospital with a supply of top-class antibiotics in the nick of time. If we hadn't, it could all have ended very differently.

Edie's lucky, in many ways, despite the tragedy that has touched her life. She's lucky because she is at the heart of a watchful community, and because she has anextended circle of friends and family who love and cherish her beyond measure. We've all been keeping an eye on her ever since, through an unofficial Edie Watch rota that we all take part in.

Other people in our isolated little part of the world, though, aren't quite so lucky. Sometimes its elderly people, like the man I've just visited – Mr Pumpwell. As well as having the most amusing name on the face of the planet, he also has type 2 diabetes, and lives on his own in a tiny freeholding miles away from any other human beings. That doesn't bother him, as he views most human beings as well below a water vole on the evolutionary scale, and prefers his own company.

He's a tough old bird and has lived that life for decades, making the land work for him, largely self-sufficient, never marrying or having kids, and only occasionally venturing into the big bright lights of the village itself. He's almost eighty now, and still on his own, despite the offer of a place in sheltered accommodation.

He dismissed it, saying it was 'for old people', and stayed where he was. I suspect he's got a point. He's active and proud and he'd probably fade and wilt if he was uprooted, like a wildflower that can only exist in certain soil.

I understand that, and respect his choice, but also worry

for him. For him and the surprisingly abundant amount of people in his situation.

Some rural communities can be like this – the young ones get frustrated at the lack of opportunity, or the hard battle of farming, and move away. The older ones are often left keeping the flame alive. They're not always old, either – one of my clients is a woman in her fifties, living in a cottage in a vale so green and fertile it looks like something from one of those old Technicolor films from the olden days.She's a widower, living with her adult son with Down's Syndrome, who has complex needs and various health problems.

Then there's a couple of new mums, out on farms where they don't have access to baby groups or day centres or places like the Comfort Food Café, struggling with a double dose of motherhood and loneliness. There's also a man called Charlie, whose seventy-seven-year-old wife has Alzheimer's, coping alone after the unexpected death of their daughter.

All of this sounds a bit grim, but it isn't any different than anywhere. I know from working in London that life in the big city can be just as isolating, just as much of a struggle, especially with the added pressures of urban poverty and air quality that suck the life out of you.

Here, though, I do at least feel like I can make a difference. It wasn't entirely intentional – I didn't sit down and make an action plan – unsurprisingly – it simply happened when I started delivering prescriptions. Katie's learning to drive now, but until she can get behind a wheel on her own, she keeps the shop open while I do my visits.

In the early days, I'd stick to filling the prescriptions that the GPs sent over, then either popping them through the letterbox or dropping them off with a quick hello. Bit by bit, though, it changed and grew and became something much more time-consuming but also much more satisfying.

It started with Mr Pumpwell offering me a cup of tea, and me staying for a chat. Then one of the young mums asking me to take a look at some nappy rash. Then I began talking to Charlie about his wife's condition, and about Lynnie's, and suggesting ways he might be able to get more help.

Over the months, it's become something of a lifeline – not only for the clients but for me as well. I've always struggled with being stuck in one place for too long, and doing this helps me to get out and about, spend time both on my own and with other people, and to feel useful. I've only recently started to realise the importance of that – of feeling useful.

Coming back here - helping look after Lynnie, starting the pharmacy, making friends - has changed the way I view the world. Before, I'd have been horrified at the idea of being trapped here, in this situation, with all these responsibilities. I'd have done anything to escape such a terrible fate.

But now? Now I see that it took me a long time to grow up. I'm not all the way there yet, but I'm doing my best – and I'm coming to understand that being useful isn't a death sentence where joy and fun are concerned. It's something we all need – it's the reason why Laura freaks out about not being able to work full-time at the café, and Lynnie insists on trying to cook for us, and Zoe's getting worried about her step-daughter Martha going off to university this year.

So, yeah, I might have started late, after decades of utter uselessness, but now I'm trying – and these rambling visitations in the depths of Dorset are a big part of it.

They also mean that I have a chunk of time to let my mind wander. My life is busy, with Lynnie and family and Finn and running a small business. There's not a lot of unscheduled downtime. I've learned over the years that my brain works at its own pace – there's no use trying to force myself to pay attention, or fix something, or come to a conclusion. It simply doesn't work.

But if I give myself a bit of space, and let the thoughts and events percolate through the many layers of illusion and mazes of procrastination, I get there in the end. I see things more clearly and make decisions, or simply amuse myself by planning practical jokes I can play on my siblings. Nothing keeps the spirits up like cling film on the toilet seat, does it?

* * *

Mr Pumpwell is my last visit of the day, and I am driving across an especially lovely stretch of road alongside Eggardon Hill. Eggardon is an old Iron Age fort, strikingly weird and beautiful, with views over all the tumbling fields and out to sea. It's also one of those places that Lynnie used to treat as some kind of spiritual mecca when we were kids, telling us stories about its folklore and history. She's not the only one to feel that way– for as long as I can remember there've been legends attached to it, everything from ghosts to UFOs.

Some people don't like it, and say it has a bad energy, and share tales of how their cars stalled unexpectedly or they saw dead birds fall from the sky. Maybe I'm more in tune with a bit of bad energy, but I've always loved it – it looks different every single day, depending on the way the sun hits it, or the cloud cover, or the colour of the sky.

Today, like everything else around here, it's bathed in dazzling yellow sunlight, the distant sparkle of blue waves beckoning as I drive towards the coast. The view gives me a bit of a natural high, as does knowing that my next stop – quite legitimately – is at Briarwood.

An alarmingly high number of the brainiacs seem to have asthma, or eczema, or allergies. Maybe there's a scientific study to be had there – maybe they've spent more time indoors because of those things, and ended up as whizzkids. Or maybe spending all their time indoors being whizzkids didn't help. Who knows? Anyway, I have several white paper bags to drop off, and as it's my last visit of the day, it'll give me an excuse to see my handsome Viking Star Lord.

It's been over two weeks since I bared all on the Cliffside. And by that I mean emotionally – it was too cold to get naked physically.

On the night, Finn didn't react with big speeches, or pep talks, or further queries. He could obviously tell that unstoppering that particular bottle of homebrew had unsettled me, and was wise enough to not push me any further.

What he did do, and what he has continued to do, is be even more . . . Finn. By that I mean he's been kind and strong and funny, and done what he has this amazing skill at doing: allowing me to be myself without making me feel crappy about it.

Don't get me wrong, he calls me out on any self-indulgence, or any time I get ridiculous. But he also knows the difference between me being a bit on the wacky and confused end of the spectrum, and me genuinely being worried or anxious. It's like he's some kind of mind-reader.

I still can't figure out quite why he'd be interested in reading my mind – I'm more of a cult classic than a best-seller – but I'm not complaining.

On the whole, I've felt better since I talked to him about things. Like a weight has been lifted, or a boil's been popped.

I've also spoken to Willow and Van, and while I wouldn't say it gets easier to remember, it definitely gets easier to describe – I've got the condensed version down to tweet-size now. Plus, I seem to be able to talk about it more dispassionately, without the snot and the tears.

So far, nobody has condemned me, or called me names, or chased me out of the village with a pitchfork. I don't know why I thought they would – nobody gets through life without making at least one big mistake, do they? Admittedly, in my case it seemed to be a decade or so of making mistakes, but ultimately I hurt nobody but myself.

Talking it through with Finn has at least made me consciously reduce the amount I blame myself for hurting Seb. All these years, I've felt bad that I hadn't been able to help him – that in fact I'd made it worse. Then I ran away, and that can't have helped either. It all made me feel cowardly and weak and without any value at all.

But, as Finn calmly said when I raised this, Seb was already well on his path when we first met. He could have married Mother Theresa and not have changed course. Most importantly, he's made me realise that everything that happened with Seb is in the past – and I can't let it affect my future, or my present.

And my present, I think, as I pull up and park on the gravel driveway in front of Briarwood, is damned good. I'm healthy, I've cut down to one ciggie a day, Lynnie's symptoms are manageable, I have my work, my friends, and my man. I'm satisfied in a way that I don't think I've ever been before, and am fighting the urge to expect some kind of diary irony. I don't want to carry on spoiling what I've got by worrying about what I might lose.

I grab my container full of prescription packages and go into the building. I've seen several other cars parked outside, so I'm expecting company.

What I'm not expecting is to be confronted by the combined menfolk of Budbury prancing up and down the hallway like they're performing some kind of impromptu fashion show.

They're all here: Finn, Becca's partner Sam, Cal, Tom, my brother Van, and Matt, Laura's soon to be husband.

They're all also wearing outrageously pink suits. I stop dead in my tracks and stare at Sam as he strikes a pose, hands on hips. I burst out laughing, because why wouldn't I? These men are all amazing in their own way. Sam looks like a surfer and works as a coastal ranger; Cal is a rugged cowboy type of dude; Matt is a vet; Tom is a millionaire inventor, and Finn is . . . well, perfectly Finn.

They all look different – different hair colours, different builds, different heights but seeing them all en masse, dressed head to toe in pink, is breathtakingly silly.

'I'm sorry,' I say, putting my packages down and surveying them all in various stages of embarrassment, 'did I interrupt a flamingo convention?'

Sam responds by standing on one leg and flapping his

arms about while I walk around, examining them all. The suits are all different – Sam's a bit seventies, Matt's a classic wedding outfit with tailcoat, Finn's very well tailored – but they're all very, very pink. Different shades, but undeniably pink. Even their shoes are pink – ranging from Tom's Converse to Van's spray-painted steel-toed boots to Matt's petal-pale dress shoes.

I knew this was happening, but it's the first time I've seen it in reality – and it is nothing short of spectacular.

I walk over to Matt, take his sheepish-looking face between my hands, and give him a big kiss.

'Laura,' I say to him, 'is a very lucky woman. You all look amazing.'

'Yes, well,' he replies, flustered, looking over my shoulder in a bid to avoid eye contact. 'We couldn't have done it without your sister and your mum.'

This all started that day in the café, when Becca revealed that Laura's dream wedding was entirely pink. Due to the advanced state of her baby-growing venture, and because Cherie loves to organise a good party, the wedding planning has been left to her friends. And her friends – me included – decided that if Laura wanted a pink wedding, then she'd darn well get a pink wedding.

Willow and Lynnie, who were always more artsy and craftsy than me, have been busy with dye packs, creating these dream outfits for the men – and the fact that everything's been home-coloured has resulted in a splendid range of different pinks. Finn's, I notice, is at the pastel end of the colour chart – and it actually goes well with the golden skin and the blue eyes and the blond hair. The man would look good in a suit made entirely of used kebab wrappers, damn him.

'Go on then,' I say, nodding down the hallway. 'Give me a proper show!'

They all take turns parading down the wood-panelled corridor, some doing it with more style than others. Matt and Tom, both on the quiet and shy side, are clearly mortified to be the centre of attention. Van does it like he hasn't a care in the world. Finn gives me an extra over-the-shoulder wink when he reaches the end of his runway, and Cal and Sam ham it up like the big show-offs they are.

Once I've finished laughing, I ask: 'Is everyone sorted now, then?'

'Yep,' says Sam, undoing his jacket. 'Frank and Joe have theirs. The kids are all going to Primark in town at the weekend. You ladies, I assume, are well on your way to pink fashion glory.'

'Kind of. If by that you mean looking like complete tools. At least in mine and Zoe's case – have you any idea how bad gingers can look in pink? We're the ones making the real sacrifice here . . .'

Van snorts, tugs off his hot pink tie, and says: 'Gingers don't look good in anything, sis. Right, gotta go – that garden won't weed itself . . .'

I try and trip him up as he walks past, but he's too experienced in my evil ways – he easily dodges my not-so-subtly outstretched foot, and blows me a huge raspberry as he clomps off towards the exit.

One by one, the other men follow him, getting back to their real lives, to jobs and responsibilities that don't involve them being forced to dress like a giant human candy floss.

Eventually, I'm left with Finn – which is how I like it. Our eyes meet across the hallway, and he raises one eyebrow. He hasn't taken his jacket off – I suspect he knows he looks good in it.

'Deliveries for me?' he asks, eyeing the box full of prescriptions.

'Not all for you – unless you're one of those people who's allergic to the twenty-first century and needs to live in a bubble. Can you pass these out to the gang later?'

'I can do it now if you like,' he replies, a small smile tugging at the corners of his lips.

'Not right now, no,' I say, closing the distance between us.

'Oh, why's that?' he asks, the smile growing as I start to unbutton the jacket, and then the shirt that lies beneath it.

'Because you look so hot in pink.'

'I know.'

'I know you know . . . and I find your arrogance irresistible.'

'It's not arrogance,' he says, slipping his fingers into my hair, 'it's confidence. Would you like to discuss the difference between the two somewhere more private?'

'I think I'd like that very much, now you mention it,' I reply, leaning into him. He might be dressed like Barbara Cartland, but he's all man.

'In that case, come into my office,' he answers, taking my hand and leading me down the hallway behind him. 'Just promise me one thing . . . ?'

'What's that?' I ask, blatantly admiring the rear view as I go.

'If we ever get married, we get to ban pink all together . . .'

I smile as I follow him into his office. Not so long ago, a sentence like that would have churned up so many feelings I'd have felt the need to run outside and chug away on twenty Marlboro. These days, it only makes me grin.

'No problem,' I say, closing and locking the door behind us. 'If we ever get married, I'm thinking Viking horns and feasting halls.'

Chapter 8

There are only two days to go until the wedding, and the latest meeting of the Emergency Dream Wedding Planning Committee is taking place at the café.

Actually, I think, looking around me, it's less of a meeting and more of a craft convention. Today's project, ladies and gents, is hats. Exciting stuff.

Laura herself is off with Willow at our cottage, getting fitted for her dress, which Willow has made for her. Given the advanced state of the bride's belly, and the astonishingly limited range of Big Fat Pregnant Wedding Dresses available on the high street – gap in the market there – she needed to have one put together just for her.

I know, from her complaints in the pharmacy, that the dress has involved 'about three miles of fabric' – but I also know, from seeing the work in progress at home, that it's absolutely gorgeous. Much as she sees herself as disgusting right now, she's truly beautiful – her skin is glowing, her hair is rich and shining, and her boobs are the size of small moons. They're so magnificent she should plant flags on them and give them names. She doesn't look like a beached whale, like she's always saying – she looks like an earth goddess.

While she's taken care of, we're all sorting out our head-wear. The café has closed an hour early, but it's busy because of the nice weather, so Cherie has let the teenagers have a pop-up shop in the garden. I can see them all out there: Lizzie and her boyfriend Josh, her brother Nate, Martha and her chap Bill.

Lizzie is quite the entrepreneur, and has set up trestle tables with slices of cheesecake and wrapped sandwiches, and a couple of chiller boxes crammed with cloudy lemonade and cream soda and other pops. Looks like they're doing well, and the tables and chairs out there are almost full. Lizzie's negotiated a 20 per cent of the takings deal in addition to a flat-rate payment of a tenner each, so she's highly motivated. She even sent Nate down to the beach with a big container of ice lollies to sell earlier.

I've joined the party a bit late after keeping the pharmacy open as long as possible. It was nothing more than an excuse, as I'm nowhere near as good at handcrafting as the rest of my family. My headdress, I have insisted, will consist of nothing more intricate than a pink hairband. Given the colour of my hair, that will look quite silly enough, thank you.

Now I'm here, I see everyone has done fine without me. Lynnie, despite her Alzheimer's, comes alive when she's doing things like this. She actually leads workshops at the day centre she attends, and was the kind of mum who could whip up a fancy-dress outfit for school using nothing but a needle, a thread and an old duvet cover.

She's at the head of one of the long tables, a conch shell mobile dangling above her bushy grey hair, busily using a glue gun and masses of pink fluff to make fascinators. There are pots of sequins, and tubs of glitter, and rolls of lace and brocade laid out in front of her as she decorates the wire shapes. Everything, needless to say, is in shades of pink.

Becca and Zoe are busily coating Matt's currently grey top hat with swathes of pink felt, and Katie, her mum Sandra, and Saul are making up small pink bags of party favours containing tiny packets of Love Hearts, sugared almonds and those incy-wincy bottles of bubbles in the shape of champagne. Little Edie is sitting on Big Edie's knee, and the two of them seem to be randomly sticking discarded scraps of pink material onto cardboard squares.

Cherie is leaning against the counter, still wearing her flour-dusted apron, her mobile phone tucked under her chin as she speaks to the florist about the fact that only pink flowers are allowed.

I wander over towards her, as she is very near to a large tray of home-baked scones, and nod my hellos as she finishes her conversation.

'Just the girl!' she announces, as she automatically goes to the coffee machine to get me a mocha.

I look around to check she was talking about me, and raise my eyebrows in a query. I can't ask her what she means, as my mouth is busy having a scone-inspired orgasm.

She places the drink next to me, spritzes it with squirty cream, and folds her arms across her ample bosom. She's an intimidating woman in many ways, Cherie, not least of which is her sheer size, and for a moment there I find myself feeling like I did throughout my teenaged years – casting my mind back over recent behaviour to see what I was about to be told off for. I can't think of any misdemeanours, but Cherie knows all.

'A little bird called Katie tells me you've been performing some kind of community service, delivering the prescriptions and visiting folk in need?' she says.

'Um, kind of,' I reply, swallowing the last of my mouthful and wiping the crumbs from my chin. 'It's no big deal – mainly I just drink free tea and listen to people.'

'Well, that is a big deal to some, isn't it? It's one of the reasons I made this place into what it is. But I've always been aware of the fact that not everyone can come here, for whatever reason. I can't figure out everyone's comfort food, or sit them down for a natter, or stuff them full of carrot cake, much as I'd like to. So I was thinking . . .'

She pauses, getting distracted by a sudden whoosh of

glitter flying into the air, coating the bookcases in pink sparkle. She shrugs it off, and continues: 'I was thinking that maybe we could work together on it.'

'What do you mean?' I ask, wondering if Cherie's secretly a pharmacist in disguise.

'I was thinking I could make up some care packages for the people you visit? Nothing extravagant. Maybe some cake and home-made bread, and fruit loaf, and biscuits, and muffins, and whatever the day's special is?'

'Nothing extravagant though, eh?' I say, grinning. Cherie is, to put it tastefully, comfortably off. To put it less tastefully, she's minted.

Her late husband provided for her extremely well, and in addition to owning the café and the Rockery, she has a part-share in the pharmacy and goodness knows how many other ventures that we don't know about. Frank, her husband, owns the biggest farm in the area, and between them they're the most unlikely property moguls the world has ever witnessed.

But what she does have, she shares – she's legendarily generous, and always community-minded. A capitalist with a heart.

'It's not caviar and venison, my love, is it? Just a few treats . . .'

I nod, and turn it over in my mind. I see where she's coming from, and it's a lovely idea – but it might need to be handled sensitively as well.

'That's a nice thought, Cherie,' I say eventually. 'But you do know most of these people aren't actually starving? They might see it as charity.'

'Ha! They won't say that once they've tasted the fruit loaf!' she scoffs, waving her hands around. 'But . . . all right, I take your point. It wouldn't be charity, though – more a way of saying hello, letting them know we're here if they need them. Maybe I could get Lizzie to run up some flyers for the café and include them in the boxes, so it looked like I was marketing the place as well? Do you think that would help? Make it look like I was doing it for nefarious reasons?'

'It might, yes,' I reply, giving it some brain power. 'Especially if we include the word "nefarious" on the flyer. Look, most of the people I see would be delighted with it, and not over-think it at all. But a few of them are old school, they have a lot of pride and they might see it as a threat to their independence. They'd hate to think that anyone was feeling sorry for them.'

'I understand that, sweetness,' she replies firmly. 'I'm married to Frank – the man who insisted on carrying on working through a broken arm one harvest. People round here can be like that. So we mustn't step on anybody's toes . . . we'll do it subtle, like? Then I was thinking, if that went well, I might start organising some kind of social here at the café, hire a minibus to bring people in and back again, get everyone together . . . what do you think?'

I lean forward and give her a kiss on her wrinkled, sun-weathered cheek.

'I think it's a lovely idea, but we need to take it one step at a time. You could maybe start with the mums – some of them are desperate for a bit of company.'

'Marvellous,' she says, smiling delightedly. 'We shall make the world a better place, one cake at a time.'

'You should make that your corporate motto,' I say, sipping my coffee. 'The Comfort Food Café – making the world better, one cake at a time.'

'I think we probably should!' she replies, laughing. 'But for the time being, I'm trying to make Laura and Matt's wedding better, one shade of pink at a time. I've had a complete fail on finding a pink pony, which is probably for the best as it'd be hard to get a carriage up the hill – but I have hired a pink limo to pick her up from the Rockery. And I've told the registry office people they have to wear pink too – it's the same people who did mine and Frank's wedding, so they weren't surprised to get a weird request . . .'

'I bet they weren't.'

'I tried to book that singer Pink to do the reception, but apparently she's busy . . . I got a tribute act instead, she's called Ponk. Should be fun. And there's pink champagne, obviously, plus the pink ten-layer cake she mentioned, and Willow's made pink coats for all the dogs. We decided pink kittens were too much of a health and safety hazard.'

I nod wisely, as though I'd have come to the same conclusion myself. I wouldn't, of course. I'd have been busily trying to spray-paint kittens for a week.

Cherie blows out one long puff of air and looks momentarily tired. She's such a force of nature that it's easy to forget sometimes that she's in her seventies.

'Crikey, this wedding lark is quite the business, isn't it?' she asks, looking around at the hive of pink industry that surrounds us.

I spot Lynnie placing a wobbling feather-laden fascinator on Big Edie's grey permed head, and Saul sneakily eating the Love Hearts, and Becca trying on Matt's pink top hat and it falling down to her chin and entirely covering her face.

'It is,' I say, laughing. 'But heck – she's worth it, isn't she?'

'Laura?' answers Cherie, smiling. 'Oh yes. She's worth her weight in gold, that one – which really is saying something at the moment . . .'

Chapter 9

When the big day itself arrives, I suspect we all do the same thing as soon as we wake up – look through the windows and peer up at the sky to see what the weather's like.

I see Lynnie and Willow both out in the garden doing the same, and then they hold hands and do a little dance around our friendly neighbourhood scarecrow. He's dressed in a suit himself to mark the occasion, complete with pink carnation in his lapel.

The sunshine is warm and plentiful, the sky that perfect shade of vivid blue that makes the whole world look like an Impressionist painting. When I join the ladies outside, clutching a mug of coffee to give me a kick-start, I can hear the chaffinches and wrens and blackbirds joining in with the celebration.

Lynnie insists we do a few sun salutations to begin the day and, much as I groan about it, I do feel better afterwards. More awake. More alive. Lynnie, unfortunately, has one of her memory time-slips while she's doing her yoga, and becomes convinced that we are strangers and she is leading us in a class. That's okay – we're used to that, and it's easiest to play along. It makes her happy.

Because of that, though, we have to handle preparations for the wedding carefully. We can't expect her to remember that it's Laura and Matt's day, and wear the right clothes, and come peacefully with us when we set out for the café.

Willow is better at all of this than me – probably at everything – and has already prepared. The day of the hat workshop, she'd asked me to take some photos, which she printed off. Then she stuck them into Mum's notebook – part diary, part aide memoire – along with some details about the wedding, and who will be there, and what will happen at it.

Lynnie carries on for a few more minutes, as if she's there to give us a yoga class, and seems to expect us to leave – 'before the children get home from school'. We don't argue with her, but Willow asks her to look at the notebook.

I try not to stare as the familiar process takes over – the slow spread of recognition and remembrance in her expressions – and instead am thankful that it works. Last year, when she was ill with the cancer, it didn't; she was in too much discomfort, and it threw everything else out of kilter. Now, it does – although for how long, none of us can say. Pondering that particular question is likely to result in a migraine, so I don't. Instead I smile and ask Lynnie if she can help me find my pink hairband.

Willow sets off earlier than us, heading over to the Rockery to help Laura get ready. Matt's staying at Frank and Cherie's farm for the night, and I suspect he's well off out of it. Laura was in a bit of a state the day before, when she called in to get her blood pressure checked. It was fine – a tiny bit up, which is to be expected – but she was definitely on the agitated end of the spectrum.

Once Willow has left, taking Bella Swan and Mum with her, I potter around the house, joined by Van once he wakes up and drags himself out of the cocoon of his camper van. He staggers into the kitchen in his boxers and a T-shirt, scratching his groin and putting the kettle on, hair all tufted up and yawning so wide I can see his tonsils.

'My God, Katie's a lucky woman!' I say, poking him in the ribs and darting away before he can retaliate.

'I know, I keep telling her that,' he replies, giving me a lazy grin and leaning against the countertop. He smells like a geriatric hamster.

I take pity and make him a coffee, handing it to him as he yawns again.

'Big day,' he says, nodding in thanks. 'Wedding.'

'Yes, I had remembered. It'll be fun! There'll be booze and cake and dancing and a huge pregnant woman in a fancy dress . . . maybe it'll be yours next, who knows? Looking at you right now, it's hard to imagine that Katie could possibly resist your charms.'

He rubs sleep out of his eyes and laughs.

'Could be you too, sis, the way things are going with you and Finn . . . We've come a long way, haven't we? Feels like one minute it was all backpacking and sweltering airports and sleeping in tents in far-off lands, and now we're back here. With proper jobs, and proper lives. Almost like grown-ups.'

He looks genuinely confused by this, and I know exactly what he means. Like myself, Van did a lot of travelling before Lynnie's siren call pulled us homewards. He left his life in Tanzania to come here – and it wasn't an easy transition for him.

'Well, only one of us has a proper job,' I reply patronisingly. 'You're only the random bloke who builds walls and cuts down trees. But . . . yeah. Kind of like grown-ups. I don't regret it though, do you?'

'Nah,' he says, smiling, his eyes distant. I guess he's thinking about Katie. 'Not one bit. And we're not that much like grown-ups . . .'

He throws a soggy dishcloth in my face, splattering me with lukewarm water, before dashing off to get the first shower.

'Bastard!' I yell, chasing after him and arriving at the bathroom door in time for it to slam in my face. I hear him chortling away to himself as he locks it, and shout: 'I will have my vengeance, in this life or the next!'

'Are you quoting *Gladiator* at me?' he shouts back.

'Yes!' I reply, threateningly. 'And look how that turned out!'

'Um . . . yeah, kind of–he died. Now, bugger off and let me get ready.'

I pull some faces at the door for a while, then do as he says. I fill in a bit of time catching up on some emails, and flirting with Finn through a series of sexy emojis, and answer the phone to Robert, Willow's dad.

Robert is a new addition to our lives, but we don't see him often. He lives in a commune in Cornwall, and we only very recently found out he was Willow's dad. Long story, but my mum had a fling with him while he was a teenager, right after my dad died. It was all very scandalous, a kind of hippy version of the *Jeremy Kyle Show*. It took them both a while to decide what to do about it, but they've since been tested, and – it's essential to say this in a Darth Vader voice – he IS her father.

They speak to each other on the phone, and every now and then she drives over to visit him. He's never been here though – Lynnie seems to have completely buried the whole thing under layers of Alzheimer's and deliberate forgetfulness. It must run in the family, this whole pretend-it-never-happened-and-it'll-go-away thing.

Once Van's done with the shower – sneaking back to the camper van so I can't ambush him with a frying pan on his way out – I get changed into my wedding outfit.

I have to say, as I stare at myself in the mirror on the back of the wardrobe door, that I've looked better. We went for a deep pink, which makes me look a little less like something out of a horror film, but it's not good. The dress itself is okay – a kind of sixties vibe swing affair – but the colour? Not something I'd choose.

I remind myself, slipping my headband on, it's not about me. Today's about Laura, and nobody will care what I look like. My hair, I think, looks good – I blow-dried it straight, and it's almost to my waist now – but the pink strap holding it back doesn't add anything other than nausea.

I slip my trainers on, carrying my proper pink shoes in my bag to put on after the walk, and wait for Van to knock for me.

When he does – dressed in his pink suit and pink work boots – we both stare at each other in horror. I mean, I look bad – and normally this kind of outfit would be enough for him to feast upon with a month's worth of mockery. But he looks bad too, and he's clearly not comfortable with it, and it seems that we cancel each other out.

'Truce?' he says, holding out a hand.

'Truce,' I say, shaking it. 'Until the wedding is over and we both look like human beings again.'

'Yes, he agrees, heading towards the footpath across Frank's fields. 'Once we look like human beings again, we can start acting like monsters.'

The ten-minute walk to the café is sublime. The sun is shining, the breeze is gentle, and it's so, so quiet. Right until we get to the pathway that leads up the hill to the café, we don't talk, don't make any noise, don't so much as hum a catchy ditty. Van and I have both lived in big-sky places in Africa and South America, and sometimes being here can feel claustrophobic – but on days like this, with the sea sparkling in front of us and the gulls wheeling overhead, it just feels glorious.

The pink theme for the wedding starts as soon as we reach the path. The handrail has been twined around with flowers made of pink paper, and rose petals have been scattered along all the steps. By the time we reach the top and emerge into the garden, the whole world turns pink.

The small stage-like pergola where Matt is standing is painted a very pale shade of pink, its wooden roof over-hanging with heavy boughs of blossom-like flowers. Matt himself is wearing the morning coat I've already seen, along with the felt-coated hat and the pink shoes.

He looks a bit nervous, staring out at the small crowd in front of him without seeing any of them, Frank at his side as best man.

Most people are here already, sitting on chairs that have been arranged around the existing tables, not quite in neat rows, but scattered in weird shapes and circles. Van heads straight for Katie, who – being a petite and pretty blonde – looks gorgeous in pink, damn her. I spot Zoe, wearing her pink trouser suit, fascinator fighting a losing battle to stay upright on her ginger curls, sitting with Cal and Martha.

I meet her eyes and grimace. She returns the look, and

shakes her head, gesturing down at herself in disgust. Gingers united. We should probably form some kind of support group.

Becca looks alarmingly sexy in her tight pink sheath dress, and I see Sam's gaze linger on her in a way that suggests he might have noticed too. Little Edie is a natural in pink, being a toddler girl, and big Edie looks like a small cupcake sitting next to them.

Cherie – dressed in a tie-dye kaftan and shiny patent leather boots – is up at the front, chatting to the lady who will be doing the service, and glancing into the café as she does it.

Willow's plan was to get Laura and Lizzie, her bridesmaid, here earlier than everyone else, and to blindfold her as she walked through the garden so she couldn't see anything beforehand. She won't be expecting all this pink, and I hope she likes it – some of us have sacrificed our dignity for her childhood fantasy.

Laura, in fact, will be the only person here not dressed in pink – her gown is in a deep shade of magenta. An unusual choice for a wedding dress, to be sure – but it was a compromise. Initially she wanted to wear black, 'because it's slimming'. We kindly pointed out that there was nothing on earth bar a cloak of invisibility that was going to make an eight-month pregnant woman look slim, and she settled on this, with much humphing and moaning.

I only hope she's calmed down, and is able to enjoy the

day. It's actually rather magical, all of it – her story. The way she lost her first husband and came here to heal. The way she found love again when she never expected she would.

Thinking about it is making me feel a bit mushy, so I look around automatically for Finn. No sign of him yet. I take a seat next to my mum, who seems happy enough in her favourite pink feather boa, and Tom, who looks so embarrassed in his outfit that I fear his face out-pinks his suit. I pat his hand and tell him he looks gorgeous. Which he does, in his own sweet way.

After a few minutes, the music starts – some kind of gentle violin melody that wafts around the garden from speakers set up on pink-painted poles – and we all turn our heads towards the café doors. The conversation dies, and after a false alarm where Willow sneaks out, bobbing her fashionably pink head in apology, Laura emerges on her dad's arm.

Her parents are from Manchester, but as both their daughters and all their grandchildren and grandchildren-to-be live here, they've settled in Applechurch, the next village over. Her dad looks proud as can be, holding her hand over his arm as they step through the doors, Lizzie by their side.

Both Lizzie and her granddad are dressed in pink, which must have confused Laura no end when she saw them. Lizzie is usually a fully paid-up member of the black eye-liner emo clan, so this is quite the turnaround for her – a simple pale pink dress with lace sleeves, which looks gorgeous. Her dad is wearing a lightweight linen suit in pastel, which makes him look like he might have been a spy in a musical version of 1950s Vienna.

Laura herself looks amazing, and a communal cheer goes up as she walks alongside the chairs and heads to the pergola. It seems to lift her spirits and she raises one hand and gives us all a wave as she makes her way carefully along the grass, grinning in surprise and amusement at all our outfits.

Her dress is mainly satin, but with a little chiffon cape 'to hide my fat arms and shoulders', she'd said. She doesn't look fat, though – she looks round and strong and magnificent, her curls pinned up and trailing around her face, her cheeks as rosy and pink as her dad's suit.

Any doubts she might have had, any insecurities she might have felt, seem to evaporate the moment she lays eyes on Matt. He's stopped fidgeting, and stopped looking awkward, and stopped looking around as though he's trapped in some kind of nightmare.

He's stopped doing anything other than look at Laura as she climbs the small steps up to meet him, then he holds his hands out to hers.

They both smile, and it's so lovely, so sweet, that I feel tears prick at the back of my eyes. They're like living proof that happy endings are real, and even now – after almost three years together, and with twins on the way, they look at each other like they've only just met and fallen in love.

As the registrar starts the service, I feel even more emotional. The part about the rings being a symbol of eternal commitment, and the tender way Matt places the ring on Laura's finger, finally pushes me over the edge. I let the tears fall, glad to notice that I'm not alone as I gaze around at everyone else.

Becca's in floods, Laura's mum's a goner, and Cherie is holding her cheeks in her hands as she weeps.

My mum passes me a tissue in a rare moment of traditional mum-like behaviour, and I'm carefully scooping off mascara as Finn finally appears. He's snuck up from the back, and edges into the chair next to me.

He slips his hand into mine, and whispers: 'Sorry I'm late. Minor crisis back at the Bat Cave.'

I nod, unable to quite formulate words amid the floods, and he looks at me.

'Are you all right?' he murmurs, gently wiping the tears from my cheeks and kissing my nose. 'You look beautiful, by the way.'

I stare at him incredulously, wondering how he can possibly think I look anything other than horrific amid all the pink and the snot and the blubbing. I see, though, that he means it. That he is looking at me in the same way that Matt looked at Laura. In a way that I don't think anyone has ever looked at me before.

'I love you, Finn,' I say simply, whispering the words into his ear, only realising the truth of them once they spill out.

He smiles, still calm, still steady, and places an arm around my shoulder to pull me in tight.

'And I love you too,' he replies quietly. 'Even in pink.'

I tear my gaze away from him – from this beautiful man who has helped me change, helped me grow, helped me face my past – and look back up at the wedding.

Just in time, the registrar announces that Matt and Laura are now man and wife – and the whole crazy pink garden goes absolutely insane. There are hats and fascinators and hankies thrown up into the air amid the cheers, flying up and fluttering down like plus-sized confetti. There's applause, and yelling, and everyone is on their feet.

Laura and Matt turn around and face us all, holding hands, grinning like teenagers, and take a bow.

There are more cheers, and Cherie fires off a confetti cannon and showers everyone with pink fluff, and the dogs bark along, and we're all swept along on a wave of joy.

Finn stands up and pulls me to my feet. He ignores the crowds, ignores the cheers, ignores the confetti, and takes me into his arms. He kisses me long and hard and so well I feel giddy, and have to sit back down again afterwards.

My mum pats me on the arm, looks at me approvingly, and says: 'The Angel of Light has pink confetti stuck in his hair.'

Chapter 10

The party gets properly started once Matt and Laura have completed all their paperwork, and the tables of food are unleashed on a hungry crowd. It's still only lunchtime – Laura insisted she had to do it early because she'd be ready for bed by five, and nobody argues with the bride. Especially a bride in her condition.

Cherie, as she tends to do for events, got somebody else in to do the catering – weird for a café, but it means they all get to enjoy themselves rather than spend the whole day replenishing salad trays and topping up trifle bowls.

What she did make, though, is the cake – an utterly splendiferous thing that is wheeled out from the kitchens on its own trolley. There are indeed ten layers, and it is indeed very pink. Laura gasps in amazement when she sees it, her eyes going wide and her hands flying up to her cheeks as she takes in the ever-decreasing circles of iced sponge and the tiny figures of her and Matt on the top, accompanied by a miniature version of their black lab Midgebo.

'Oh my goodness!' she says, as a thousand phone cameras click photos of her. 'It's absolutely perfect! The cake, the outfits . . . all of it!'

She turns around and smiles at us all, eyes suspiciously wet, and adds: 'I can't thank you all enough. This is all so brilliant!'

Matt nods in agreement, and looks happy because she's happy. I'm fairly sure getting decked up in a pink top hat and tails was never part of his life plan, but sometimes these things just sneak up on you and you have to go with the flow.

Distinctly uncomfortable with all the attention, he takes off his hat, gazes around, and finally settles his eyes on his new wife.

'Yes, thank you, all of you,' he says, smiling at her. 'And most of all, thank you to Laura – the most beautiful bride the world has ever seen.'

She blushes, and harrumphs, and wiggles her huge body around, and yes – looks truly beautiful. And truly happy.

After many more photos, mainly orchestrated by our own semi-pro photographer, Lizzie, we all descend on the groaning buffet tables and fill our boots. And our plates.

The food is luscious, as you'd expect, and Cherie and Sandra are busily going around with trays of champagne to hand out.

Finn picks up two glasses, and hands one to me. We've not had a minute to discuss our mutual dropping of the

L-word earlier, which is probably a good thing – it also means I haven't had time to over-think it.

He raises his glass in the air and says, for my ears only: 'To Matt and Laura. And to us.'

I clink my glass against his, and we both down them in one. I have no idea why we do that, but it clearly seems appropriate, and makes us burst out laughing during the ensuing head rush.

We wander back outside, where people have pulled the chairs to huddle around the existing tables, and listen to Ponk as she launches into 'Get the Party Started'. Clever. Ponk is actually called Jackie, and lives on the outskirts of Bristol with her husband Kevin, a very round man who does a Meatloaf tribute act. They must have some terrific karaoke nights round at their house, I reckon.

We take our seats at a table with Mum and Lynnie and Big Edie. Bella Swan is curled up in a ball beneath us, managing to look dignified despite her pink coat. Bella is an elder stateswoman of the dog world, and pretty well behaved. The other two – Midgebo and Tom's multi-breed hybrid behemoth Rick Grimes – are prone to acting like hooligans, especially around tables of food, so they're safely away in the doggie crèche field, sadly poking their snouts through the fence trying to see what all the fuss is about.

Laura had refused to do a 'first dance', on the grounds of her bulk, but we all cheer as she manages to trundle up to the front, dragging Matt behind her, and bop around to the song. Becca and Sam join in, and the ensemble mass of the village teenagers throw themselves into it with mosh-pit abandon. The party is well and truly started.

Willow and Tom join us soon after, and Mum sips her champagne as she looks around, surveying the dancing and the people and the pinkness of it all.

'This is very beautiful,' she announces finally. 'You could almost reach out and touch the happiness, couldn't you? What a nice wedding to be invited to.'

Something in the tone of her voice implies she's not quite sure whose wedding it is, or why she's been invited, but she also sounds calm and mellow and relaxed, which means that we can be all of those things as well.

I feel Finn's hand resting on my thigh, and place mine over it. I'm feeling like I could reach out and touch happiness myself, but I settle for his fingers twining into mine. Pretty much the same thing.

Willow is looking at me with her eyes narrowed in suspicion, and I glance around, wondering what's going on.

'What are you looking at?' I ask, possibly a bit belligerently. She is my little sister after all – can't have her thinking I've gone all soft, can I?

'I'm looking at you,' she says, pointing one long finger at me accusingly. 'You look . . . really, really happy! And you're not smoking, and not messing with your hair, and not biting your nails, and not fidgeting. What's going on?'

I feel everyone's eyes on me and Finn, and realise she's right. I am still and calm and almost normal.

'Nothing's wrong,' I reply, smiling pleasantly to freak her out, 'I'm just . . . in a good place right now.'

She snorts and laughs and answers: 'In a good place? You look like you're in some kind of nirvana . . .'

I wink at her, and Finn puts his arm around my shoulder, and Mum chips in: 'She's in love, Willow. Can't you see it?'

Willow blinks a couple of times, and stares at me some more, and nods.

'As a matter of fact, I can. No wonder she looks weird . . .'

While I am enjoying confounding Willow and her expectations of me, I'm not especially enjoying being the centre of attention – so I stand up, drag Finn to his feet, and head off to the impromptu dance floor at the front of the garden.

There are a lot of people up and dancing now, all dressed in pink, and I can only imagine how weird it must look. A passing drone taking spy footage would be extremely confused at this heaving mass of colour.

I give Laura a hug of encouragement as she's shuffling from side to side among the dancers, and tell her she looks gorgeous.

'I'm not so sure about that,' she says, slightly out of puff, 'but I'm glad you're here. You know, just in case my waters break!'

I try to keep the look of horror off my face – that would

be unprofessional – and hope she's kidding. She's provisionally got a C-section booked nearer her due date, which I know she's desperate to avoid. She has a thing about hospitals, absolutely hates the places, and I have a sneaking suspicion that she's hoping to go into labour at home and have some kind of miraculously easy birth where she ends up pain-free and tucked up in bed with twins and a cuppa after an hour of delicate pushing.

She knows, of course, that in the real world, at her age and so long since her last baby, that twins are unlikely to make it so easy for her – but a girl can hope.

'Never fear,' I reply, gripping her hand in reassurance, 'Auburn's here! We didn't cover home births on my course, but I'm sure Matt could help out . . .'

She grins, and does a little spin, and then adds: 'I think Matt's already helped out quite enough, thank you. But Cal could. He delivered Becca's baby when Little Edie arrived in the café. He was brilliant, loads better than a doctor . . .'

I glance over at Cal, who is wearing a pink cowboy hat to go with his suit. He's busily leaping up and down with the teenagers, like people do to that 'Jump Around' song, and I'm guessing he's already well on his way to hammered.

'Yeah, it'd be fine,' I say to Laura, adding a silent prayer that it doesn't come to that.

She finally gives up on the dancing, and heads back to the café for a 'little sit-down'. Matt, of course, follows her immediately – he's not the kind of man who would stay on a dance floor of his own free will.

Ponk has moved on to 'What About Us?' now, and everyone is singing along. Finn is with Sam, both of them doing very passable man-dancing, busting out some impressive spins and in Sam's case a high kick as well. Surfer dudes, having fun.

I shimmy over to them, and we dance and laugh and smile and the world feels so free and full of potential, I feel like I might burst. Or even worse, start crying again.

I'm here with a man I love, surrounded by friends and family, on a glorious day full of celebration and community. Somehow, no matter what mistakes I've made in the past, I've fallen on my feet here – and I know exactly how lucky I am. Somewhere out there, there's an alternative Auburn, in a parallel universe, drinking cheap sherry from a plastic bottle and living in a squat.

When I'm all danced out, I go back to the table and sit down with my mum and Willow. Edie is up and boogying with the best of them, her pink tights flashing as she defies her age and cuts a rug.

Mum seems happy enough, her fingers tapping away on the tabletop, smiling as she watches Katie and Van dancing together, Saul perched on his shoulders. I glance at Willow, and she grins: all is well in Longville world.

'There's an Angel of Darkness at the top of the steps,' says Mum, completely out of the blue. Her voice is calm, and she's gazing off in the direction of the head of the path.

Willow and I both frown in bafflement – she can be a bit on the random side, and in fact always was, even before the Alzheimer's – and follow her line of sight.

I have a chicken drumstick halfway to my mouth when I see him. I drop it back down, and gulp in air, and stare so hard my face feels frozen in place.

Willow looks from him to me, concerned and confused, and raises her eyebrows.

I ignore her. I don't have any breath to spare for talking right now, as I watch him, standing still at the edge of the crowd.

I notice a few other people staring at him as well, which isn't surprising – he's the only person here not dressed in pink. In fact he's dressed all in black, as usual.

I stand up, and take a hesitant step in his direction. I'm kind of hoping he'll disappear in a shimmer of sunlight, and it will all have been some kind of mirage, but as I walk towards him, he remains distressingly real.

His eyes meet mine as I put one foot determinedly in front of the other, and he smiles. It's a good smile. He always had a good smile – it got him out of trouble way too many times.

His hair is shorter than I remember, but still flopping over his forehead. He's bigger as well – he was always rail-thin, in a hard-living chic kind of way, but now he seems to have bulked out a bit. His eyes are exactly the same – a brilliant splash of hazel-green amid smooth olive skin.

After what feels like a three-hour moonwalk, wading through the mud of my own disbelief, I finally reach him.

'Seb,' I say, my voice wired and stretched, barely audible over the music and the ringing in my ears. 'What are you doing here?'

Chapter 11

'I happened to be passing,' he says, grinning at me in that oh-so-familiar way. The way that used to make my heart melt into a puddle, and forgive him anything. This time, it just makes my heart melt in anxiety as I glance behind me to see if Finn's spotted us.

This is not what I expected to be doing today, and I'm fresh out of witty repartee.

'Come with me,' I say firmly, striding off down the steps and assuming he'll follow. I don't know what he's doing here, and I don't know how I'm going to handle it, but I do know one thing: I can't let him bring his Angel of Darkness drama to Laura's wedding and spoil the whole day. There's alcohol up there, and the Seb I knew would make short work of it.

The music fades the further away from the café we get, until, after what feels like an hour of climbing down steps, we reach the small car park by the bay. I see Laura's pink stretch limo there, the driver looking at his phone as he waits to take Laura and Matt on their one-night honeymoon, and I feel a weird collision of worlds.

Today was supposed to be all about the pink pink, and now I'm standing here, with my black-shrouded estranged husband, feeling the sunshine but not feeling it; hearing the sounds of children playing on the beach but not hearing them.

I continue to ignore him, slip off my shoes, and walk out onto the sand. It's busy down there, dogs and kids and picnics and ice creams, people skimming stones into the waves and hunting for fossils on the cliffsides, and I walk along for a few minutes until I find a quiet spot in the shade.

I whirl around, and find him way too close to me. So close I can see the changes in his face: lines where there were none; laughter creases around his eyes; a hint of something more mature. I realise that when I met him he was only a boy – and at some point between then and now, he's turned into a man.

A man who I desperately wish wasn't here.

'Seb, I'm going to ask you again – why are you here?'

He frowns, and I see him examining me in the same way I did him. It's been so long. So much has happened, undoubtedly to both of us.

'You look good, Auburn,' he says, reaching out to tuck a stray strand of hair behind my ear. It's too familiar. Too close. Too much like the way we used to be.

I slap his hand away, and take a step back. I need some distance before he casts his spell over me.

'Yeah, well, I feel good too – or at least I did until five minutes ago. Why, Seb? After all this time?'

I hear a hint of pleading in my voice, and hate myself for it. I hate the fact that he has this power over me – this ability to make me someone I don't want to be.

'I think you can probably figure out why,' he replies, his eyes pinning me down. 'Years go by, and I hear nothing from you. Then you ask for a divorce. I thought perhaps we should see each other, talk it over, before we take that final step.'

I laugh bitterly, and shake my head.

'Final step? It's just a technicality, Seb! Just a piece of paper. Everywhere that matters, we were divorced years ago. I've moved on. I'm sure you have, too. There's . . . no need for this!'

He sees how upset I am, and looks . . . concerned. That's a change of pace for him. Usually, if I got upset around him, he'd react with contempt, or annoyance, calling me a drama queen, frustrated at my humanity getting in the way of his good time. Resentful of anybody taking the attention away from his place at centre stage.

'There might not have been any need for you, Auburn, but there was for me,' he says, his tone level and not at all contemptuous. 'And as for moving on . . . yes, of course. Both of us have. But that doesn't mean I don't think about you. That doesn't mean I haven't thought about you every single day since you left. Can you say honestly that you haven't? We have unfinished business, and I needed to see you again, querida.'

'Don't call me that!' I snap, feeling some angry tears spike behind my eyes. I haven't cried angry tears in a long time, and the vast majority of them were reserved for the man standing in front of me.

I'm angry because he's here. I'm angry because I'm not handling it well. Mainly, I'm angry because he's right – I have thought about him every single day since I left. Not always in a complimentary fashion, but he's always been there, at the back of my thoughts, a shadow in the corner of my mind's eye.

It's only very recently that I've started to evict the ghost of his memory from my mind – and now, just as I get to grips with that, the real bloody thing is standing here in front of me, on a beach in my home town, apparently expecting some kind of reunion.

I take a deep puff of fresh air and channel some of the breathing techniques Lynnie used as a painkiller when we were kids. Wasp sting? Deep breaths in and out. Splinter removal? Deep breaths in and out. Phantom husband back from the dead? Deep breaths in and out.

As ever, it works a bit better than I'd expect, and I manage to rally my thoughts enough to talk.

'Seb, you've got to understand that this is a big shock to me. You've planned this, and presumably had the plane journey to think about it and how it might go. I haven't.'

'No, I understand that, Auburn. But I didn't have much time to plan for you leaving me, either. Or for you asking for a divorce after all this time. Both of those things came as a big shock to me, too. Look, I didn't come here to upset you, or hurt you, or break your life – I honestly didn't.'

He sounds genuine, and I find myself staring into his eyes, looking for signs that he's lying – that he's convincing me again. Persuading me against my better judgement.I see nothing but sincerity, which is somehow even more alarming.

'Then why did you come, Seb?' I ask. 'Because you're doing all of those things, whether you intended to or not. I don't understand what you're hoping to achieve here. Is it some kind of misplaced machismo, refusing to accept that I got away? Are you going to hold me hostage over the divorce, refuse to sign the papers? Because I'm telling you now, that won't work . . .'

'Nothing so dramatic, my love,' he replies, slipping in yet another term of endearment to entangle me. 'I'd never do that. I understand why you left, and you did the right thing for both of us. And if, when we've had time to talk properly, you still want a divorce, then it's yours.

'I came here to do something much simpler, Auburn – I came here to apologise, and to ask for your forgiveness. It's long overdue, and I'm only sorry I didn't do it sooner, but . . . well, we were maybe both working on ourselves, yes?'

Working on ourselves. Right. Well, that's one way to put it, I suppose. And I definitely have been – and definitely continue to. As for him . . . he looks better than ever. He looks well fed, and clear-eyed, and clean in all kinds of ways. He looks like a new and improved version of the man who broke my heart.

'Okay,' I say, biting my lip in frustration. 'Apology accepted. You are forgiven. Now will you go away?'

He laughs out loud, and the sound of it whisks me back into a time machine: back to the days when he laughed all the time. When I laughed with him. When we were both so young, so arrogant, so sure of our place in the world.

'Eventually,' he says, sounding amused. 'I promise. But I'm here for two weeks, and all I ask is that you spend some time with me. That's all.'

That's all? That's everything, in my world. I don't have a lot of spare time, and what I do have, I like to spend with Finn. My boyfriend. The man who told me he loved me today. The man who's waiting up those steps, in a pink suit, probably wondering where the hell I am. I have no idea how I'm going to explain all of this to him.

'How did you find me, anyway?' I ask plaintively.

'The address was on the divorce letter,' he says, shrugging. 'And this is a very small place. I'm staying in a cottage at a place called the Rockery, and when I asked in the village, everyone knew where you'd be. A wedding, yes? A pink wedding?'

I harrumph a little at the thought of him staying at the Rockery. Cherie's holiday cottages are usually booked up way in advance, but of course Laura's recently moved out of her cottage, Hyacinth, and into Matt's, Black Rose – conveniently freeing up space for my hopefully soon-to-be-ex hubby.

'Yes,' I reply, gazing back up at the café, perched on the cliffside. 'A wedding. A good friend's wedding, where I was enjoying myself with my mother, and my brother and sister, and my boyfriend.'

I stare at him when I say that last word, maybe hoping that he'll get the hint and announce that he's leaving. Or act like a jerk about it, and make it easier for me to ask Cherie to kick him out.

Instead, he smiles tenderly and says: 'I'm glad you're with your family. I'm glad you're happy. And if this is the man you're meant to be with, then I'm even glad you have a boyfriend. I'm not here to destroy your new life, please believe me.'

I give him a cynical look that tells him very clearly that I have my doubts on that front, and he adds: 'I know. And I don't blame you. The way I was, all those years ago . . . the lies and the games and the damage I caused. I gave you no reason to ever believe me again. But I see that you've changed, Auburn, and I accept that. Is it so hard for you to imagine that I have as well?'

He's being so damn reasonable that I'm getting even more deflated. This whole thing would be easier if he acted like the monster I remember him as so capable of being. But in the same way that he looks the same but different, he's behaving the same but different – still the flirtatious tone, still the verbal caresses, still the slightly accented but perfect English that used to drive me wild – but combined with a brand-new sense of honesty and openness that I've never seen before, and don't know how to deal with.

Yes, he's right. He's definitely changed. But I don't want it to be any of my business – I want this new and improved version of Seb to be far away, in another land, with another woman, living a life removed from mine.

I hear my phone beeping in my pocket, and know that it will be Finn, or Willow, looking for me and checking that I'm still alive. Or Laura, telling me that her waters have broken over the wedding cake and I need to deliver twins. Even that would be preferable to this.

I shake my head, and decide to take the only sensible course of action.

'I've got to go,' I say. 'Back to the wedding. Back to my life. You stay here, do you understand? Do not follow me. Do not bring your whole Angel of Darkness aura into the pink paradise on the top of that hill. I'll find you later, and we'll talk, and then hopefully you can get on the next flight to Barcelona tomorrow. Understood?'

'Sure. Understood. I'll give you a call.'

Ha. He even has my phone number, presumably also from those pesky divorce letters.

'If you know my number, why didn't you warn me you were coming?' I ask.

'Because I knew you'd say no, querida, and I wasn't willing to let that happen without the chance to see you again.'

I would have said no, he's right. And that would have been so much easier.

He's smiling again, amused by how flummoxed I am, so I turn around and make a dignified exit. Or as dignified an exit as a woman dressed in a pink dress stomping through sand can possibly make.

Chapter 12

Every step I climb back up to the café leaves me more breathless, and more anxious. It's not a physical thing – I'm fit enough to walk up a hill despite my bad habits – it's an emotional one.

Seeing Seb has completely turned everything upside down. The simple joys of life I'd been relishing only minutes ago now feel at risk, jeopardised by his presence. Jeopardised by the effect his presence might have on me.

Already, I feel tangled up in his web – even if he is only here to apologise, to find some closure, to talk, I feel threatened by it. Threatened by him, and me, and by the spectre of the past tumbling into the present and messing everything up.

I reach the top of the steps and stand beneath the wrought-iron archway that welcomes visitors to the Comfort Food Café. I catch my breath, and look out at the dance floor. At Sam and Becca doing a comedic bump and grind, and Cherie wafting the arms of her kaftan around like Kate Bush, and Cal's pink cowboy hat getting thrown into the blueness of the sky, floating back down into his hands as he leaps to catch it.

I glance around looking for Finn, and instead find Willow, heading towards me in long strides in her pink Doc Marten boots.

'Who was that? Where did you go? What just happened?' she asks in a rush of concerned words, hands on her hips.

She sounds on the aggressive side, but it's only because she's worried about me. I smile as calmly as I can, and say: 'That, sister dearest, was an almighty dose of diary irony hitting me in the chops.'

'What?' she replies, frowning, 'Diary irony? What does that mean? Are you all right?'

'I'm not sure. I think maybe I was feeling a bit too happy. A bit too settled. So the universe had to come and knock me down a peg or two.'

'That's daft,' she says, reaching out to hold my hand. 'You shouldn't see the universe as your enemy. Was that . . . your ex? Or am I being mad and imagining things?'

'Yeah. It was. Weird, huh?'

'Weird, definitely. What did he want? And do you want me to track him down and assassinate him with my bare hands and a hair clip?'

I have to laugh at that. She looks completely serious about it, even though with her pink hair and height she'd hardly be the world's most anonymous secret killer.

'Not yet,' I reply. 'Though I might take you up on it at

some point, sis. Look, I'll talk to you more about this later, but I kind of need to go and find Finn, and have an intensely awkward conversation that I don't want to have.'

She nods, and pulls a sympathetic face.

'I can imagine. But it'll be fine – he'll understand. I think he was looking for you inside . . .'

I give her a quick hug to reassure her, and head off into the café. That's not quite as easy as it sounds, with so many now quite drunk people between me and the door, all of whom seem to want me to stop and dance.

I'm not exactly in the dancing mood, but manage to keep a smile plastered to my face as I make my way past them and into the building.

Inside, the café has been decked out in pink, with pink streamers and paper roses draped over all the dangling mobiles, and all the tables covered in pink gingham cloths. A few people are in here, having a sit-down and a break from the dancing, and I spot Laura and Matt crashed out on the comfy sofas by the bookcases in the corner.

They're both eating wedding cake, and look extremely content to be sitting together, watching the world go by. There's no sign of any imminent twin arrival, and I give them a little wave as I walk by.

I find Finn with Frank behind the counter, wielding a hammer as he helps fix the coffee machine again.

'Can't you persuade Cherie to replace that antique?' I ask as I approach them. 'It seems to break every other day.'

Frank looks up and grins at me, his blue eyes sparkling beneath a thick thatch of silver hair.

'Sentimental value,' he says, pointing at the side panel and telling Finn to 'whack it there'. Finn obliges, there's a hiss and a gurgle, and Frank nods his head in satisfaction.

'She's right as rain now,' he says, patting the top of the machine. 'Last another lifetime, she will.'

He gives us both a little salute, and walks off to wash his hands in the kitchen. I'm left with Finn, who is still holding the hammer, and looking at me cautiously.

'Are you okay?' he asks gently. 'Because you don't look it.'

'Oh. How do I look?' I ask, as he hooks the hammer back over the nail where it lives, ever-ready to be used in coffee machine assault and battery.

'You look,' he replies, turning around and gazing at me, 'like you've seen a ghost. Do you want to sit down? I can get you a coffee if you like . . .'

I shake my head. I don't think I need to be more wired right now. I can already feel my insides sloshing around like a bag of full water balloons, and I've bitten my lip so hard I taste blood. I desperately want to sneak outside and smoke twenty cigarettes, possibly all at once, but fight it down. Luckily, I don't have any, which helps the whole battle.

Without saying anything further, Finn reaches out and takes me into his arms. He holds me tight, rests his chin on the top of my head, and squeezes me so securely that I feel at least some of the tension fizz out of me. I breathe out, heavily, my face resting against his chest, the smell of his clean shirt and his body calming me even further.

'Whatever it is, it'll be okay,' he says, the words low and steady in my ear.

I nod and mumble something vague in response, and after a few moments of wallowing in his embrace, pull away and look up at him. He's tugged his tie loose and undone the top button of his white shirt, and he looks supremely dishy. It's a tribute to his handsomeness that even in a state of stress, I can make time to have a little lech.

I take his hand and lead him over to one of the small tables in the corner of the room. As soon as we're settled, I decide to plunge right in before I lose my nerve or even the ability to form sentences. I can already feel my toe tapping furiously on the floor, which is often a sign of a full-on meltdown fast approaching.

'Seb's here,' I say simply. 'You know, Seb, my . . . husband?'

He blinks, twice, in rapid succession – which in Finn world is a very extreme reaction. I see him school his face back to normal as he asks: 'Right. I see. And what does he want?'

He sounds calm, but I can't tell how real it is. Maybe he is totally fine with it, and I'm over-reacting, as usual.

'I don't know . . . to talk, he says. To apologise. To make amends for everything that happened . . .'

'Okay. And how do you feel about that?'

I reach out across the tabletop, and place both my hands over his. I look him straight in the eyes, and reply: 'Unhappy. Confused. Surprised. Annoyed. All kinds of things. But what I definitely don't feel is pleased to see him. Hopefully he'll be gone before too long, and we can get back to normal.'

Finn squeezes my fingers, and turns his face away to look out of the window. He's usually Mr Eye Contact, so that feels weird. Like he's avoiding me. Like he doesn't want to show me how he feels until he's had the chance to think it all through and see it from every possible angle. Usually I like his measured approach to life – in fact I marvel at it, it's so different than mine. But right now, I just want to feel like things are okay between us.

'I didn't invite him, Finn,' I say, keeping my voice even and trying not to show how much I'm freaking out inside. 'I had no idea he was coming, and would have stopped him if I did. I'm with you, and I'm happy with you, and I don't want you to feel bad about this. To feel . . . threatened in any way.'

He turns his gaze back to mine, his eyes so intense and so blue they make Paul Newman's look dowdy. He smiles, and says: 'I don't feel threatened, Auburn. I feel . . . concerned. Not about him, but about you. About how this will affect you, and us. Even talking about your life with this man was a head-fuck. Having him here will be far worse.'

Finn never swears. He's too much of a gentleman. The fact that he does belies the level tone of voice he's using, and I hate the fact that he's upset. He doesn't deserve it – any of it.

I start to spiral a little at that point, finding myself treading familiar paths that all end in the one destination: the one where I decide he doesn't deserve to be lumbered with me, becauseI'm not good enough for him, and I'm a natural disaster in human form, and I'm probably going to mess up his life.

I want to argue with him, and tell him he's wrong, that it'll all be easy and sorted and there are no complications to deal with – but I can't.

Instead I nod and blink away tears, and reply: 'I can see why you think that. You might be right. All I can say is that I'll talk to him, and try to get rid of him, and put all of this behind us. It might . . . well, it might even be good, in the end.'

I haven't expressed that very well, but I can tell he understands.

'It might,' he says, smiling gently at me. 'Seeing him again might prove to you that he's only a human being, like the rest of us. That he doesn't hold this superpower over you. That he's in the past.'

I'm pathetically grateful for that small speech, and for the effort he's making to help me through this. And I also think, genuinely, that he's right – I need to put Seb in the past, as a real-life living and breathing human person, not some creature from legend. He isn't an evil god, or an Angel of Darkness, or a super-villain – he's simply a man I used to love.

'How long is he staying for?' Finn asks.

'Two weeks, he says – but I'm hoping he won't be here that long. He seems . . . different.'

'In what way?'

I hesitate, pondering my answer. 'It's hard to put my finger on. Older . . . maybe less of a dick?'

Finn laughs abruptly, and it breaks some of the tension from the conversation.

'Well, less of a dick is always good,' he says, grinning at me. 'And two weeks isn't that long. But take it one step at a time, be honest with me about what you're feeling, and don't expect me to be perfect, okay? Beneath this calm exterior lies a normal bloke – one who gets jealous and doesn't always react rationally when it comes to the woman I love, and the man she's unfortunately still married to.'

I pull his face towards mine, and kiss him, long and hard.

'I love you,' I say, enjoying the sound of that on my lips and refusing to let Seb's sudden appearance ruin it. 'And you're not a normal bloke. You're the best bloke in the world.'

Chapter 13

I spend the night with Finn, because I think we both need the closeness and the reassurance.

The wedding party lasts until almost midnight, despite the fact that the bride and groom were whisked away in their pink limo by tea-time, and we all disappear off in different directions, across fields, into the village, to various farms and cottages, and in our case, all the way up the giant hill to Briarwood.

It's a long walk, but I'm both tipsy and adrenalised, and we make it home with several impromptu snogging sessions in hedgerows and country lanes. It seems as good a way to break up the journey as any.

By the time we get to Finn's flat, we're both tired, a bit less tipsy, and in my case have a scraped knee from an unexpected encounter with a kerb. What can I say? The pavement somehow leapt up at me, out of nowhere.

We don't even make love, we just fall into bed, wrapped in each other's arms, clinging on tight. I wake up that way too, my head on his chest, one arm slung across his waist, sprawled in a mess of sheets.

I stare at him while he's asleep, and try to stay very, very still so I don't disturb him. I like to do this – to admire the very bones of him, to look at his face, to gently touch the golden blond stubble on his jaw, and feel jealous of his eyelashes. He's a beautiful man, and sometimes I feel like I need to store up these images to keep in my mind-bank for later. Especially the morning after the wedding, when it feels like so much has happened.

I'm busily logging the sensual curve of his lips when he makes me jump by suddenly talking.

'Are you staring at me while I'm asleep?' he says, eyes closed. 'That's creepy.'

'I was,' I reply, 'but you're not asleep any more, so it isn't creepy. It's just . . . appreciative.'

'Right . . . well, thank you. Exactly how appreciative are you feeling?'

We spend the next hour or so demonstrating our mutual appreciation, before I finally drag myself out of his bed and into the shower.

When I get back, he's drifted off to sleep again, long limbs relaxed and languid, tan against the white of the sheets.

I sit beside him and place a little kiss on his forehead, not wanting to wake him, but feeling the need to say goodbye in some way.

He lazily opens his eyes and smiles up at me, one hand reaching out to stroke my hair. The sunlight is peeking around the edges of the curtains, and his face is striped in pale yellow.

'I love you,' I say simply, kissing the palm of his hand.

'I know,' he replies. 'I love you too. It'll all be okay, don't worry.'

He sounds confident and reassuring, but I can't help feeling a bit shaky about everything. Perhaps because I start from more wobbly foundations than Finn, or perhaps because I know myself too well – I am supremely gifted at screwing things up.

I give myself a pep talk as I leave, doing the walk of shame out into the morning light, and tell myself that two weeks of Seb will not in any way be able to negate what Finn and I have. And, in fact, if I have any control over it at all, he won't even be here for two weeks. Seb and I meant a lot to each other in another lifetime – but now, we don't. Simple.

I am so buoyed up by this pep talk that when I check my phone and see a text from him, I don't even freak out. In fact, I reply immediately, telling him I'll see him for lunch the day after – today, I'm otherwise booked looking after Mum while Willow and Tom spend some time together.

I make it home in record time, having decided right then and there that I'll take up jogging as a form of stress relief. I must have looked quite fetching, streaking through the fields in my pink dress and trainers, hair flying all over the place.

It does kind of work though – by the time I get back to our cottage, I'm completely incapable of worrying about anything more pressing then breathing, which certainly boots Seb out of my mind. Clearly all I need to do is keep myself in a suspended state of near physical collapse for the next fortnight and everything will be completely fine.

I spend a busy and relatively pleasant day with Mum, walking back across the fields to the café to help with the post-wedding clean-up. Saul is there with Katie, and Mum and him team up with bin bags and recycling boxes, while I help Cherie and Frank fold up all the extra chairs ready for the hire company to collect.

The garden's a bit of a pink war zone, covered in confetti, party-popper silly string and abandoned pink paper plates, and not especially helped by a galloping Midgebo, who stayed with Frank and Cherie overnight whileLaura and Matt had their one evening away.

The real honeymoon, Laura insists, will be taken in approximately three years' time, once the babies are old enough to not poo their pants and to sleep through the night and to possibly stay with someone else for a few days. Until then she seems to be anticipating a bleak regime of fatigue, chronic exhaustion and shuffling around in a zombie-like state. That seems overly pessimistic to me, but she's had two babies already, so she's coming at this from a position of superior knowledge.

I keep my mind occupied while I work, rehearsing speeches that I'll give to Seb the day after. Really good speeches, full of logic, super-calm, delivered with the perfect combination of conviction and civility. I've done this before, and it's always so annoying how the other party never seems to play along with the script.

I also realise, as I overhear a snippet of conversation between Cherie and Zoe, that I'm not the only person thinking about Seb this morning.

'Spanish, apparently,' Cherie is saying, scooping used plates into a bin bag. Her hair's tied up in a shabby bun, and her cheeks are rosy from the sunshine and the cleaning.

'On his own?' replies Zoe, sounding intrigued. 'No wife or kids of dogs with him?'

'Nope. Doesn't even have a Spanish name – Seb Martin. You wouldn't even suspect until you met him, and even then, it wouldn't be obvious where he's from. He has that slight accent that makes him sound a bit exotic and glamorous, and he looks . . .'

Cherie trails off as she says this, straightens up, and rubs the small of her back to relieve an ache.

'Looks what?' Zoe insists, 'Hideous? Frightening?'

'No,' Cherie replies, grinning. 'The opposite. A touch of Antonio Banderas. And a big dollop of Enrique Iglesias.

All dark and mysterious, but with these bright eyes, all gold and green and pale brown . . .'

'Cherie, I think you might need a sit-down,' says Zoe, laughing. 'You've gone all giddy! What would Frank say?'

Cherie snorts with amusement, and carries on cleaning.

'He'd offer to dress up like a matador and dance the paso doble around the bedroom!' she says. Crikey. As Frank is in his eighties, and Cherie in her seventies, I can only admire their energy levels.

I hover in the background as they chat, pondering whether to step in and confess all or not. It does feel weird, letting them continue to chat about Seb like this, but it would also feel weird to march up to them and say 'Hey! That's my hubby you're talking about!'

In the end I decide that pretending not to have heard is probably the best thing in the circumstances. Cherie would be upset if she knew I was upset about Seb being here. She obviously had no clue who he was when she rented him the cottage, and had no clue who he was when he came to collect the keys, and no clue who he might be married to. You don't automatically assume that stray Enrique lookalikes are wed to your mates, do you?

I am, however, compelled to listen in when I hear Zoe ask Cherie what he's doing here – handsome Spaniards don't usually come to our quiet part of the world on their own, and Zoe has a suspicious mind.

'Maybe he's on the run from a crime syndicate,' she says, staring off into the distance. 'Or a Mexican drug cartel. Or perhaps he's a spy, under cover . . .'

'Why would a spy be interested in Budbury, my love?' asks Cherie, obviously amused.

'No idea. But a lot goes on beneath the surface of these sleepy little places – look at the Wiltshire poisonings then other year! Dorset could be a hotbed of espionage for all we know . . .'

I can't help smiling at the thought, as I glance around at the various villagers present today. They all look a bit hungover and sweaty, and are dressed in shabby jeans and joggers and flip-flops and walking boots. It's not exactly a scene from *Casino Royale*.

'Sorry to rain on your parade, Zoe, but I don't think he's a spy,' says Cherie, as she ties up a full bin bag and lobs it onto a table.

'Why not?' replies Zoe, sounding extremely disap-pointed.

'Because he told me he was here for personal reasons. And when I got a bit nosy – it seems I'm prone to do that – he gave me this dreamy smile and said he was looking for a lost love he's never quite given up on.'

'Oooh . . . a lost love! That sounds almost as exciting as looking for stolen plutonium!'

I've done a good job of listening in sneakily so far, standing just enough far away to hear but not be that noticeable, keeping busy with my sweeping brush and not looking at all interested in their conversation.

Hearing myself described as a lost love, though? As a lost love he's never quite given up on? That's an eavesdrop too far. That's enough to make me drop the brush, go light-headed, and rush into the café to lock myself in the ladies' loo.

I sit on the closed lid, and put my head in my hands, and take some deep breaths. This would all be so much simpler if he really was a Russian spy, looking for pluto-nium.

Chapter 14

I get into the pharmacy later than usual the next day, as it's my turn to drop my mum at the day centre she goes to a few times a week. Willow has a big cleaning job on, and Van is working with Frank and Cal at Frank's farm.

I'm not feeling spectacular. I had a sleepless night, my brain on overtime, working in some kind of evil tag team partnership with my body to make every muscle tense and strung out. When I did snatch sleep, it was riddled with those lovely anxiety dreams where you're trying to walk through sludge in high heels or trying to open doors with keys that never fit. You know the ones.

Katie has opened up for me, and as I nudge back the door and hear the familiar ding-dong of the old-fashioned bell, I am already looking forward to coffee and maybe a whistle pop. I am prepared for the necessity of starting my day with sugar and caffeine to give me a kick-start.

What I'm not so prepared for is the sight of Seb, kneeling in front of a hugely preggers Laura, massaging her legs.

Katie meets my eye and shrugs as I walk in, then makes

the universal 'cup to lips' symbol that offers me coffee. I nod, and blink, and temporarily freeze on the spot.

Laura is making noises that by rights nobody but Matt should hear, groaning and sighing in what I have to presume is pleasure.

Seb, dressed in black jeans and a snug-fitting black T-shirt, is chatting to her as he works, in a tone of voice that is kind of hypnotic. Maybe, I think, that's his job now – he's a stage hypnotist, and before he leaves Budbury, we'll all be squawking like chickens every time we hear the word 'roundabout' or something.

He doesn't look behind him, but I'm guessing he knows I'm there from the fact that Laura notices me and says: 'Auburn – you must keep this man around! The Budbury pharmacy needs a massage therapist!'

I sit down, perched on the arm of the red velvet sofa, and he smiles up at me, still working on Laura but shifting his attention in my direction.

'Well, it looks like you're enjoying yourself,' I say, which is something of an understatement.

'I am. I'm sure Matt'll forgive me for saying this, but it's definitely better than our honeymoon night . . . that was mainly me passing out after dinner, then waking up with heartburn every ten minutes for the rest of the evening . . .'

She's had her eyes closed in ecstasy, but suddenly pops them open again when she realises she might have sounded a bit disloyal.

'Not that I'd change anything,' she adds hastily. 'I mean, Seb is wonderful with his hands, but Matt is the best.'

She blushes bright red, and I take pity on her and laugh. Seb always was good with his hands, I think, feeling a touch of a flush on my own cheeks as well. Whatever problems we had in our relationship, the sex wasn't one of them – in fact that was the last thing to work.

I shut down this train of thought, as I am also feeling a bit disloyal, and say: 'Seb, could I have a word with you? When you've finished?'

I head out to the small stockroom at the back, passing Katie as I go. She has a mug of tea for Laura, and a coffee which I take from her hands.

'Who is he?' she asks in a whisper, glancing over at Seb as he gives a very relaxed Laura a final pat on the knee. 'He turned up not long after we opened. Laura had called in for a natter, like she does, and they got talking, and before you know it, he was down on the floor rubbing her legs!'

'Yes, that's one of his skills,' I say a tad bitterly. 'Making women feel so comfortable they let their guard down . . .'

Katie doesn't answer that, and I see the concern in her eyes as she stares at me over the clouds of tea steam.

'Sorry,' I add quickly. 'Ignore the angst. That, Katie my dear, is Sebastian – my husband. Technically at least.'

'Oh! Right . . . wow. That's . . . odd. What's he doing here?'

'Looking for missing plutonium,' I say wisely, not exactly helping her feel less confused. 'Or something like that. The truth is, I haven't a clue. I was supposed to be meeting him later, but there you go. He never was very predictable. I better go and see what he's up to . . . What time is it, anyway?'

'Five past ten,' she says, her eyes darting to the clock on the wall above my head.

'Well he's only two hours early I suppose . . . I'll get rid of him for now, but will you be okay over the lunch hour?'

'Of course,' she says, nodding. 'Not a problem. By the way, Mr Pumpwell was in hospital over the weekend – he slipped and fell down some steps.'

I make an 'eek' face in response – the steps in his home are steep and made of stone and look like something out of a gothic horror story.

'Is he all right?' I ask.

'Reading between the lines, he's not brilliant – he's hurt his back – but he discharged himself from hospital as soon as he could, and got a cab home. They gave him some high dose codeine to take with him, but he might need some more. His GP's going out there today and says he'll send over any prescriptions later, if we can deliver them.'

For a blessed moment, all thoughts of Seb and his guerrilla massage warfare are bumped out of my mind, and I mentally schedule in a trip to see Mr P that afternoon. The stubborn old sod would have discharged himself even if he'd lost a leg, I suspect. He'll be worrying about his animals and his land, and won't be giving a second thought to his long-term health. He has that fatalistic outlook that a lot of older people have, the 'when your number's up, it's up' attitude.

I nod, and tell Katie that's fine, and I walk back into the stockroom. I'm so tired it's all I can do to keep my eyes open. Ironically, after spending the whole night trying and failing to get to sleep in a nice comfortable bed, I now feel like I could arrange myself on one of the metal shelves we use to store toilet roll and manage to drift off.

I sip my coffee while I try to plan what I might say to Seb. I don't have long, though, as he strolls right in almost immediately, looking around in curiosity.

The stockroom consists mainly of shelving units piled with boxes and plastic pallets, a small kitchen area with a sink and the all-important tea- and coffee-making facilities, and two doors that lead to the yard out back, and to the loo.

I gesture for Seb to follow me outside, as I'm perfectly well aware of the fact that voices carry from the stockroom out into the pharmacy. Everyone in the village will know soon enough who Seb is, but for the time being, I'll at least try to keep it private.

The yard is tiny and not especially picturesque. Katie has placed a few potted plants out here, and there's barely enough room for a patio table and two fold-up chairs. It's mainly the place where I sneak out for cigarettes – although I've been doing a lot less of that recently.

Being here with Seb, though, automatically has me reaching into my pocket for a pack that isn't there. He sees me do it, and grins.

'I've given up too,' he says, 'but there are some occasions when it would feel so right, aren't there?'

'Yep. So, apart from your impromptu pregnant lady fondling, why are you here? I thought we said we'd meet for lunch.'

I keep my tone civil and polite but firm – not wanting him to knowhow shaken I am by being around him, in case it gives him any ideas about his lost love still having feelings for him.

'I was just passing – honestly this time! I didn't even realise it was your place until I saw those pictures on the walls, the ones of you and – Katie, is it? – and your names underneath. I was only planning to have a look around, and I got chatting to Laura, and Katie, and . . . well, here we are.'

I'd like to call him a liar, but it's all perfectly reasonable. Lizzie designed the poster for us when we first opened up, me and Katie smiling down from the wall, trying to look all reassuring and professional, listing our various services.

'I'm impressed,' he says, when my only response is a nod. 'You've done well. I wouldn't have expected this to be your dream job . . .'

He's smiling wryly at me, and I know exactly what he means – it's a not-so-veiled reference to our former lifestyle, when prescription drugs were viewed mainly as potential highs.

'I'm not sure it ever was my dream job,' I reply, shrugging. 'But I'm good at it, and it's useful, and it helps people, which I've come to realise is important to me these days.'

'Me too,' he answers, his eyes never leaving mine and making me feel under way too intense a scrutiny. The yard is too small, and he is too close, and I am too befuddled.

'Are you a masseur then?' I ask, raising my eyebrows. It sounds ever-so-slightly naughty and suggestive, which would be exactly how I'd picture him ending up.

'Not the kind with happy endings,' he replies, sounding amused. 'Mainly sports massage. I do a lot of work with football clubs, tennis pros, that kind of thing. And some voluntary work at a few clinics and shelters.'

'Saving the world one rub-down at a time?' I ask cynically.

He doesn't look offended, and simply says: 'If you want to put it like that, then yes. But in my own way, I'm helping – people in rehab can benefit from it, and at the shelters it's sometimes the only human contact homeless people get. So no, maybe not saving the world – but making a bit of a difference to their world.'

I feel immediately shitty for the tone I used. He isn't bragging, or trying to impress, or buttering me up. And I do know how important human contact can be – I see the benefits it brings when I do my home visits, so I really shouldn't be mocking.

'Right,' I say, desperate to bring this conversation to a conclusion. 'Great. Well, look, I have work to do – can we go back to the original plan, and I'll meet you for lunch in a couple of hours?'

Instead of waiting for a reply, I go back inside, bid my farewells, watch him say goodbye to anow very relaxed Laura, and usher him out of the front door.

I fight the instinct to lock the door behind him, and take a few huge breaths to calm myself down as he walks away. I put on my 'everything's fine' face and walk back towards my friends.

Katie is making herself busy dusting shelves that are already spotless – she's one of those women who cleans when she's unsure of herself, just one of the things that make her a superb employee – and Laura is holding her tea in both hands, resting the mug on the round mound of her belly. She'll miss that extra table when it's gone.

I decide that the quickest way for everyone to find out about Seb will be to tell Laura. She can keep a secret when she needs to, but she's also a key branch on the village grapevine, and will spread this particular gossip effectively and quickly, thus saving me the job of repeating myself over and over again and answering loads of questions and or listening to women compare him to Enrique Iglesias or other Latin love gods.

'That,' I say, flopping down next to her, 'was my husband. Feel free to tell everyone, you'll be doing me a favour.'

She does a cartoonish double take, and her jaw drops open.

'Seb? The massage man? He's your husband? The one you're trying to divorce?'

'The very same.'

'But . . . but . . .'

I watch her as the cogs turn in her brain, and I see her both ask and answer the question that immediately springs to mind: Why would I divorce a man like that? A man who looks so beautiful, and has magic hands, and is so ridiculously charming? Because there must be more to it than meets the eye . . .

'Well,' she says, firmly, 'all relationships have their stories, don't they? And I know everyone thinks I'm obsessed with happy endings, but I'm not so naive as to think all marriages are made in heaven. And anyway – I bet Finn can give great massages too!'

He can, as a matter of fact, even without the professional training. I plant his image firmly in my mind, and use it as a kind of talisman to ward off evil spirits.

'I feel awful now,' continues Laura, plaintively. 'I feel a bit like I've betrayed you somehow . . .'

'Don't be daft,' I say as decisively as I can. 'You had no

way of knowing. And even if you had known, so what? He's only here so we can . . .sort a few things out before we go ahead with the divorce.'

'Oh. Right. Is it complicated?' she asks, raising her eyebrows. 'Is there shared property, or . . . a pet? I'm assuming no kids?'

'No kids. And no pets.And . . . well, no shared property either. But I suppose we need to have a proper talk before it all goes ahead. At least he thinks we do, which is why he's here.'

'And what do you think?'

She's looking at me with deep concern, her pretty face serious.

'I think I need to get some work done,' I reply, dismissing the whole question. It's too complex, and I'm too tired, and the Seb effect has left me feeling ever-so-slightly unhinged.

She nods, and accepts this, although she clearly knows there is more to be discussed at some point or another.

'Fair enough,' she responds, gearing up to perform the seventeen-point manoeuvre that is Heavily Pregnant Woman Standing From Low Sofa. 'I need to get on anyway . . .'

By this, I suspect she means 'get to the café to tell Cherie all about Seb', which all fits into my evil masterplan.

I help her to stand up, then wave her off, watching her toddle down the street as I wonder what to do next.

As the answer to that question seems to be 'I have absolutely no idea', I am way too thrilled when a pharmaceutical rep appears unannounced on the doorstep, wanting to talk to me about my current stock of laxatives. I end up keeping her there for an hour, examining the various benefits and costs of her new range, and ultimately order way more than the combined bowels of Budbury will need in a year, purely out of gratitude for having something else to do.

I fill out a couple of prescriptions, help Katie check stock, and ping off a couple of texts to my nearest and dearest. I even jump in front of the till and serve some passing tourists from our fine selection of postcards – all pictures taken by Lizzie – in an attempt to keep my head straight.

By midday, when I set off for lunch with Seb, I'm almost feeling normal again – although that goes right out of the mental window as soon as I arrive at our designated meeting spot and see him sitting in the beer garden, leaning back with his eyes closed, sunlight shining on his dark hair, looking like a cat soaking up the rays.

I walk towards him, giving myself a big telling off as I do. Something about being near him knocks me off balance, makes me feel edgy, tense. Not quite normal. I recognise it as the way I felt for all the years I was with him, and wonder how I managed to escape without becoming a complete basket case. Maybe I didn't.

I also wonder, as I approach him, if it will ever go away – or if he'll always have this kind of hold over me. Maybe, if I see him every day for the next two weeks, I'll get used to it. Maybe familiarity will cure me. Maybe I'll be able to shake off the Seb effect, and react to seeing him in exactly the same way I do when I see Scrumpy Joe, our local cider maker, or Frank, riding round on his tractor.

It's a nice prospect, but I'm not quite there yet, I think, as I feel my heart racing and my blood pressure undoubtedly doing something quite unhealthy inside my veins.

He waves at me when he notices me walking towards him, and I see that he's already bought me a glass of something wine-like. I decide I won't drink it, because I want it too much – it would soothe my nerves and act like a legal anaesthetic, but drinking for need is a slippery slope that it took me a while to climb back up from. Whatever the outcome of him appearing in my life again, I won't let it take me down in that way. In any way.

It's early for lunch, and only a few tables are taken, mainly by older couples or young families trying to keep toddlers entertained with bowls of chips while they get a few minutes to sink a pint. This place – the Drunken Sailor – is a good twenty-minute drive away from the village, and mainly used by tourists and visitors.

It felt a bit safer meeting him here, rather than anywhere local – a bit less likely to taint my home turf with his aura.

It's also in a very picturesque spot perched on the cliffs

like the Comfort Food Café, but further along the coast, with views down over Lyme Bay, which is looking especially splendid in the sunlight today. The air feels warm and comforting, and it's reaching the glorious stage of the year where everything is green and lush and it's hot enough to start leaving coats at home.

He stands up and leans in for a kiss. I dodge it with as much style and grace as a baby elephant, and sit opposite him on the bench, feeling a blush sweep over my cheeks. The fact that I'm blushing makes me embarrassed, so I blush even more. His little smile tells me he's noticed, and I wonder if it would be possible to shove him off the edge of the cliff accidentally on purpose.

'Hi,' he says simply, gesturing at the wine. 'I got you a drink.'

'Thanks, but I'll fetch a Coke in a minute. I don't have a lot of time.'

'That's okay. Has the new Auburn given up on drinking as well?'

'No, but the new Auburn is driving, and it's only lunchtime, and she has a lot to do today. The new Auburn has a drink whenever she wants one . . .but she's learned to control it.'

She also, I think, seems to have started talking about herself in the third person, which is weird.

'I'm a lot more in control these days,' I say, putting third-person Auburn in a cupboard. 'It's intentional. I was a mess by the time I . . . by the time I came back to the UK. It's taken me a long time and a lot of effort to get . . . well, less messy.'

He nods, and leans back, stretching long legs out in front of him. I hastily rearrange my feet, worried about even our footwear connecting.

'Maybe that's where I should start,' he says, fixing me with a no-nonsense look as he notices how nervous I am. 'By telling you that I'm not here to mess you up again. I promise you, 100 per cent, that's not what I intend.'

I nod, and look away. He sounds sincere, but even if he's being truthful, it doesn't help that much – because whether he intends to or not, this is all making me feel a bit of a mess. I'd been strong and hopeful and optimistic before – and now I'm biting my nails and feeling nostalgic for the days when pubs used to have cigarette vending machines on their walls. It might not be intentional, but having him this close is unnerving.

'So, a lot has happened since then,' he says, when I don't reply. 'For both of us. Maybe we could start by sharing that?'

'You go first,' I reply quickly, not at all certain of how much I want to tell him about my life.

He laughs, and one of the mums at the table next to us gazes at him, glass of lager paused halfway to her lips as she stares. He has that power, Seb – he draws in the admiring looks, and women behave like horny bees around a honeypot. The woman's toddler daughter throws a chip at her face with perfect timing, and the spell is broken.

'Right . . . well, there was rehab. My parents insisted on that, and I was in no position to argue. When they told me you'd left, that nobody could find you, I didn't believe them. I thought maybe you'd gone off to party somewhere, forget all about me for a weekend, but that you'd be back. That we'd try again.

'It was only when I got back to the flat and saw that your things were gone that I accepted it. I was still bruised from the crash, and you'd gone, and I guess I was having the mother of all comedowns . . . I kind of lost the will to fight them on the rehab front. So, I was in a residential place outside Madrid for two months. That was fun.'

'Was it?' I ask, refusing to apologise for my disappearance even though something very English in me automatically wants to.

'No, it wasn't. There was a lot of talking therapy, and group therapy, and family therapy. It was . . . hard. It made me see myself in a way I didn't want to see myself.'

'Did it work though?' I say, knowing how hard that must have been for him. Heck, how hard it would probably be for any of us.

'Eventually. Not to start with though – going to rehab because you don't have the energy to fight it probably isn't the best of starts. There were . . . slips. I relapsed a couple of times. It didn't quite take hold until I actually wanted it to. I'd go through the motions and pass all the tests and convince everybody that I was fine. But until I genuinely wanted to do it, it was all empty words. Short-term promises. I always fell back, was always looking for some way to fill the missing part . . .'

I see him falter, and hope he's not about to make some big claim that the missing part was me – because that simply isn't true. I was as much a symptom of his problems as a cause.

'To start with, I thought maybe it was you I was missing – but obviously, it wasn't. And it's not fair for me to have even thought that.I suppose things properly changed when I started my training. Initially it was physio, then I decided to specialise in massage therapy. I had a reason to get up in the morning, which give me a reason to go to sleep at night, and a reason to stay sober. I moved out of the flat and back home with my parents, and stopped seeing our old crowd.'

'That was a good move. There's no way you could hang around with the twenty-four-hour party people and live a normal life. And I can't believe you stayed in that flat for so long . . .'

He shrugs, and replies: 'It was easy. Or I thought it was anyway. With hindsight? Not the brightest of decisions. So, once I'd moved, and was training, and working, and exercising, and drinking kale smoothies, and doing everything right, it became easier to say no to all the things

I used to say yes to. And it became easier to be open with the people around me, to explain why I didn't go boozing after classes, or join in with social events so much, or trust myself with anything stronger than a bottle of lavender oil for a while . . .'

I have to laugh at the image that immediately pops into my mind, and I say: 'Be honest – did you ever sniff the lavender oil?'

'Hey, I'm only human!' he replies, holding his hands up in guilt. He smiles at me, and for a moment – one tiny, teeny weeny moment – I remember how special a woman can feel when bathing in the brilliance of one of Seb's smiles.

I don't smile back. It would be a step too far, too soon. Instead, I ask: 'And that was it? You were miraculously cured?'

'It wasn't miraculous, it was a lot of hard work. And I know myself a bit too well to use the word "cured". I view it as being in remission . . . hopefully for the rest of my life. It helped that I finally told my parents everything – about that night. The night of the accident.'

I look away and study the child at the next table instead of meeting his eyes. She's colouring in a printed sheet that has line drawings of dinosaurs on it. It looks peaceful, and I wonder if I could ask the staff for one myself. It would definitely be more calming than this conversation, or the memories it's triggering.

I don't like thinking about all of this stuff. About the night of the accident. About the look on his parents' faces in the hospital. The way they were so disappointed, so angry, so worried. It felt unfair at the time, and I suppose deep down, it always has. I had plenty of things to blame myself for, but driving that car wasn't one of them. Accepting it had felt like a kind of penance, I suppose. A dumb way of making up for my mistakes.

'Right. Well. That's good. They hated me so much . . .'

'I know. And it wasn't fair, and it wasn't healthy – while they could hate you, they could let me off the hook again, couldn't they? If they could blame all the bad things on the wife, they could allow me to escape the consequences. Even I started to see that, and I started to feel guilty about it.'

'Guilty?' I say, my eyes wide in disbelief. 'You?'

He nods. 'It was quite the novelty for me. I didn't like it at all – but once it started, I couldn't stop it. It's like after years of telling myself everything I did was okay, I suddenly realised it wasn't. I realised how much I'd done wrong. How badly I'd behaved. How much I'd hurt you. The way I'd deceived my parents. The damage I'd done. So I told them – I had to.

'My dad was furious with me. My mum . . . well, she did a lot of that shout-talking that she does, ranting away and waving her arms and crying, but she was always ready to forgive. That's what mums do, isn't it?'

I nod. It is, I think – although in Lynnie's case everything is a grey area.

'I bet they still hate me,' I reply, smiling bitterly, staring at the wooden grain of the tabletop, and wondering why I even care what his parents think.

'My mum probably does . . . but then again, I suspect she'd hate any woman I brought home with me . . . Not my dad though. He didn't hate you, Auburn.'

I notice the use of past tense, and lift my gaze back to Seb.

'What happened?' I ask, feeling a swell of sadness at the look on his face, and the failed attempt at a nonchalant shrug.

'Heart attack, a year ago. It is what it is.'

I reach out and touch his hand, just once, just lightly, and say: 'I'm sorry. I always liked your dad. How's your mum coping without him?'

He laughs, and squeezes my fingers before letting them go.

'Oh, as you'd expect– wearing black. Going on a lot of holidays with her other merry widow friends. Constantly harassing me about the fact that she wants grandchildren.'

She was always doing that, I remember – she even asked if I was expecting on the day of our wedding, her tone somehow managing to combine both horror and hope. Seb's in his mid-thirties now – young for a man, but in her eyes, maybe time is running out. Being a matriarch to only one must be disappointing for her.

'I can imagine. Does she . . . know you're here? Doing this?'

'Yes,' he answers, surprising me. He sees my look, and continues: 'No more lies. That's kind of a rule with me now. So yes, I told her. And yes, she was about as happy with it as you'd imagine.'

'Did she throw any plates?'

'An ashtray. Kind of at my head, but aimed just far enough away to miss.'

I laugh, and can perfectly picture the scene.

'Why now, though, Seb?' I ask, changing the subject. I don't want to think about his dad, or his widowed mum. I don't want to feel sorry for him, and sucked into his life again. 'Why didn't you try and find me earlier, if you were so sorry, and wanted to make amends?'

'Well. That's a complicated question.'

'No it's not.'

'Okay, maybe it's a complicated answer then . . . Look, I did consider it earlier. My therapist thought it would be helpful if I could track you down, say my piece, move on. But I never quite felt ready. I never felt strong enough.

'Then my dad died, and that . . . changed me. Made me think about things even more. So when your divorce papers arrived, I took it as a sign. A sign that I should finally come and see you.'

'You do realise that's not the purpose of divorce papers, don't you?' I say. 'Traditionally they're issued to mark the end of a marriage – not as a cue to re-start one.'

'Ah, yes – but I'm not a very traditional person, am I? Those who know me well might even say I can be deliberately awkward about these things. So, the divorce papers. My dad. Time. Therapy. All of it, I suppose – all of it combined somehow added up to me getting on a plane to London and coming here and finding you. To be with you again, to tell you . . .'

He pauses, and runs his hands through his thick hair, and takes a deep breath. I should probably step in and make it easier for him, but I think I need to let him say his piece. Get it over with, for both our sakes.

'I genuinely am so very, very sorry, Auburn, for everything,' he says. 'Not just that one night, but the whole thing. The way I manipulated you and lied to you and dragged you down with me when you were trying to change. I knew you were, and I resented it – I was a child who didn't want anyone else to have the sweets I couldn't have. All you were doing was trying to help me, and I even resented you for that.

'Later, after the first few attempts at my own rehab, I still didn't think it would ever happen for me. I still didn't believe in my own ability to change, to be better. I still didn't think it would ever stick. So I decided the very best way I could show I was sorry was to leave you alone. To give you a chance to live without me. To let you heal. Does that make any sense at all?'

I have to admit, it kind of does. Even now, after all this time, sitting here with Seb is knocking me off balance. If he'd reappeared in my life a month after I left – heck, a year after I left – things could have gone very differently for me.

I always found him so stupidly hard to resist, and it was only putting an ocean between us that allowed me to move on. If he'd done then what he's doing now – turned up on my doorstep in all his glory, begging my forgiveness – then maybe I would have weakened. Maybe I would have plunged straight back into the whirlpool, and drowned for good that time.

'Yes,' I say quietly. 'It does make sense. And . . . thank you. I needed that time. I needed to be away from you. I needed to see who I could be without you. I'm sorry I did it the way I did, but I felt like I had to escape. Does that sound awful? It probably does. But I think you get what I mean.'

He nods, and smiles gently, and replies: 'I get it. You needed to leave. I know that, and even though it hurt at the time, it was the only thing you could have done. For both of us. And who you are without me seems . . . good. Better than good. You have your work, your home, your family. This beautiful place where you live. You seem . . . a lot more together.'

'Ha!' I say, snorting. 'Well, I could hardly be less together, could I? But yes . . . I am. It's not been easy. It's taken time. There are complications – family stuff. Me stuff. It's probably never going to be easy – I'm not made that way – but I'm making it work. I am.'

'And are you happy, Auburn? Here, with this life?'

'Yes,' I say firmly, not willing to give him an inch for fear of him taking quite a few miles. The new Seb might not be as reckless as the old one, but he could potentially be every bit as dangerous.

'I am,' I repeat. 'Very happy. With my family, and my job, and my boyfriend.'

'Ah. Yes. The boyfriend . . . is it serious?'

'It is,' I reply. 'He's . . . calm. And steady. And kind.'

'That sounds exciting,' he replies, a touch of sarcasm tinging his words.

'And gorgeous and ripped and looks like a Viking warrior and is brilliant in bed,' I add. For balance, you understand.

He laughs, and I have to join in. This is so very, very weird – extolling Finn's virtues to my estranged husband in a beer garden.

'That's more like it,' he says, grinning. 'I'm happy for you.'

'Good. Not that I'd care if you weren't. What about you? It's been years. I assume your libido hasn't been in rehab as well. Any sign of those grand-babies your mum wants so much?'

He gives me a crooked smile, and a feral look in his

eyes tells me that no, his libido is still very much intact. He replies: 'Of course there have been other women. As you say, it's been years.'

I can't think why I asked the question, or what I hoped I might gain by it. Why I was even interested in Seb's love life.

Whatever my motivations or expectations, what I actually get is a sudden and blinding lightning bolt of jealousy that comes from nowhere, and leaves me feeling raw and jagged. Feeling jealous is wrong, and it's inexplicable, and it's completely inappropriate, so I try very hard not to let any of that momentary surge of emotion show on my face.

The look he gives me tells me I haven't quite managed, and he adds: 'Nobody special though, in case you were wondering.'

'I wasn't!' I say emphatically. 'You could have shagged your way around the whole of Europe for all it matters to me!'

Clearly, I'm protesting too much, and I hate the slightly smug way he raises his hands in surrender. I hate the fact that I felt jealous, even for a nano-second, and I hate that he knows me well enough to read it.

I hate everything – but mainly the fact that Seb still has this power over me. We've sat here, and had this conversation, and it's taken around twenty minutes. During that twenty minutes, I've felt sad, scared, anxious, amused, challenged, and jealous. All of the stuff is here, and a lot of it is completely unrequited.

This is one of the things about Seb and me that made it so hard to get away the first time. He makes me feel so much, almost against my will. Nobody has ever been able to pull my strings quite like this man, and it looks like I haven't quite cut all of them yet.

'I'm getting a drink,' I announce, standing up abruptly and stomping off to the bar inside. I need a few seconds away, to decompress and level out. I need a large Jack Daniels and Coke, but I settle for the latter half only, taking my time before I go back outside again.

When I do, I see that the little girl from the next table is standing by his side, showing him her colouring in. He's making appreciative noises, and ooh-ing and aah-ing at a bright pink T-rex, and it's all disgustingly sweet. She waddles back over to her watchful parents as I sit down, and I deliberately make no reference to it at all.

'Okay,' I say, stretching the word out and hoping I sound calm and in control. 'So now we've caught up. I'm genuinely glad you've sorted your life out, Seb, and I'm so sorry about your dad. And I appreciate your apology. But ultimately, it changes nothing – I still want a divorce, and I don't think there's any need for you to stay here any longer.'

He ponders this, his eyes fixed on mine as he sips his water, and eventually nods.

'Like I said, Auburn, I'm not here to mess things up. Or to stop the divorce. I'm here because I wanted to see if there was anything left between us, before we finally make it official. To see if the spark that drew us together in the first place is as bright as I remember.'

'Seb,' I say, exasperated, 'the spark that drew us together never even existed! We were both . . . young. Stupid. Drunk. High. What we thought we had together wasn't even real – it was based on a mutual love of a lifestyle that we now both know wasn't sustainable. In fact it was probably going to kill us just in time to join the 27 Club. It wasn't a spark, it was . . . one of those raging bush fires that kills hundreds of people!'

He nods, and lays his hands on the table placatingly.

'I understand that,' he replies gently. 'And so much of what you say is true. But not all of it . . . not everything. There was something, Auburn – something between us that was special. Pure. I'd never met anybody before you who had that kind of effect on me, and certainly not since. You're the only woman I've loved and wanted to share my life with. I'm not ready to throw that away so easily. And deep down, I don't think you are either. Not yet.'

I close my eyes and take a deep breath, trying not to explode. I'm not only angry with him, I'm angry with myself. I'm angry with myself because maybe, just maybe, there's a tiny part of me that thinks he's right. That we have unfinished business. That I still care. That I still haven't quite managed how to learn how to live my life free of his influence. That so long as he can keep pulling those strings, there will always be a part of me that's a puppet.

That was easier to cope with when he was hundreds of miles away, in another world, another lifetime. When I had him all boxed away in a file marked 'ancient history'. Now he's here, all tall and dark and handsome and saying all these things. Confusing me and befuddling me and saying too many things.

Things that I want to dismiss, to ignore, to deny. But I can't quite do that – because if I do, I'll always feel like a coward. I'll always feel like I ran away rather than facing the pain head-on. I'll always feel like he's part of me – and I don't want him to be part of me.

Ironically, I'm coming to the conclusion that the only way to make sure he doesn't stay a part of me is to let him at least try. Giving both of us the opportunity to realise that it's totally, completely, 100 per cent over. Giving my relationship with Finn a fighting chance, by having enough faith in it to confront this.

I look up, into the gold and the green and the brown of his eyes, and shake my head in frustration.

'And after this visit? After you've found out whatever it is that you need to find out? Once you've finally accepted that there's nothing left between us, between the people we are now, accepted that it's over? Then, Seb, you'll leave?'

'I'll leave,' he says solemnly, crossing his chest in a gesture I associate much more with his very Catholic mother. 'I promise you that.'

Chapter 15

I call at the café on the way back to the village. I completely
failed to eat lunch during actual lunchtime, and don't
even feel much like it now. But I know that if I let my
blood sugar do insane things, then the rest of me will
follow, and do even more insane things.

Laura has been busy. By the time I make it to the top
of the hill and through the doors, it's obvious that my
secret husband is a secret no more.

'Auburn!' bellows Cherie, as soon as she sees me. 'Do
you want me to boot him out of the Rockery? Heck, do you
want me to boot him out of Budbury?'

I look at her, the best part of six foot and a force to be
reckoned with, and decide she probably could boot him
out of Budbury if she tried. I grin, and shake my head,
and say: 'No, but thanks for the offer. It's always good to
know I have back up.'

'Damn right,' she says, reaching out and pummelling
my shoulder in a way that's probably supposed to be jokey,
but is actually quite painful. 'Always. What can I get you?'

'Whatever. I'm not hungry, Cherie, but I need to eat. Keep myself on the straight and narrow.'

She looks at me in mock horror, obviously finding it hard to imagine a world where someone isn't hungry, and sets about gathering up various food items while I perch at the counter. There are quite a few people in today, enjoying the sunshine for walks along the coastal paths and calling here for a drink or a snack. It's unusually busy, and I see my sister bustling around serving and taking orders.

Zoe, who runs the Comfort Books store next door, slinks into the stool next to me and gives me a nudge. She's practically a midget, and her legs swing in the air rather than touch the floor.

'I hear your husband's turned up,' she says, raising her eyebrows and grinning. It's good that I'm giving people such comic relief, I think – spreading a little joy in the world one disastrous life choice at a time.

'He has,' I reply simply.

'And I hear he's a sexy Spaniard.'

'He is,' I say. No denying it.

'And didn't you have a fling with that dance teacher last year – Mateo? Wasn't he Spanish too?'

'His family was from Portugal.'

'And Finn's part Danish?'

'Yep.'

She grins some more, and nods, and adds: 'Wow. I can guess which way you voted during Brexit.'

I groan, roll my eyes, and deliberately kick her tiny feet off the stool foot-rest.

'You look like a ventriloquist's dummy, sitting on that stool,' I say, as she rearranges herself.

'True,' she replies, laughing. 'It's my sexiest look. Anyway . . . now I've taken the urine out of you for a bit, are you okay? Must be weird having him back here. Anything I can do to help? I read a lot of crime fiction. I can come up with many ways to kill someone quietly and dispose of the body.'

'It's super sweet of you to offer, Zoe, but I don't need the ginger assassin's services yet. I think . . . I think it might be a good thing that he's here.'

I'm feeling my way around this whole situation, and testing the words out on Zoe. Maybe before I use them on Finn, who knows? Although he's usually ten steps ahead of me on the whole 'what's-good-for-Auburn' front anyway.

'How so?' she asks, looking up at me quizzically.

'So I can finally put it all behind me. It all ended a bit dramatically, you see – no time for goodbyes or heart-to-hearts or soul-searching. And I thought that was fine – but maybe it's not. Maybe things that happened to us in the past actually affect our present.'

She widens her eyes, and makes a fake-impressed face.

'Really?' she says, sarcastically. 'You think so? That's quite a revelation. I think you should call the International

Ruling Council of Psychiatrists and Brain Fiddlers and tell them about this breakthrough you've made.'

Cherie pauses in front of us and places a tuna and cheese panini in front of me with a small bow. I scoop off a tiny bit of tuna, and flick it at Zoe's face.

'I'm sorry,' she says, wiping it off with a napkin without complaint. She lives with a teenager and an Australian cowboy – she's probably used to food fights. 'My default setting is mockery,' she adds, balling up the tissue. 'Seriously, though, you might be right. In fact, you're definitely right. We all have stuff, don't we? Stuff from the past that we think is dead and buried and every now and then it sneaks up on us and whacks us over the head with a cartoon mallet. Maybe this is your chance to whack it back. Put it in its place.'

'That,' I say, between chews, 'is the cunning plan.'

She takes advantage of the fact that I'm busy eating to carry on talking at me.

'If it was me, it wouldn't go to plan,' she says, shrugging. 'Nothing in my life ever goes to plan. I didn't plan for my best friend to die and leave me to raise her daughter. I didn't plan for Martha to go off the rails and have to move her here to get her away from the city. I didn't plan to fall for her biological dad, or to stay here. But . . . I suppose it's worked out all right, all things considered. I'm sure it will for you as well. Just . . . I don't know. Have a bit of faith, I suppose.'

I nod, and chew, and eventually speak: 'That's what I'm telling myself. A little faith. And now . . . I must leave you, my sinister-yet-wise dwarf friend.'

I climb down from the stool, leave some cash for Cherie, and give Willow a wave as I make my way through the crowded tables to the garden.

There's an honesty box set up out there for people who don't want to come into the café, and I leave a fiver in exchange for two small packets of Laura's home-made white chocolate-chip cookies. It's more than the going rate, but all the extra cash is donated to the day centre my mum attends, so it's a win-win. Biscuits, and a good deed, all at the same time.

I leave the van in the car park and walk back to the pharmacy, enjoying the fresh air and the sunshine, and hoping the exercise will stop my brain going into overdrive. The more I use my legs, the less I use my imagination, which in current circumstances can only be a good thing.

Katie is gazing out of the window sipping a mug of tea when I arrive, and instantly looks guilty when she spots me. I can tell from the lemony fragrance in the air that she's cleaned the whole place, and I also spot that she's rearranged the nappies. A new supply of nail varnishes has been unpacked and arranged on the display cabinet, and I have a sneaking suspicion she's hoovered as well.

'Slacking again, are we?' I ask, mock angry.

She looks momentarily taken aback, then she remembers

that she's a mouse that can roar, and I see her search for a suitable retort.

'Fiddlesticks!' she says grandly, looking proud of herself.

Well, that told me. I smile, and wave the cookies in front of her face.

'I brought treats,' I say, tearing open the bag and offering her one.

'How did it go?' she asks quietly, as she fishes a crumbly cookie from the bag and nibbles at it. 'If you don't mind me asking.'

'It was . . . okay. Not easy. But okay. We caught up. It was all fairly civil.'

On the outside, at least, I think. Inside, it's left me feeling raw and vulnerable, and I'm sure Seb isn't on top of the world either. Revisiting your past disasters is never pleasant, especially when we have so many to choose from.

'Oh, good. I was a bit worried.'

'Listening out for sirens, were you? Police helicopters hovering overhead perhaps? Thought you might see my photofit on *Crimewatch*?'

'No! Well . . . maybe a bit. It's been quiet here.'

I nod, and eat my cookie. It's often quiet here. It's one of the reasons I like it. At first, I thought I'd be bored – I was used to working in an inner-city pharmacy in London, which has a completely different customer base and a lot more people queuing up for their methadone prescriptions.

I suppose accepting the quietness, and the slower pace of life, has all been part of the last year's self-development. Being willing to be still, and enjoy the calmness in a way I never have previously. I think, in some ways, I always needed to be hectic before to keep me distracted from the way I was feeling. It helped to chase away the ever-lurking sense of pointlessness.

Now, I don't need so many distractions. I've found a place where people accept me, and more importantly, where I'm starting to accept myself. Seb being here might disrupt that, but I hope it's only temporary – and once he's gone, I'll feel even better. Maybe I'll start meditating, or yogic flying, or become a self-help guru, or . . . well, maybe I'll be able to stop and smell the roses. That'll be enough. I do like the smell of roses.

'I think I might shut up shop early,' I announce to the non-existent crowds of customers. 'Katie, you're off to get Saul from school anyway soon, aren't you? I think I'll give Mr Pumpwell a call, see how he's getting on and how hard he pretends he's not in pain, and then . . . well . . . then I'll smell the roses for a bit.'

Katie's head is perched to one side, and she's looking a little confused. I realise that my interior monologue just became exterior, and shake my head.

'Don't worry about it. I'm fine. What have you got planned for the rest of the day?'

She blushes slightly, and gives me a small smile.

'Ah. Is Van coming around for his tea?' I ask. 'Followed by outrageously wild sex?'

I know that'll embarrass her, which is most of the fun. Sure enough, she looks horrified, then folds her arms over her chest and replies: 'I wish! With a four-year-old in the house, it's not so much outrageous as very, very careful . . . although we've already decided we're going to say we're playing Twister if he ever catches us at it . . .'

'You can't say that to Saul,' I insist. 'He'll want to join in.'

She ponders this, and I can see she agrees. Back to the drawing board.

'Bring Saul round to the cottage for a night,' I say, as I shoo her towards the back room to gather her belongings. 'We'll look after him for you, while you and my brother dearest play Twister. You could even go away for the night. Stay in a hotel, drink room service champagne, wear those little slippers with the cardboard feet . . .'

She nods as she slips on her jacket and picks up her bag.

'We did get one night together last month,' she says, 'where my mum took Saul to Bristol to see her sister. We played an awful lot of Twister while he was gone.'

I decide that the Twister analogy is working well for me, even if not for Saul. It allows me to think about my brother and Katie's physical relationship in a way that is both suggestive in a *Carry On* film fashion, but also deliberately obscure. I know he's a grown man, but I don't like to have those images in my mind. It'd be weird if I did, I suppose.

'How is your mum?' I ask, as Katie waits for me to sort the lights and lock up. Her mother, Sandra, moved to Budbury shortly before Christmas after splitting up with her dad. After a brief attempt at a reconciliation, they now seem decidedly apart – which has come as a big relief to Katie, who was raised with the two of them re-enacting World War II around her.

'She's good, thanks,' Katie replies. 'I think she might move back to Bristol soon though. It's been nice for her, staying in Cherie's flat over the café, working there – it gave her time to regroup. But I wouldn't be surprised if she makes the devastating announcement that she's leaving before long.'

I can tell from the tone of voice that Katie will be far from devastated – in fact she'll probably throw a party. Sandra is quite the drama queen, and Katie is the complete opposite.

We leave the pharmacy together, making small talk as we walk to the van, and I drop Katie off at Saul's primary school in the next village. The school gates are milling with mums, some with pushchairs, all gabbing away as they wait for their offspring. It looks like hell, and I wish her luck as I pull off into the road again.

I head towards Mr Pumpwell's cottage, deciding that I might as well visit him in person so he can't lie as easily.

He's the kind of man who, if asked where his pain lies on a scale of one to ten, will always answer with zero, and will call a broken vertebra a 'crick in the neck'.

I park outside his cottage and beep the horn twice to give him my usual warning. The cottage isn't especially pretty or chocolate box – parts of it are very old, parts of it added on higgledy-piggledy as the need arose over different generations.

I can hear the various noises of the animals as I walk towards the cottage door, and wonder if he's managed to get out to feed them. This used to be part of a much bigger farm, owned by Mr P's parents and their parents before them and . . . well, you get the picture. Once it became clear that Mr P wasn't going to carry on the family line, he made the practical decision to sell off a lot of his land, keeping enough acres around him to maintain his solitude, but easing the burden of daily life.

Now he has some chickens, a pen of pigs I suspect he keeps more for companionship than bacon, and randomly a very old, very ugly donkey called Belle, who routinely tries to bite the hand of those who feed her.

I knock on the door, wait a couple of beats, then open it anyway, shouting: 'Yoo-hoo! I'm a burglar coming in to steal your priceless cuckoo clock collection!'

The door opens straight into the kitchen, which is all stone floors and exposed brick walls and low-flying beams that were designed for function more than beauty. Also, I remember as I duck, designed for midgets. The ancient Aga is the dominant feature, along with a massive Belfast sink and a battered kitchen table that's seen its fair share of action.

'Through here, Miss Burglar!' I hear him call, and smile in relief. I suppose a part of me had been a touch concerned that I was walking in on an Edie-with-pneumonia style situation like last year.

Thankfully not – Mr P is sitting in his armchair, his feet propped up on a boxy stool, listening to the radio and looking rested. His skin is a little on the grey side, and I can tell he's in pain, but he doesn't seem to be at death's door yet.

'Priceless cuckoo clocks, eh?' he says, his eyes crinkled in amusement. 'That'd be just the thing! No such luck, though, maid – you'll have to settle for the priceless company of an old man instead.'

Mr P is nearly eighty, and frankly he looks it. He has one of those weather-beaten, creased-up faces that people get when they've spent their whole lives outside, squinting up at the sun, beaten down by rain, blown around the fields. He also has one of the thickest Dorset accents of any of the people around here, probably because he's lived most of his life in isolation, doesn't watch the TV, and regards town centres as distilled evil.

'That'll do for me,' I reply, perching myself on the big

bay window ledge. 'So I hear you've been stair-surfing, Mr P? And that you refused to stay in hospital?'

'Bah! Bloody stairs . . . made for smaller feet than mine, they were. Anyway. Fuss over nothing. I'm right as rain.'

'Really?' I say, screwing up my eyes in disbelief. 'Because as a trained professional, looks to me like you might be in some pain . . .'

'How do you reckon that, then, clever clogs?' he challenges, looking unconvinced.

'Years of training,' I reply. 'Coupled with the fact that I've never, ever seen you sit in that chair, or have your feet up. You're usually on the move, or in the kitchen, or outside. Unless you've suddenly gone soft on me, then something's hurting.'

He pulls a face, and says: 'Are you going to carry on wittering or will you put the kettle on, woman?'

'I'll put the kettle on,' I answer, standing up to do exactly that. 'And if you need me to, I can go and feed the animals – or in Belle's case, throw food and run. Then in return, you can thank me by taking some pain relief, okay?'

'I'll think about it,' he mutters sourly, gesturing for me to leave the room. I know he doesn't want me to see him struggle to his feet, so I oblige, and by the time he shuffles through I have the tea brewing. He likes it so thick the spoon stands up on its own.

I stay focused on the tea while he settles himself down

onto one of the wooden chairs, trying not to groan as he goes.

'So, you remember Cherie, at the Comfort Food Café in the village?' I say, placing the tea in front of him.

'Grand-looking hippy type with all the hair? Moved here a few years ago?'

'Yep, that's her – although to be fair it was a few decades ago. Well, anyway, she was saying the other day she's thinking of doing some outside catering, or selling Comfort Food Café goodie hampers, and she wanted to practice by sending some to people who live outside Budbury. All for free, obviously. What do you think?'

He sniffs, and sips his tea, and raises one bushy grey eyebrow.

'Depends,' he announces, 'on whether her food's any good or not, don't it? I've lasted this long without a food hamper, can't see why as I'd change now.'

'Believe me, it's good. And it's free. If you don't like it, you can give it to Belle. Now stop moaning, you nasty old coot.'

'I'll stop moaning when you stop bossing, madam!'

We snap and snark at each other for another half an hour or so, which is our usual style, and I do as I said I would and go and tend to the animals. I'm not the kind of woman who's ever likely to live on a farm and milk cows, but you can't grow up like I did – in rural Cornwall and Dorset – without learning a few things about livestock.

And even if I didn't, Mr P was on hand to give me rigid instructions and glare at me through the kitchen windows.

By the time I've finished, to his satisfaction, he finally relents and agrees to take a painkiller – and I notice as he does that the pack he brought home with him from the hospital pharmacy is completely untouched. I gently explain to him that taking them isn't a sign of weakness, or a signal for social services to swoop in and put him in a home – it's merely a way of giving his battered body the respite it needs to properly heal.

'There's no medal for sheer awkwardness,' I say, as he swills down the tablet with yet more tea.

'If there was, I'd have a cabinet full!' he acknowledges, grimacing as he swallows.

I check he has everything he needs before I leave, making a mental note to bring him one of the catalogues I have that feature recliner chairs and the like, and head off towards Briarwood. Willow is picking Mum up from the day centre, so I'm free for the rest of the day. Yippee.

It's a pleasant drive, and I concentrate on living in the moment rather than allowing Seb to intrude on my thoughts. I can't smell any roses, because I'm in a van, but I look out of the window at the rolling green hills, and the kestrel I see hovering over one of the fields, and the wooden sign by the road advertising home-made honey. That sign always makes me laugh, because the hand-painted picture makes the hive look like a giant pile of poo. Small pleasures.

It's almost five when I reach Briarwood, and it feels as though all the sunshine and heat of the day has been building up to a lovely, sultry finale. I stand and stretch, turning my face up to bathe in the light, eyes closed as I soak it in.

'You look like a sunflower,' says Finn, sneaking up on me and snaking his arms around my waist. I lean back into him, and let my head rest against his chest.

'I've been called worse,' I reply, holding onto his hands and smiling as he nuzzles my hair. 'How are you?'

'Good, thank you. An exciting day today – one of the junior genius brigade shorted all the electrics in the building. Nobody could do anything after that, so they kind of declared it a public holiday, and had a giant picnic instead. I got an electrician out this afternoon and it's all sorted now.'

'Never a dull moment at Professor Tom's School for the Gifted and Talented, is there? So, have you got anything else to do today, or can I tempt you out for a walk? I'm feeling very at one with nature today, Finn. I think I might become a Druid.'

'You'd look good in the gown. And yes, you can tempt me – it's too beautiful to be indoors. Anyway, I wanted to show you this little waterfall I found in the grounds . . .'

'Waterfall, not pond?' I ask, turning to face him. He

looks supremely lovely in the sunlight, laughter lines crin-
kling around the blue of his eyes.

'Yes. Definitely not pond. Why?'

'Because,' I say, shaking my head as though he was stupid
not to have figured it out, 'the pond belongs to Willow
and Tom. And when I say "belongs to", I mean they've done
the deed there. And much as I love my sister, I don't want
to share her sex pond.'

'No,' he says, grinning. 'When you put it like that, I
completely agree. Give me five minutes to grab some picnic
leftovers and get changed.'

I lean against the front of the van, listening to insects
buzz around the lavender pots and wondering what they're
saying to each other, until Finn emerges. He's changed into
a pair of well-worn Levis and a pale blue T-shirt, and has
a rucksack on his back.

'You look like an explorer,' I say, as I follow him off
into the thick greenery that surrounds Briarwood. 'You
should maybe get a pith helmet, or a bullwhip like Indiana
Jones.'

'Wasn't he an archaeologist?' Finn asks, as he leads me
along a path that gets more and more narrow as we go.

'He was. But don't spoil my fantasy, okay?'

He laughs, and we carry on walking. Briarwood is set
in acres of garden and woodland, some of it tamed and
cultivated, some of it not so much. The more formal
gardens immediately around the house lead off, on a

variety of paths, into the deeper countryside that circles it.

When we were kids, and Mum was working here all those years ago, this was our unofficial playground for a couple of summers. We climbed the trees, played hide and seek in the woods, had picnics in the small, shaded, bluebell-drenched dells, and in Van's case, brought girls out to his secret camp to drink cider and snog.

It was all very Swallows and Amazons, with hindsight. Or borderline neglect, depending on your viewpoint. As we all survived the endless days of unsupervised roaming, I'll go with the Swallows and Amazons perspective. It wasn't the easiest time in my life, being a teenager, but there were benefits.

As we delve deeper into the undergrowth and further away from both the big house and the road that leads to it, the atmosphere starts to feel more and more jungle-like. The overhead leaves and trees are thick and lush, dripping shades of green, the tree trunks surrounded by giant ferns and scatterings of brightly coloured wild-flowers.

The sunlight is partially blocked by the boughs, but the air remains warm despite the shade. We walk single file as the path narrows to nothing more than a rarely used trail.

'Hey, Indiana,' I say at one point, 'did you bring your machete?'

'No need,' he shouts back, glancing at me over his shoulder. 'I thought we could use your cutting comments!'

'Sorry?' I reply, grinning. 'I can't hear you. I'm too busy looking at your arse!'

He gives it an obliging waggle, and I follow him through to the end of the current path, where it starts to widen again. I can hear the sound of fresh water gurgling and bubbling, and it's the sound more than anything else that sparks a memory. A distant image of the gang of us as kids, from Van as the elder statesmen at fifteen or something like that, then me, and Angel, and Willow when she was maybe seven or eight, scrawny and scrappy.

A hot day, possibly a series of them, just like this. Us finding the waterfall. Van bringing rope to tie to one of the tree branches that dangles over the water. Us taking turns to swing out and jump off, splashing into the pool. Willow being terrified but goaded into doing it anyway – we were always so vile to her, the runt of the litter. Now she's the toughest of the lot, so it must have been character building.

I pause behind Finn, and remember what we called it.

'The Bibber,' I say out loud, recalling the word.

'The what?' he asks, looking back at me.

'The Bibber. It's what we called this place, when we were little. It's an old Dorset word, means something like shivery, or cold. The water in there is really chilly, and after we'd jumped in, we'd all sit around the edge, shaking. So we called it the Bibber . . .'

'Ah. I see this is not the virgin territory I'd assumed?' Finn says, smiling gently as I reminisce.

'No. In fact there might even still be a rope swing if we're lucky . . .'

We both make our way out into the clearing, which is decidedly smaller than I remember it. Or maybe I'm bigger, who knows? And yes, I can see the frayed tip of the old rope swing dangling from the branch, looking a bit creepy now.

The foliage is dense here, and the thick canopies of leaves and boughs make it shady and cool. The Bibber is exactlyas I remember it – a perfect cascade of white-frothed water bubbling over the rocks and tumbling into the pool.

The pool itself is tiny – I recall it being so deep I couldn't put my feet on the ground. Poor Willow, who could barely swim at the time, was forever spluttering and flapping her skinny arms, determined not to ask for help.

It's quiet out here today, the mellow sounds of birdsong and the gentle hum of insects almost lost amid the splashing water – but back in those days, it was raucous. Four feral children, filling long hot days, hooting and hollering and yelling.

Finn looks at me, takes in the expression on my face, and asks: 'Happy memories?'

'Yes,' I reply, snapping back to the here and now, 'on the

whole. Life with Lynnie as a mother was never exactly normal – but it could be a whole lot of fun. Anyway . . . last one in's a nincompoop . . .'

I race towards the edge of the pool, eyeing the clear water as I go, shedding my trainers one at a time in an elegant hop. I know it's going to be freezing in there, but I can't resist. I wriggle out of my jeans and T-shirt, unhook my bra, wave it around my head with a rebel yell, and let it fly. I wince as it snags in a tree branch, knowing I'll have to go and retrieve it later, but it makes a statement.

Finn's right behind me, laughing along, and just about beats me to the prize – damn him and his lack of fiddly underwear. Men have it so easy.

He jumps in, and I pause, waiting for the inevitable reaction. I get it, and point a finger at him as his face changes from amused and excited to rigid with the sudden shock of cold. He gulps, and his eyes widen, and I say: 'Ha ha! Serves you right, you nincompoop! Told you it was cold . . . what's happened to your Viking heritage now, big man?'

I dip a toe in, feel the pierce of it, and decide that jumping in is the only way – if I try to do it inch by inch I'll never make it.

'Honestly?' he says, grimacing as I make a splash landing opposite him, 'I think Norse raiders crossing the North Sea would sob if they fell into this!'

He reaches out and pulls me towards him, crushing my

flesh into his. I can feel the goosebumps on his chest, and we're both shivering while we giggle. I wrap my legs around his waist, and kiss him, long and hard.

I can't touch the bottom of the pond, so he holds me up while we kiss and splash and play around and generally behave like naughty teenagers sneaking away from the adults.

Eventually, after what feels like an hour but might only be five minutes, I pull away from him, treading water to keep myself warm.

'When I imagined this,' I say, slicking back my wet hair, 'it was very erotic. It was like something out of a romantic comedy movie, where we declare our love under the waterfall before we tenderly take each other in a gentle yet possessive way?'

'Like, I'm just a boy, standing in front of a waterfall, freezing my bollocks off?' he replies, grinning and reaching out to touch my hair.

'Yeah. That kind of thing. But it's actually just bitterly cold, and I keep choking every time I'm under the waterfall, and I sort of think . . .'

'That we should get out and continue this on dry land? That would be the Viking way.'

I nod in relief, and we both clamber out of the water. I suddenly have the realisation that it's going to take ages to drip dry, and consider shaking myself off like Bella Swan does after she's had a bath.

Finn, however, has other ideas, and he strides naked and rather sublime over to his rucksack. He unzips it, emerges with two towels, and passes one to me, a slight smirk on his face.

'Goodness me,' I say, accepting it gratefully and wrapping its fluffy contours around my shivering body, 'you really are the best man in the whole wide world, aren't you?'

'You can thank Det Danske Spejderkorps for that,' he says, the words coming out but the meaning remaining obscure.

'Danish Boy Scouts,' he supplies, towelling dry his hair and grinning. 'I spent quite a few summers with my grandparents when I was a kid. I guess I still try to always be prepared.'

He proves his point by unpacking the rest of the bag – a blanket for us to lie on, a couple of bottles of Scrumpy Joe's cider, and a random selection of Scotch eggs, sliced chicken and a tub of cupcakes. Marvellous. He even has a bottle opener for the cider.

We're both shaking, despite the warm evening air, so we agree to cuddle on the blanket while we warm up, vowing to revisit the whole taking each other in a gentle yet possessive way later on, when we can move our extremities. In all honesty, even if we had sex right now, I probably wouldn't be able to feel it – which would be a waste.

We drink and snack and chat, and gradually look a bit less blue. He tells me about his day, and recounts some stories about his summers in Denmark, and his Granddad Christian, and eventually, after a particularly exciting tale involving a boat trip and an aggressive bull seal, I find myself noticing the way his flat stomach feels beneath my hand. The strong line of his nose; the sparkle in his blue eyes; the way his fingers are twined in my hair.

I'm guessing he's noticing a few things about me as well, and liking what he notices, as his hands start to roam and his leg accidentally finds itself splayed across my body and his lips are soon on mine. Then we stop chatting, and start loving, and it is absolutely exquisite. Maybe it's the setting, or the warmth of summer, or just how it is when you're with someone you love. Whatever the reason, it's wonderful.

'Would it be embarrassing if I used the word "wow" about that?' he asks, when we're both lying, pleasantly exhausted, on the blanket afterwards.

'No,' I reply, grinning at him in a way I suspect might fall into the category of 'adoring'. 'I think it would be an entirely appropriate usage of the word. It was indeed wow. Only problem is, we now have a ten-mile jungle trek when all our limbs are in a weakened state.'

'I'd say it's maybe two miles, tops, but yeah . . . I know what you mean. And it's starting to go a bit darker now as well. I think we need to rest here for a while, though, don't you? Just lie here, and stare at the sky, and talk. Tell me about your day – you've already heard all about mine.'

I've not exactly been dreading this moment – more that

I've been avoiding it. I've been so busy living in the present that maybe I convinced myself the rest of the day didn't even happen. Now he's asking me, though – well, I can't lie, can I? He's been so understanding about this whole Seb situation – this whole me situation – and the one thing he asked for was honesty.

'Well, I visited Mr Pumpwell at his cottage,' I say, building up to it.

'Oh – how is he? Didn't you say he'd had a fall?'

'He has, but he was pretending like it never happened. He wasn't that convincing, as he was clearly in a lot of discomfort. I made him some tea, fed the donkey, and persuaded him to take some pain relief before I left. So that was good. And before that . . .'

I taper off slightly, suddenly wondering how this will go. Suddenly feeling like I've done something wrong.

'And before that?' he prompts.

'Before that, I had lunch with Seb. Well, not lunch exactly. I met him. At a time that happened to coincide with the period of the day when people usually eat lunch.'

I feel him stiffen slightly beside me, and not in a good way. I wait, my eyes screwed up in anticipation.

'Okay. Right. Well, how did that go?'

'It was awkward. And weird. But . . . I think you were right, when you said it'd be good for me. I mean, it didn't feel good – it felt odd and unsettling. But I think we maybe need to sort some stuff out.'

Finn is quiet, and his fingers stop twirling in my hair, and I recognise the signs of him processing tricky news and trying to decide how to respond.

'What kind of stuff?' he asks, finally.

'Well, we caught up. His dad died, which is really sad – his dad was nice. And he's been clean for years, after a variety of stints in rehab. And he works as a sports massage therapist. And . . . and he said he wanted to be sure there was nothing left between us before he gave up on our marriage.'

When I say it out loud, that last sentence is actually a bit of a humdinger. It even feels that way to me, never mind Finn – so I totally understand that yet another silence kicks in.

'I see,' he says, pulling away from me and sitting upright, gazing out at the woodland around us. 'And what do you think about that?'

I'm at such a loss here – completely out of my depth. I feel like a teenager again, trying to navigate my way through emotional currents I don't understand. I want to reassure him – but I also want to be honest, like he asked. It kind of feels like whatever I do will be wrong.

I sit up too, and hold his hand.

'I feel . . . a bit off balance? I don't love Seb, Finn. I really don't – I can promise you that. I wouldn't lie to you, ever. But I did love him once, and we never finished things off properly, and part of me thinks it would be healthy if we did. So I agreed to him staying, and spending some time with him, and then he's said he'll leave.'

Finn nods, and is suddenly so fascinated by the activities of two woodfinches pecking at my bra on the tree branch that he can't meet my eyes. I feel wretched, like I've somehow wounded him without even meaning to.

'You said you were fine with this,' I add, squeezing his fingers. 'You said it would be a way to put him in the past, to prove he doesn't have a hold over me any more.'

'I did say that, you're right,' he replies quietly, finally turning to look at me. He's smiling, but it looks sad on him. 'I did say that, and I still think that's true, but maybe I underestimated how much this would knock me for six. I believe you when you say you don't love him – but I can't help feeling . . . edgy. And I kind of wish you'd told me about this before we lived out that whole rom com scene.'

I frown, confused now.

'What do you mean? Before we had the wow sex?'

'Yes, before we had the wow sex. Because the wow sex now feels a bit weird. Like you've come straight from seeing your ex-lover, and current husband, to me. I can't quite get a handle on the logic of it, if indeed there is any logic, but it doesn't feel good.'

'I didn't come straight to you from him! I went to the café first and threw tuna at Zoe's face, then I went to the pharmacy and talked to Katie about her love life, then

I visited an old man and his donkey! And anyway – all I did with Seb was sit in a beer garden and talk. We didn't even sit on the same bench. No parts of us touched!'

He shakes his head, and manages a little laugh.

'I'm not suggesting otherwise. I know you too well to assume you'd have spent a steamy morning with him getting naked – I do trust you! I just . . . well, this is strange for me, but I can't understand the way I'm feeling. All I know is thatI'm feeling it.'

I sigh, and feel desperate to fix this – but I have no idea how to. I'm angry with Seb for turning up here and ruining my life, and angry with myself for not getting things right yet again, and if I'm honest, a tiny bit angry with Finn for reacting like this – which isn't fair at all. He's not a robot, he's a man, with emotions and fears and anxieties. Maybe I've expected too much of him.

'Okay,' I say, blowing out a big breath that I wasn't aware I was holding. 'I'm sorry. The very last thing I'd ever want to do is upset you. But it's hard to get a grip on some of this. You're so . . . calm. Usually. If you'd ranted and raved and told me you didn't want me to see him, I wouldn't have seen him. But you didn't even seem that upset . . . you were all calm and Bjorn Borg about it!'

'Bjorn Borg was Swedish,' he says, automatically correcting me in a way that I find infuriating.

'I know he was!' I snap back. 'That's not the point though, is it? Look, Finn . . . I love you. I want to be with you. I want to build a future with you. And just to be clear, again, I don't love Seb. I don't want to be with him, and I don't want to build any kind of future with him beyond the next two weeks. Less than that, even, now, it's, like ten days or something. But I want to work my way through this maze, and when I do, I want us to be even better and stronger than we were before. Does that make sense?'

He stands up, and starts to gather his clothing.

'It does,' he replies, as he pulls up his Levis. 'It does make sense. And I think it's the right thing to do, and I'm going to be waiting for you at the end of the maze, Auburn. But . . .'

He pauses as he tugs his T-shirt over his head, his blond hair popping out the other side.

'But what?' I ask, standing up and facing him. Generally speaking, during a spirited debate like this, nothing good ever follows the word 'but'.

'But for me to get through this with myself intact, I think perhaps we need to leave the wow sex alone for the time being. It might not make sense to you – but I need you to accept it.'

'Just the wow sex?' I ask plaintively, as I follow suit and reassemble myself into knickers and jeans and trainers. 'Can we still have mediocre sex, or downright rubbish sex?'

He stops, and grins despite the seriousness of his mood, and says: 'Since when did we ever have rubbish sex?'

'Never . . . but I'd be willing to start if it meant we could be together!'

'No,' he says firmly, squashing the towels and blankets back into the rucksack with way too much force. He might sound steady, but he's clearly not feeling it. 'No sex at all. It's too confusing. I want our sex to always be wow, and always to be followed by feeling great about life, and each other – not like this. So no sex at all. Anyway – like you say, it's not long. I just need . . . a clear head.'

He's stopped what he's doing, and is looking at me warily, like I'm a volcano that might pop at any minute. He might just be right.

I'm bewildered and hurt, and feel cut adrift in a sea of conflicting emotions. He isn't ending anything, and he says he loves me, and the sensible part of me knows that we can get through this – that it's not the biggest deal in the whole wide world.

Somehow, though, it feels big. It feels like a rejection, and it stings. I'm in pain and I'm frustrated and I don't want to say anything that's going to make this worse.

'I'll see you tomorrow,' I say, striding off towards the path.

'Don't get lost' he shouts after me, sounding concerned. 'And you've left your bra!'

'I'll be fine!' I yell back, stomping away through the greenery. I take a different path, because I don't want him following me all the way back to Briarwood. 'I know these woods like the back of my hand!'

Chapter 16

I soon realise that that is one of the most stupid phrases ever invented by humankind. I mean, who actually knows what the back of their hand looks like? Not me, that's for sure.

After angry-walking for twenty minutes, I also realise that I'm completely lost. I'm crying, and I'm tired, and I have a nasty scratch on my cheek from a vicious and totally unprovoked attack by a bramble bush. I keep swiping the tears and the blood away, and keep marching, convinced that I'll soon emerge from the wilderness.

After the best part of an hour, I'm starting to think that I never will. That I'll be like one of those old soldiers you read about, who live wild in the hills and think they're still at war decades after a peace treaty, sleeping under the stars with a billy can and a machete.

My phone is no use at all, either flickering in and out of signal range or displaying a map made entirely of green. In the end I use it as a torch, helping me pick my way through the treacherous tree roots and through thickets of fern.

Eventually, I reach the pond. Willow's sex pond. This, at least, I recognise – though even then it takes me another half an hour to make it back to Briarwood. By the time I emerge onto the gravel pathway, I'm drenched in sweat and ready to climb into my van and sleep for a thousand years.

I am, however, at the very least a lot calmer. Maybe the whole back-to-nature thing was cathartic – it gave me time to have a weep, do some swearing, kick some innocent tree trunks, and come to the conclusion that although life is hard and often sucks, it's all the better for the thought of a hot shower and a slice of cake.

I walk towards my van in the now mainly dark evening shade, and see that Finn's lights are on. I stand still for a moment or two, then shrug and walk towards the house. I need to be a grown-up – and also to use the toilet.

I push open the door to Briarwood, and make my way along the corridor to his apartment. I can hear the sounds of loud techno music competing with the sound of even louder Nirvana, and laughter and chatter floods from the rooms up the stairs. There's a slight smell of sulphur on the air, which I put down to one of the inhabitants' experiments, or possibly a Satanic visitation.

I pause outside Finn's door, catch my breath, and knock once before opening it. He's not in his office, but before I can go into his rooms he emerges, looking concerned. His hair is damp but tidy, and he's barefoot – so at least one of us has had a shower.

'Auburn,' he says, sounding relieved. 'I was just considering coming to look for you. I saw your van still there, and was worried you'd been eaten by wolves or something. What happened to your face? It's covered in blood.'

My hand goes up to my cheek defensively, and I realise what a mess I must look. My hair is damp from effort and tangled around my face, and my skin is covered in smears of dirt, blood and tears.

'Nothing. A nasty bramble, that's all. Can I use your loo?'

He nods, and gestures behind him, and I quickly go about my business. This might make me a very shallow person, but there are few better feelings in the world than finally getting to let loose a wee you've been holding in for too long, are there?

I grimace into the mirror when I see that I look even worse than I imagined, and give my face a quick swill. The cut has stopped bleeding, and I know it'll heal up nicely. If not, it'll give me a jaunty pirate air.

When I come back out, Finn is holding my bra towards me, having clearly retrieved it from the tree branch before he left the Bibber.

'Thank you,' I say, with as much dignity as a braless woman can muster, taking it from him.

'Did you get lost?' he asks, smiling gently.

'No! I . . . experimented with my sense of time and place. Anyway. I wanted to pop in and say I'm sorry. For whatever it is I've done. And I don't want this to go wrong, and I don't want things to be weird between us, and I don't want us to be angry with each other. So I'm sorry, okay?'

He nods, sits down on the sofa, and pats the space next to him.

'Are you sure?' I ask. 'I smell really bad.'

'Not as bad as a bull seal,' he replies, which is fair enough. 'Come and sit with me.'

I sink gratefully onto the couch, and he slips his arm around my shoulders and snuggles me into him. I could very easily pretend everything is fine right now, and fall asleep.

'You know that thing you said about me being like Bjorn Borg?' he asks, making sure I don't snooze off.

'Yes. Sorry about that.'

'No need to apologise. What do you actuallyknow about Bjorn Borg?'

'Next to nothing,' I reply, frowning in confusion. 'He was a super-duper tennis player in the olden days. He was always ice-man calm and never shouted at bad line calls. And my mum fancied him.'

'Seriously? Lynnie fancied Bjorn?'

'Oh yes,' I say. 'I think it was the short shorts . . .'

'Good to know. Or weird to know anyway. Well, Bjorn

Borg was famous for being calm on court, and never losing his temper, right? The thing is, when he was younger, he was the opposite. He almost had to give up tennis because he couldn't manage his anger, and got into trouble for shouting and smashing his racquet and that kind of stuff. He wasn't always the ice man – he used to be so ferocious that at one point he got himself suspended from the game.'

'Okay,' I mutter, not at all sure where this is going. Maybe as well as the no-sex rule Finn's now going to instigate a 'no interesting conversations' rule.

'I'm telling you all this for a reason.'

'Good. I was starting to wonder.'

'The reason is this – when you called me Bjorn Borg, you were kind of right, on both counts. I wasn't always this calm and steady version of myself, Auburn. This is the version of me that I've got now, after years of work and effort. The version of me that existed when I was a teenager, and into my early twenties, was wild. I had the world's worst temper, and it got me into a lot of trouble.'

I look up at him, my interest well and truly piqued, and reply: 'Tell me about it.'

'It started when I was about fourteen or fifteen. I've told you the history of my parents – the affairs, the divorce, my life as a human pawn in their battles. I suppose all of that contributed, along with a hefty dose of incoming testosterone that was normal for that age. I'm afraid to say I was a bit of a monster – always getting into fights, rising to every bait, losing my rag at absolutely anything.

'I was expelled from two schools, and it was only spending those summers shipped off to see my grandparents that kept me calm enough to finish my A-levels. I was always angry – sometimes on the outside, but always on the inside.'

'That's awful, Finn. What a horrible way to live. Did it get any better when you were older?'

'I got better at hiding it. I didn't go off to university, though, because I couldn't handle the thought of communal living. I started working on a farm in Northumberland, which helped – being outside helped, as did being physically tired. But it didn't ever quite go away, and it's the main reason things didn't work out with Cara, the ex I told you about.'

He has mentioned Cara before, but not in any detail.

'Tell me,' I urge, placing my hand on his thigh. 'You've never told me much about her.'

'Ha!' he says, snorting with amusement. 'I don't think you're in any position to comment on that, as you didn't tell me much about the fact that you were married!'

'That is a fair point. But tell me anyway – just because I'm rubbish doesn't mean you have to be.'

'Okay – well, we met when we were twenty-one. She was the daughter of the family who owned the farm, but she'd been away at college for years. We were together for about four years, I suppose, on and off. We lived together for the last year of that. I can say with the wonderful power of hindsight that we were disastrous for each other – we were too much alike.

'She had as much of a temper as me, and we argued all the time. It was never a happy or settled kind of relationship. And the more things were going wrong at home, with her, the more things went wrong elsewhere – I'd go to the village pub and end up having a fight with some other macho young farmer type, or I'd get drunk and start one with a stranger. On one memorable occasion I even managed to get into a scrap at the village fete, and crashlanded in the middle of the prize jam table.'

'Good lord!' I say, in almost mock-horror. 'What did the vicar say?'

'The vicar was none too pleased, now you mention it – his wife had won first prize for her Damson Delight. Anyway, it took a while for everything to fizzle out between us, and I'm not proud of the fact that it took her to finally have the courage to end it. We never fought physically – although there was the occasional flying teapot – but the verbal rows were enough, it was draining for both of us, and eventually she sat me down and said she couldn't live like that any more. That she wanted to have a family of her own, and we just weren't ever going to be in the right place for that to happen.

'I have no idea how long I'd have carried on like that.

Until some disgruntled clergyman did me in with a candle-stick in the library, I suppose.'

I nod, and try to imagine that Finn. The reckless Finn, fighting his way through life, so miserable and raw with inner pain that it constantly spilled out into violence. I struggle with that, because he's so different now, but I'm forever grateful that Cara had the strength of mind to finish it. If she hadn't, I wouldn't be with him now. Funny how many stars have to align to bring two people together. I only hope it takes even more stars to break them apart.

'So what happened after that?' I ask. 'How did you get from there to here, both physically and, you know, mentally? Because you're describing someone I don't recognise. I know the old me – the old me I told you about, who travelled the world and randomly got married and was a complete fuck-up – is different than the me I am now. But at least I think I'm probably just about recognisable?'

'Only the good parts,' he says kindly, kissing my head. 'The parts that are spontaneous and fun and adventurous. Well, it didn't happen overnight – it wasn't like a film, where I had some revelation and went on a retreat to live with Buddhist monks in Tibet or anything. I just . . . moved away. Saw a counsellor. Had some long overdue conversations with my parents. Spent a lot more time in Denmark. Went back to college to get my qualifications – basically, I looked at where I was, and where I wanted to be, and got help to make it happen.'

'Actually, that does sound a bit like something out of a film . . .'

'It does a bit, doesn't it? Or some kind of hideous self-help book. But the sessions with the counsellor helped. At her suggestion I took up boxing for a while, which was a good way to release a lot of anger. And eventually, after a lot of talking, and a lot of thinking, and a lot of listening to my wise old granddad, I let go of my anger. I didn't even notice it happen – but I finally realised one day, when someone cut me up at a roundabout in Bristol, that I wasn't furious. In the old days I'd have wanted to get out of the car and beat them to a pulp with a baseball bat.'

I shake my head, and feel super impressed. I've been on my own journey of self-improvement, but I've never done anything sensible like see a counsellor, or take up a sport. I just kind of floundered my way through it all, smoking fifty cigarettes a day.

'So now, I try to stay calm,' he says. 'I try to think before I react. I try to understand my feelings, and where they come from, and what they might provoke. It's not always easy, but on the plus side, I'm now really, really good at dealing with dickheads at roundabouts.'

I shake my head in admiration, and reply: 'Finn, you are amazing. That is so brilliant. And so brave. I'm . . . well, I'm sorry if all of this stuff – this stuff with me and Seb – is rattling your sense of zen or whatever. I don't want to be responsible for upsetting you, or taking away your balance. That's not fair to you.'

He nods, and holds me tighter, and replies: 'I know you don't, and don't worry: I love you. You love me. We will get through this. But I need to be aware of what I'm feeling, and understand why I'm feeling it, and avoid doing things that compromise me.'

'Hence the no wow sex rule?'

'Hence the no wow sex rule. I have faith in you, and us, and I'm sure this will all sort itself out – but just ignoring it, and ignoring the way it affects me, isn't the way forward. Seb has found his way back into your life. He's here, and the rabbit's out of the hat. Even if he left tomorrow, it would be there, hanging over us – or me, at least. I'd be wondering if it had stirred feelings up in you, wondering if you were thinking about him, wondering if he was ever going to come back. It'd be like trying to manage a relationship between the two of us with a silent partner looming in the background.'

That sounds pretty ominous, but Isee what he means. And of course, he's right. This won't be easy for either of us – or for Seb, I suppose, but I'm less worried about him. It won't be easy, but I think it's necessary.

'Okay,' I say, sighing as I realise I need to get up, go home, and get some rest. 'I understand. And I have faith too. I was just . . . upset, earlier. This is all messing with my nerves as well. But yeah, all right – I shall go along with the no sex rule. I promise I won't turn up wearing a busty Bier Keller serving wench costume and seduce you or anything.'

He laughs, and then looks a little distracted.

'No,' he says, a moment later, 'please don't do that. Because it would definitely work – maybe at a later date, Fraulein?'

'Ja, meinen pumpernickel. Definitely. Can I just ask though . . . I know the no sex rule. But that doesn't mean we can't see each other, does it? Because I'll miss you if it does. I might start stalking you, and secretly hiding in the shrubbery with a pair of binoculars just to catch a glimpse.'

'Don't be daft,' he says, standing up and helping me to my feet. 'Of course we can see each other. And you'd never be able to hide in the shrubbery – your hair is not exactly tailor-made for espionage.'

Chapter 17

A few more days of my allotted Seb time pass relatively quickly. He has wormed his way into my life, and even found a wary welcome at the café. I know that if I told them he was evil, they'd all band together and black-list him; possibly perform some kind of Wiccan ritual with burning branches and chanting. But he's not evil. He's not even bad. He just brings chaos, at a time when I thought I'd put it behind me.

I live in a bubble of anxiety about the two men in my life meeting, but so far it hasn't happened. Finn has stuck mainly to Briarwood, and although he hasn't said it out loud, I think it's because he wants to avoid a scene. And to give me space.

Seb has charmed Sandra, Katie's mum, into complete submission – but she was an easy sell. She even fancies Alan Sugar. He's won Edie over by talking about his granddad fighting in the Spanish Civil War, because she's old enough to remember it. And Little Edie is completely smitten with him, the junior trollop, climbing onto his lap whenever she can, wrapping her chubby fingers around his and calling him 'Bebby'.

Willow treats him with polite distance, which must be hard as she's desperately nosy about it all, and Laura has, with my permission, sunk into a state of deep love with his massage techniques.

Interestingly, it's only the menfolk who seem to be able to resist his charm – Matt and Tom remain quiet around him, which isn't unusual as they're quiet around most people; Van is civil but not overly friendly, and Sam and Cal haven't even invited him to the pub – which is quite the insult for them.

They all chat to him, and none of them has punched him, but I sense an underlying hostility that probably stems from their solidarity with Finn. It's a weirdly subtle display of male bonding, and kind of sweet in its own way.

My mum, though, is the one who really despises Seb. I can't work out whether it's some scary sixth sense she's got, or an Alzheimer's thing where he reminds her of someone from the past. Either way, she literally hisses when she sees him. The other day she presented me with a home-made bundle of herbs in a small bag to wear around my neck on a leather thong, explaining that it would help 'protect my aura'.

It smells rotten – I think she may have got her herbs mixed up as it pongs of mould – so I only wear it when she's around, to stop her freaking out.

I've generally managed to keep my cool around him, and am trying to strike a balance between engaging with this whole process, and not getting in too deep. I've also managed to avoid spending too much time alone with him, and none after dark – which is a silly distinction as he's not a vampire or anything, but most of my associations with Seb come from night time. Clubs and parties and late-night walks and hours spent in bed. None of which is good to remember when you're trying to keep your cool.

Tonight, though, I'm scheduled to have dinner with him at Hyacinth House at the Rockery. It used to be Laura's cottage, before she moved in with Matt, and I hope that gives it a bit of good karma.

I gave him two rules when I agreed: one, that I wouldn't be drinking, and two, that he had to keep his clothes on. That second sounds a bit weird, but Seb always had a habit of walking around naked, and even used to cook that way. It seemed very dangerous to me, but somehow he always emerged unscathed from his naturist omelette-making sessions, despite his lack of regard for health and safety.

I drive over to the Rockery, which is a little way inland from the village itself, and leave my van on the communal car park. I decide to call in at Black Rose first, which is the cottage where Matt and Laura and Lizzie and Nate now live.

I knock on the door, and within about one second, Matt has pulled it open. He stares at me for a moment in what looks like blind panic, and ushers me in.

'Are you okay?' I ask, concerned. 'Is Laura okay? What's happened?'

My head is, understandably, filled with potential scenes of disaster – Laura in labour on the kitchen floor while Midgebo licks her face; Laura screaming in pain; Lizzie and Nate with their shirt-sleeves rolled up ready to deliver their new siblings . . .

'I'm fine,' he says quickly, shaking off the look of shock and horror on his face. 'Laura's fine. I just . . . she made me watch a video, Auburn. A video of a woman giving birth to twins.'

I burst out laughing, and punch him on the arm – in a kind way, of course. Matt is big and brawny and must have pulled numerous baby animals out of various creatures, but for some reason this has clearly pushed him over the edge.

'Matt!' I say, still laughing. 'You're a vet – a man of science! You of all people should understand the birthing process. I can't believe you're being such a big wuss!'

'That's what she said,' he replies sheepishly. 'And you're right. Technically, I understand the process. But . . . well, it's different with cows, all right? I'm not married to a cow. I'm married to Laura, and I love her, and the thought of her going through all of that . . . uggh!'

He physically shudders, and I reach out to pat him reassuringly on the shoulder.

'She'll be fine. You'll be fine. Just keep an eye on her – you know what she's like about hospitals. I reckon she's going to try and sneak them out at home. And home births are great – in the right circumstances, and when they're planned. Probably not so ideal for her, but don't tell her I said that.'

Before he has a chance to reply, the woman herself waddles through from the living room, hands resting on her bump, a look of complete satisfaction on her face. I can see that she has very much enjoyed sharing at least some of her pain with her husband, and who are we to begrudge her that?

'Auburn!' she says in surprise. 'Do you want to watch the video?'

'Nope,' I say, quickly and firmly. 'I'm having dinner with Seb, and don't want all the bloody vaginas to spoil it. Just thought I'd come in and say hi on my way.'

Lizzie comes pounding down the stairs, all bouncing blonde ponytail and black eyeliner and exuberance. She's seventeen, Lizzie, and well on her way to being cool – so it's nice to see her giddy for a change.

'Yo, Lizzie,' I say, in my best gangsta voice. She gives me a withering look that tells me I'm way too old for such shenanigans, and replies: 'Good evening, Miss Longville. Are you going to Seb's? He's cooking tapas and I'm coming to take some photos . . .'

'Oh. Right. Why? And I really hope he has clothes on . . .'

Everyone looks understandably confused by this, and I wave it away. 'Why are you coming to take photos?'

'Because Mum asked me to. She was thinking of introducing a small plate menu at the café next year and thought this might give her some ideas.'

'Not just tapas!' Laura says hastily. 'Not just Spanish! I mean, we could have small plates from around the world, like sushi, and, erm, Danish food . . .'

I roll my eyes, and give her a hug.

'It's all right,' I say, laughing. 'Finn won't think you hate him if you start serving tapas. Are you coming as well?'

She nods, and tells us that she's nipping to the loo first, as a preventative measure in case she needs to go again during the thirty-second walk around to Hyacinth. Matt trails behind her, looking traumatised and pale.

'How're you, Lizzie?' I ask, while we wait. 'Nervous about your exams?'

'Nah. It's next year that matters. It's harder for Josh and Martha this time, waiting to see if they've got their grades for their places at uni.'

Josh has been Lizzie's boyfriend ever since she moved to Budbury a few years ago, and Martha is her best friend. I know from talking to Willow that she's been sad about the prospect of losing both of them in one fell swoop this autumn, but she seems to be putting a brave face on it.

When I ask her about it, she grins and says: 'I'm okay. I'm looking forward to the babies coming. Perfect timing – I probably won't even notice that they're gone, but if I get sick of it all here, I can go and stay with Martha or Josh at uni for a weekend.'

'Well, I can't fault your logic, and I think you'll be the best big sister in the whole world.'

'Probably,' she says, shrugging. 'As opposed to Nate being a terrible big brother. Unless there's an X Box game about changing nappies, he's going to be totally shit at it.'

'I heard that!' Nate yells from the living room.

'Good!' she screams back. Lordy, it's easy to forget how loud teenagers can be. 'You're useless!'

We're saved from the outbreak of all-out war by the return of Laura, who is wearing fuzzy pink slippers instead of shoes.

She sees us staring, and declares: 'They're comfortable. My days of stylish living are over.'

'They were never here,' retorts Lizzie, as she leads us out of the house. 'You've been embarrassing me with your fashion sense since the day I was born.'

Laura pulls a face, and sticks her tongue out at her behind her back all the way to Hyacinth.

Lizzie knocks on the door, which must be weird as she lived there until a few months ago, and Seb opens it. Naturally enough, he's only wearing half his clothes. Low-slung black jeans are in situ and correctly buttoned up, but that's about it. All three of us stand and stare at him, and even Lizzie – who surely views any man over the age of twenty as old meat – is a little dumbstruck at the display of all that bare tanned chest.

'You seem to have forgotten your shirt,' I say politely. 'Have you run out? Would you like me to drive to the nearest retail park and buy you one?'

'You said clothes,' he replies, gesturing us in. 'You didn't specify how many. Anyway, it's hot, and there's no air conditioning in the whole of the UK, and I've been cooking . . .'

From the smells wafting through from the kitchen, he's been cooking well. I glance at the dining table, and see various dishes laid out: a cold plate of hams and cheeses and olives and tiny stuffed peppers, patatas bravas, croquettes, chorizo, gambas, breads and sauces. It's a complete feast of deliciousness, and the aromas of garlic and chilli are almost making me drool.

He grandly gestures to the table, and announces: 'Voila! All your favourites, querida!'

His dark hair is damp from a shower, and he looks insanely pleased with himself as he waits for my reaction. I nod, but stay quiet – because these are indeed all my favourites. In fact, it's like a culinary time machine, whisking me back to all those nights together. Sitting in 'that Catalan place' – our little joke, as everywhere was a Catalan place – at 11 p.m., eating and drinking and laughing. Even the smell of it all makes me feel bizarrely homesick for Barcelona, for the first time in years.

Seb is gazing at me as though we are alone, and as though he knows exactly what I'm thinking. As though he can read my mind. I feel momentarily skewered by it all, and am pathetically grateful when Lizzie intrudes by snapping photos.

She takes one of Seb and me, staring at each other, and one of her mum, who's staring at us, and finally starts taking pictures of the food. It breaks the spell, and Laura suddenly begins chattering away about the cooking, asking him for recipes, asking where he got the Manchego from, asking him if it's okay if she tries a bit.

Seb happily talks her through it, and gives her a kind of guided tour around the table, spoon-feeding her tiny tastes of everything. She sighs and moans and looks utterly satisfied with her lot in life. Lizzie takes a few more snaps, then sidles over to me, looking at her screen.

'Was he always this good at cooking?' she asks, flicking through her shots.

'No. He was okay. But not at this level . . . I guess it must be one of those things he learned how to do more recently.'

I'm feeling a bit shaky, and that's not helped when Lizzie holds up a photo to show me. It's the one of me and Seb, our eyes meeting across a crowded buffet table. It's intense, and personal, and all together not a moment that I want to be captured forever on film.

'Do me a favour, Lizzie,' I say quietly, 'and don't post that one anywhere?'

Lizzie's Instagram account is famous in Budbury – it's like a still-life reality TV show of everything that goes on in the village and the café. She raises her eyebrows at me, and I add: 'It's complicated. There's a lot of history here, and photos can look odd out of context, and—'

'You don't want to upset Finn?' she responds. Clever girl.

'Yep. That. Is that all right?'

'Course. I get it. You know, for an old person, you have a really messed-up life.'

She gives me a wink to show me she's joking – I think – and takes a few more snaps before she drags Laura away.

'Come on, Mama,' she says, leading her mother from the room – I notice as she does that she's taller than Laura now – 'it's time for your cocoa and bed. You've got a head start with the slippers.'

'It's only half past seven!' splutters Laura. 'But . . . well, cocoa does sound nice . . .'

They make their farewells, and I hear them chattering away as Seb closes the door and they walk across the path. It makes me smile.

Seb comes back into the house after waving them off,

and I immediately say: 'Go and put a shirt on, would you? Seriously?'

'Why?' he asks, grinning and looking satisfied with himself. 'Worried you won't be able to resist?'

'Yes. Worried I won't be able to resist walking out right now. Anyway . . . I know what you're doing. You're . . . peacocking. Trying to prove to me that I still want you.'

'And do you?' he asks flirtatiously.

'I want you to put a shirt on.'

He laughs and nods and thankfully complies, grabbing up a black shirt from the back of one of the chairs and slipping it on. He does it slowly though, a bit like he's an extra in *Magic Mike* and wants to make sure I've noticed how buff he is these days. I have, it's safe to say.

I distract myself by picking at the food, and am unable to restrain a sigh at the flavour of the oil I dip a chunk of bread into.

'Is that paprika?' I ask, daintily wiping a drip from my chin. 'Like they used to have in that Catalan place?'

He smiles, and replies: 'It is. They've opened a deli now, attached to the dining room – so I brought it with me in case the English savages didn't have such things.'

'We probably do,' I say, casting my eye over the rest of the table, 'but probably not in Budbury. This is . . . impressive. When did you become a chef?'

He looks genuinely pleased, and explains that it was one of the things he used to keep himself busy after his last and successful stint in rehab. That he even went on a course, and spent hours in La Boqueria market learning about produce.

I remember La Boqueria vividly – it's an ancient market on La Rambla in the city centre, packed with stalls selling everything from freshly caught shellfish to exotic fruit and hand-made chocolate. It's an explosion of sights and smells and sounds, and if you get there early enough, you can perch on a tall stool at a bar or café and lose yourself in its weird and wonderful world.

'We used to go there straight from nights out,' he says, sitting opposite me across the loaded table. 'Do you remember? We'd still be buzzing, watching the fishermen unload their hauls, drinking black coffee.'

'I remember,' I reply warily, as he serves me a small plate of patatas bravas. 'Some of it at least.'

He chats away for a while, taking a trip down memory lane, smiling and laughing as he recounts events that sound familiar but feel as though they happened to someone else.

Finally, I hold up my hand and stop him.

'What are you doing, Seb?' I ask. 'With all of this. With the stories.'

'What doyou mean?' he says, frowning at me. He looks vaguely hurt, and it's a look I'm all too familiar with – it's the one he used to make me feel guilty whenever I suggested that possibly, just possibly, our lifestyle might need a slight course correction.

'You know what I mean. You're trying to manipulate me. You're trying to make me see things your way. You're trying to make me feel like I might be a little bit crazy if I don't remember things in exactly the same rosy light that you do.

'In fact, I do remember – I remember the time you were so high you toppled right off one of those stools, and the time you tried to buy ten kilos of lobster in an auction, and the time you ended up getting punched in the face by the old man who ran the spice stall because you thought it'd be funny to try and snort some saffron. So please – don't think you can somehow persuade me that it was all so wonderful. I won't let you mess with my head any more. Those days are gone.'

Even as I say it I wonder if it's true, because my head does feel a bit messed with. He listens to my small speech and sighs, and runs his hands through his hair. I'm prepared for an argument here, but he surprises me.

'You're right,' he says, nodding solemnly. 'I did manipulate you. I did make you feel crazy, even when I knew you were right – in fact, especially when I knew you were right. And I'm sorry – it wasn't fair of me. It was a way of hiding from myself, a way of avoiding change that scared me. I see now how damaging that must have been for you.'

I stare at him suspiciously, examining his words and his expression for any sign of subterfuge. Almost disappointingly, I find none.

'Okay,' I say eventually. 'Apology accepted. Neither of us was perfect. But . . . I'm different now. You can't play those games any more.'

'I realise that, and that's not what this was about . . . honestly, I don't know what I'm doing, Auburn. Seeing you again – well, it's strange, isn't it? I came here not knowing how I'd feel when I was able to talk to you. Able to see you and speak to you and touch you. Now I can, I feel . . . like I don't want to stop. Like this isn't over between us. And all of this? The food and the reminiscing and the stories? I suppose it's my way of trying to remind you that the time we spent together wasn't always bad. That you still might have feelings for me as well.'

'I do have feelings for you Seb,' I reply quickly, stabbing a chunk of potato viciously with my fork. 'But a lot of the time they're not the feelings you're looking for – they're feelings of exasperation and frustration and worry. Occasionally affection, but that might just be heartburn . . . look, you chose to be here – I didn't invite you. It was your decision, and for some reason I'm going along with it – but I think we have very different motivations.'

'Go on,' he says, smiling sadly. 'You might as well tell me.'

'I don't want to hurt you. And I really don't want to do anything that would damage your newfound sobriety. But your motivations seem to be to start things up again – and mine are to end them.'

I've been as blunt as I can be without wearing a T-shirt emblazoned with the words 'It's all over, Seb', and I see him struggle with it. The old Seb would have launched immediately into attack mode, and by the end of it would probably have convinced me I was a misguided idiot to even consider disagreeing with him.

The new Seb, though? He sits very still, and looks upset but not angry, and reaches out to hold my hand.

'I understand,' he says simply, letting go of my fingers before it becomes uncomfortable. 'And I promise that I won't be playing any games. If nothing else, then I'd like to use this time to simply enjoy your company, find out more about your life, and if it comes to it, say goodbye properly. If this is the end of a marriage, then I'd like it to mean something – not just be one of us sneaking away in the cover of darkness.'

That, of course, is exactly what happened last time – and although I did have my reasons, I also understand what he's saying. We both claim to have changed, to have grown up – so maybe this time we can actually behave like grown-ups as well.

'All right,' I agree, after a moment of thought. 'That sounds acceptable. But I don't want you to be under any false hope, Seb. Things are different now, and they're going to stay different. Now, there seems to be a table full of tapas requiring my attention . . .'

He jumps up, and starts to serve me more food. He

seems so excited as he does it, proud of himself, and I have to smile.

He always had occasional moments like this – moments where he'd be almost child-like in the way he behaved. Discovering an especially weird seashell on the beach, or coming across the *Kiss of Death* sculpture in Poblenou cemetery, or getting engrossed in Spanish-language teleno-velas from Mexico that used to be on the TV in the afternoon. He once met a bichon frise puppy tied up outside a supermarket and sat on the floor playing with it until its owner came out.

He was always a man of enthusiasms and passions – it's just that most of the time, those enthusiasms and passions were misdirected. Now, though, seeing him like this? It forces me to remember – to remember that he is right, and that the time we spent together wasn't all bad. It's been easier to pretend it was, but as ever with bloody life, nothing is that simple, is it?

Chapter 18

The rest of the evening passed easily enough. We both made a big effort to keep the atmosphere light, and it wasn't as hard as I'd imagined it would be. The strangest thing about it all was the fact that we spent a whole night together, both stone-cold sober. That was very much a first.

I'd often wondered about that, after I left. Whether we'd even recognise each other if neither of us was under the influence. Whether we'd have anything to talk about, whether we'd like each other.

The answer to at least some of that seems to be yes. We had plenty to talk about, plenty to catch up on. As to the 'like' part – well, the jury's out on that one.

I'd called it a night pretty early, which turned out to be a good thing as Lynnie woke us up at about four in the morning, looking for Joanna. Joanna is a recurring theme in my mother's less lucid moments, and the chances are we might never find out who is she is, or was, or what she represented to her.

I know she sometimes thinks Willow is Joanna, and

sometimes when she goes off on a wander she says later she was 'going over to Joanna's house'. Lynnie doesn't have any family left to talk to, and she severed a lot of ties with her old life when she left the commune in Cornwall where Van and Angel and I were born.

We've talked to Robert – Willow's new-found daddy dearest – but he has no recollection of there being a Joanna there at any point. If we ask her about Joanna during one of her clearer spells, she just looks confused, as though we're being a bit weird.

Of course, there might not be any mystery here – it might be a character from a TV show, or from a book she read when she was fifteen, or her long-lost imaginary friend. One of the many challenges of the delight that is Alzheimer's is not knowing sometimes what is significant and what is not.

Joanna, last night, certainly had enough significance to have my mum up and aggravated and furious about being locked in the house. We have to lock all the doors and windows and hide the keys, because she's been too clever at slipping out in the past, and almost seriously hurt herself last year.

Now, when she can't escape, she becomes understandably frustrated – in her mind, she's a grown woman, with every right to make decisions for herself, and every right to disappear off into the night-time countryside in search of the elusive Joanna. When we won't let her do that, she gets upset and angry, and once she reaches that stage, she often forgets who we are or why we're in her house or that we're trying to help her. We become the enemy.

Last night it was so bad, we had to let her out, and silently follow her. It was like something from a bad spy movie, me and Willow tiptoeing behind in the shadows, still wearing our PJs, jumping behind trees and bushes whenever Lynnie turned around suspiciously. I think we were both kind of curious anyway, wondering if perhaps she was going to lead us to the near-mythical Joanna.

Instead, she walked into the village, and sat herself down at the bus stop, patiently waiting for a bus that was very unlikely to come at 4.30a.m.

We'd made sure she had her coat on, and proper shoes, so we weren't too worried – but eventually Willow went home and got the van, and we drove past Lynnie, beeping the car horn and waving out of the window. There was a whole charade about how we were just passing and on our way home and would she like a lift?

It was dark, and she couldn't see our hair, so she wasn't quite sure who we were – but luckily Willow had thought to bring Bella Swan with her, who went straight over to Lynnie and started licking her fingers. That was enough to trigger a cascade of real-world recognition, and her eyes went wide, and she announced that she'd love a lift home – 'public transport in this country is a disgrace, isn't it?' she asked, as dawn broke.

Now, after several coffees and an aborted attempt to get back to sleep, I'm arriving at the Budbury Pharmacy, ready to face a day of exciting prescription filling, wart examining and whistle pop exploitation.

It's almost ten by the time I arrive – Willow had an early shift at the café, and Van had spent the night at Frank's farm, to help with the arrival of twin calves. Twin calves are rare, and often complicated, and I'm sure Matt will be far better with those than he was after that video last night.

I'd let Lynnie have a lie-in – she was tired too – and then asked if she wanted to go to her day centre to see her friends. Sometimes she does, sometimes she doesn't. Sometimes she's persuadable; sometimes she acts as though you've suggested removing both her eyeballs with cocktail sticks.

Today, though, she was keen – she thinks she's leading a workshop on using dried flowers in collages. She might even be right. Either way, I'm grateful she's keen to go, and I'm able to head into work without too much stress. Just quite a lot of yawning.

When I walk into the pharmacy, I am strangely unsurprised to see a familiar tableau in front of me: Katie at the counter, sorting through piles of cleansing wipes; Laura splayed across the couch, and Seb kneeling at her feet massaging her toes.

'Good morning, Budbury!' I announce, in my best radio DJ voice. They all look up and say hello, and I wander through the room, grabbing a whistle pop on the way. Breakfast of champions.

'How are you?' I ask Laura, who appears a little pale, and not as bubbly as usual.

'Oh, all right,' she says dismissively, swiping curls out of her eyes. 'A bit tired. I was up a lot with indigestion.'

She glances at Seb as she says this, and I suspect her pregnant woman logic is blaming him for all the oil-and-spice-rich tapas she tasted.

'Sure it was only indigestion?' I ask, placing a hand on her forehead to check her temperature. 'No action down below?'

'No!' she squeaks, sounding both relieved and disappointed about that. 'And I do wish people would stop asking! I've had two babies before, you know. I'm not a novice.'

Laura is usually such a gentle soul that it's always surprising – and a tad amusing – to hear her snap like this. I hold my hands up in a placatory gesture, and make my way towards the kitchen. I desperately need my fifteenth coffee of the morning. The first fourteen were useless – this one will be the charm, I'm sure.

Seb follows me through, and suddenly the room feels too small. He leans back against the counter while I fill the kettle and rattle the mugs. He's looking all tall and big and dark and broody, and taking up too much space. If Lynnie was here she'd hiss at him like a protective goose.

'You okay?' he asks, seeing how jittery I am.

'Fine. Tough night at casa del Longville, that's all.'

That is true, but having him here isn't helping. Once we'd got the big emotional talk out of the way last night, I'd actually started to enjoy his company – which this morning, in the warm light of a summery day, feels slightly more alarming than it did at the time.

I don't want to enjoy Seb's company. I don't want to get used to him being around. I don't want to feel anything for him. What I do want, very much, is to go outside into the tiny yard and have a cigarette.

That would be a relapse too far, so I give myself a telling off, and stick the whistle pop in my mouth instead. Possibly I am swapping one addiction for another, but such is my life.

'It was nice, last night,' he says, passing me the kitchen roll when I over-pour the hot water and slush brown coffee all over the counter.

I nod, and stay quiet. It was nice, but I'm not quite ready to acknowledge that. It's weird. I only realise now that I'd spent the whole evening at Seb's without even thinking about Finn, and that makes me feel bad and guilty and anxious. Not that I did anything wrong at all, but still – it's a step away from him that I don't want to take.

This makes me feel unfairly surly towards Seb, and I'm probably about to snap at him when a shout comes from the main room.

'Auburn!' yells Katie. 'Can you come here please?'

Katie is not a woman naturally given to yelling, and although she doesn't sound at all panicked, there is an edge to her voice that makes me immediately stop what I'm doing and dash back through, followed by Seb.

Laura is sitting on the sofa, eyes wide, her mouth formed into a perfectly shocked 'O' of surprise.

'What is it?' I ask, keeping my voice low and calm.

'I . . . I think I might have had a wee on your lovely couch . . . ' says Laura, her cheeks flaring red in humiliation. I see a damp patch spreading around her, and formulate a plan of action within seconds.

'God, how embarrassing . . . I'm so sorry . . . ' she mutters, trying to stand up, looking mortified.

'Don't be daft,' I say briskly, walking towards her. 'You can wee anywhere you want, sweetie. But I somehow don't think that's what happened here. I think your waters have broken. And I don't think it was indigestion. And I think it's time to go to the hospital now, don't you?'

She shakes her head furiously, so fast her hair whips from side to side, and bleats: 'No! I'm not ready! It's not time! I want to stay here!'

Seb rushes over and sits by her side, oblivious to the leak danger, and holds both her hands in his.

'It's all right, Laura,' he says, his voice low and deep and hypnotic. She looks into his eyes, and I see how panicked she is.

'It's all going to be fine,' he says, stroking her hair and keeping her steady. 'Like you say, you've had two babies before – you're not a novice.'

'But I don't want to go to the hospital . . . ' she says, her voice trailing off and tears sprouting in her eyes. 'Can't I stay here? You have all the drugs!'

She looks at me pleadingly, and I smile as I reply: 'Not the right kind, my love, I'm sorry. And I know it's been your master plan all along to have those babies here, but it's not going to happen, all right? Katie's going to track down Matt, and we're going to drive you to the hospital, and it's all going to be good. I just need you to stay calm for me.'

She nods, and her face twists into a shocked grimace as what I suspect is a contraction ripples its way through her.

'Oh fuck!' she proclaims, in a very un-Laura like display of profanity. 'I'd forgotten how much this hurts!'

'I know,' I reply, even though I clearly have no idea. 'But you'll have all kinds of wonderful help very soon . . . Katie?'

Katie, who is a trained nurse, isn't at all fazed by the situation – but she does look concerned as she comes off her phone. She shakes her head slightly to tell me that she hasn't been able to speak to Matt.

Laura is blinking rapidly, and Seb is whispering to her, and Katie asks me: 'How many weeks is she?'

'Enough,' I reply. 'Almost thirty-four, I think. She should

be fine, that's a decent gestation for twins. But they might want to give her corticosteroids, and she definitely needs to be monitored.'

Katie nods, and I find her calm reaction is helping me to stay calm as well. Go Team Pharmacy.

'Do you think she's actually in labour, or is it just the membrane rupture?' she asks.

We glance over at Laura, who is squeezing Seb's fingers very tight and sucking in air like she's on a decompressed plane, and I reply: 'Looks like labour to me. You go and track down Matt and we'll get her to the hospital. Stick a sign on the door that says we're closed for childbirth or something.'

Katie grins, and replies: 'Maybe that could be a new string to our bow? Budbury Pharmacy – blood pressure checks, prescriptions, verruca advice, and multiple births a speciality.'

Before I get the chance to make some suitably amusing comeback, Laura shouts out to us: 'What are you two talking about? Why are you being all furtive and quiet? What's wrong?'

I pull a face at Katie, and go back to my patient.

'We're not being furtive – we're making plans. And there's nothing wrong.'

'That's easy for you to say!' she snaps back, understandably a little grouchy right now. 'Is this going to be okay? I'm too early! I know it feels like I've been pregnant forever, and I've done nothing but moan about it, but it's too early . . . and I've changed my mind!'

I bite the inside of my cheeks to stop myself from laughing, and squat down in front of her.

'It's not too early,' I say, stroking her chubby knee. 'You've done a brilliant job growing those babies, and I'm sure they're going to be fine. And . . . well, it's too late to change your mind now, so tough luck.

'Look, I can call an ambulance – but I think it'd be just as quick to drive you there ourselves. I don't want to do that, though, if there's any chance that these little ones are going to make an appearance sometime soon. Like in the next half an hour. So I need you to take a few deep breaths, think about what's going on with you, and tell me how you feel. I need you to help me make an educated decision. If necessary, we can . . . you know, have a little look. All right?'

I'm really, really hoping we don't need to have a little look. If we do, I'm passing that job onto Katie. I'm the boss, after all. One of the perks has got to be not looking at your friends' privates.

Laura nods and puffs in air, and slowly puffs it back out again. I see the tears slow down, and she finally lets go of Seb's hand. He masterfully controls his sigh of relief, and starts to rub his own hand to get the circulation back. He may never massage again.

'Okay . . . okay . . . ' says Laura, rubbing her belly. 'I

think I'm having contractions – but so far only the one. It doesn't feel like it did with Lizzie and Nate, when things were imminent. I think I'm all right. I think . . . where's Matt? Can you get Matt? I need Matt!'

'Katie's on that,' I reply, sneakily checking her pulse. 'And we'll find him, don't worry. Now, though, we need to get you moving – okay?'

She nods, and I look at Seb, and the two of us help her to her by now quite unsteady feet. She glances back at the sofa, and her hands go to her flaming cheeks.

'Oh God! What a mess! I'm so, so sorry . . .'

'I repeat – don't be daft. Now, come on, madam, your chariot awaits . . .'

We make our way towards the door, and Katie shouts out: 'Good luck, Laura! It's going to be fine! And don't worry, I'll find Matt for you . . .'

We manage to manoeuvre Laura out to the van, and after a small debate, she opts to get into the back of it because she can't stand the thought of putting a seat belt on. It's only a small step up, and we heave her in between us, Seb clambering in by her side.

There are no seat belts back there – just some random boxes and a spare stock of whistle pops for emergencies – and it crosses my mind that this isn't the most health and safety conscious choice. I now have a lot of very precious eggs in my basket. I can't crash. I can't swerve. I can't go too fast. Slow and steady wins the race.

The drive to the hospital takes about twenty minutes, with me driving like a granny on a Sunday, and all the way there I can hear Seb talking to her. She tells him how much she hates hospitals, because she killed her husband in one, which I know must sound really weird. The reality beneath that statement is that she had to make the decision to switch David's life support off after his accident, but in Laura's mind I don't think there's ever been much difference, the poor thing.

'Well today, the hospital is your friend,' I hear him say in soothing tones. 'Today, they will help you stay out of pain, and keep your babies safe, and make sure everything goes well. By the end of today, Laura, you will have two beautiful new children in your arms. It's going to be wonderful!'

She grasps onto this, and he engages her in a conversation about names, and their plans, and the nursery, and a dozen other pleasant and positive things.

I remain unconvinced that by the end of the day, all will be perfect – the babies are a bit early, and might not even be born today, and she might need a section, and they might need special care – but it would be cruel to say anything. Instead, I concentrate on driving, the low murmur of Seb's voice also calming me, and eventually pull up right outside the maternity unit with very minimal tyre screeching.

I tell them to stay where they are while I find help,

filling in the duty midwife on what's going on, flooded with a sense of relief as she springs into action. There are men and women in green uniforms and there are calm reactions and there are doctors being alerted and there are wheeled stretchers and there are lots and lots of people on hand to take over. Thank God – the services of the Budbury Pharmacist can only be stretched so far.

I stay by her side as she's admitted, her eyes wild and rolling in terror, Seb holding one hand and me holding the other. I can see the effort she's making not to panic, and I admire her so much.

Just as she disappears off into a private room for an examination, Matt arrives. He runs into the lobby, still wearing muddy wellies, looking almost as crazed as his wife.

He spots us and dashes over, his face pale and his eyes wide.

'It's okay,' I say, reaching out to place a hand on his shoulder. 'She's all right. She's getting checked over now, and then they'll come and tell us what's happening. You can go through and see her. Just . . . take a breath first, all right?'

'Yes. Okay. I can do that. I was . . . well, I was elbow deep in Bessie when Katie tried me first. Then she got Van instead. And then we drove here really, really fast. And . . . is she going to be okay? Are the babies going to be okay?'

'I'm sure they are,' I reply, putting as much certainty

into my voice as I can muster. 'They're in the right place now.'

Matt nods, and breathes, and finally seems to notice that Seb is there.

'Thank you,' he says, 'both of you. And Katie. For looking after her. I need to go and see her, but I'm . . .'

He gestures down at himself, and his muddy wellies. Seb immediately slips off his black boots and offers them up to Matt. Matt stares for a minute, looking confused, then finally nods gratefully and does a weird hopping about on one leg dance while he changes his footwear.

'Thanks. Again,' he says, looking around him for a toilet sign. 'I'm going to have a quick wash, then I'll go and find her, and . . .'

'And then it'll all be okay,' I say, hugging him briefly. 'Call us when you know anything, all right? It might be a long haul, but we're here if you need any help, or if you want us to have the kids for the night. Anything at all.'

He nods, and suddenly grins. The smile changes his face completely, transforming him from harassed dad-to-be to incredibly handsome.

'I think it's going to be a good day,' he announces, in explanation. 'Those twin calves were absolutely perfect. And the twin humans are going to be even better.'

Chapter 19

Budbury is a small place, and news tends to sweep through it like wildfire.

Matt calls me a little after eight that night, and by the time I arrive at the hospital, with Willow and Lynnie, I'm certain that everyone else will have been alerted to the good news as well. Van has come separately, bringing Katie and Saul, and I spot Frank's jeep in the car park.

We're all giddy and excited as we traipse through the reception area, doing it in pairs and not as a huge group so as not to upset any staff who might want to stop us. Laura is in her own room, but it's not huge, and it's not visiting time, and there are always rules about how many people are allowed in at the same time.

Naturally, we're about to break all those rules, and we don't care – it'd be a brave person indeed who tackled Cherie Moon. We all congregate outside the ward, with its electronic doors, me and my siblings and Katie and Saul.

Matt spots us outside, and pops his head out to let us

in. His hair is sticking out at weird angles, his shirt untucked and creased, a euphoric grin on his face.

'Quick, quick, come on in . . . there's not much room!' he says, almost giggling as he does. Giggling is not Matt's default setting, and I suspect he might be ever-so-slightly hysterical still after the drama of the day.

'We can wait,' I say sensibly. 'We can see her tomorrow. She's got to be exhausted.'

Willow shoots me a resentful stare, and is already edging towards the door, desperate to meet the new arrivals.

'No, no, she asked me to contact everyone. Said it was the Budbury way. But yes, she is exhausted, so we're setting a fifteen-minute limit.'

I can hear from the laughter and chatter inside the room that the others have already arrived, so I nod, and smile, and am filled with excitement.

We follow him through, and barely squeeze in. Zoe and Cal and Martha are here; Lizzie and Nate; Cherie and Frank and Edie, perched on a chair next to the bed. Becca and Sam are squashed in the far corner, and Little Edie is snoozing in her mum's arms, oblivious to the excitement.

Saul worms his way through the crowds, and inserts himself onto the end of the bed, crawling slowly towards Laura.

Laura, who is sitting propped up on pillows at the centre of it all. Laura, who looks pale and tired and ecstatic. Laura, who is cradling two utterly tiny but utterly perfect babies in her arms. They're both very small, and both wrapped in pink blankets and wearing weeny little pink hats, and I can barely see their equally pink faces peering out at their new habitat.

I know from talking to Matt earlier that the babies made their way into the world a couple of hours after we left. Laura was a champion, he said, his voice bursting with pride – she got through the whole thing with only gas and air, even though the doctors would have preferred an epidural in case they needed to intervene.

They didn't need to. The babies were delivered well and safe, one of them at four pound ten and the other at five pound one, a really good size for slightly early twins. Neither of them needed any special care, both of them are breathing well and have passed all their tests so far with flying colours. They're small, and they'll need to stay here in hospital with Laura for a few more days just to be sure – but they're healthy. All the signs are good.

Laura looks up and spots us lurking by the door, and the smile that spreads across her face is nothing short of serene.

'Come and meet them!' she says, making her voice heard over the din. 'Come and meet my beautiful babies!'

Willow makes a path through the many bodies, and we eventually find ourselves at the side of the bed. I reach down, and pull one of the baby's blankets to one side. I'm rewarded with the glint of one blue eye, looking up at me as though it knows all the secrets of the universe.

Lynnie is delighted to be in the company of babies, as ever, and suggests that they should be called Teeny and Tiny. She named all of us after our physical characteristics at birth, and apart from the fact that Van's funny ear doesn't look funny any more, they seem to fit. I'm definitely still Auburn and Willow's definitely still Willowy.

'That's a lovely idea,' says Laura gently, 'but we've already decided on names. This is Ruby and Rose. Ruby is the slightly smaller one, and Rose is the chubby one.'

Neither of the babies is even remotely chubby, but I suppose it's all relative. I stroke their tiny cheeks with one finger, velvety soft and peachy, and can't believe how adorable they are.

'Thank you,' Laura says, smiling up at me. 'For getting me here. And I'm sorry about the sofa. And please thank Seb for me as well, won't you?'

I nod, and kiss her curly head, and move out of the way so that the others can shuffle forward and have their turn looking at Ruby and Rose.

I make my way to the back of the room, and stand there with a stupid grin on my face as I watch the next few minutes unfold. Saul is spellbound by the babies, gentle despite Katie's worried expression. Edie is delighted, clapping her wrinkled hands together in glee every time they gurgle or waggle a tiny finger, proclaiming them the very best babies ever.

The teenagers are trying to look bored and failing, and Lizzie keeps darting back to Laura's side to check if she needs anything, so engrossed in her new role as a big sister that she seems to have forgotten to apply her eyeliner.

Cherie and Frank are standing off to one side, looking on happily, watching over it all like proud parents – which, in a weird way, they kind of are. The Comfort Food Café mum and dad, with Edie as our gran, and the rest of us interconnected and linked in so many invisible ways, like a spider web of friendship. We might not all be related by blood, but we are a family. One big, weirdly shaped, but usually happy family. It all feels like a small miracle to me.

I'm feeling a bit emotional, which I put down to a lack of sleep and a tempestuous day and the fact that I'm basically a mess. Seb was so tremendous today, and I feel like he should be here. I also feel like Finn should be here.

Thankfully, neither of them is – which means I can sneak outside and have a little cry in private.

I've only been gone for a few moments when Matt emerges from the room. He takes in my dishevelled state but doesn't say anything about it, for which I am extremely grateful.

'The babies are beautiful, Matt,' I say. 'Perfect.'

'I know,' he replies quietly, that soppy smile appearing again – I'm not sure he'll ever lose it. Or maybe he will once the sleep deprivation kicks in. 'And thank you, for everything you and Seb did. Are you . . . okay?'

'Oh, yeah,' I say, reassuringly. 'A bit tired and emotional, that's all. Is everyone ready to leave you guys to it, before the hospital management send in a SWAT team?'

'Yes. I think there may be some kind of plan to go to the pub. I'd stay here all night if I could, but I've been warned they're going to kick me out, so I might even join you all at some point. Unless I can persuade them to let me sleep on the chair . . .'

He doesn't sound even a tiny bit sad at the thought of not coming to wet the babies' heads, which is a tribute to how happy he is with his new-found fatherhood.

As he speaks, the door opens, and everyone starts to trek back out. There is a lot of hugging and laughing and kissing as the party breaks up, temporarily, and the various groups make their way to their vehicles with promises to see each other in the Horse and Rider.

I peak through the door, and see Laura still snuggling the babies, contentedly kissing their tiny foreheads.

'Better get back to it,' says Matt, patting me on the arm. 'Drink a few for me, won't you?'

Chapter 20

By the time I drop Willow and Lynnie back off at home, then walk over to the pub, it's dark and starry-skied. Especially as I lurk around in the house for a while, drinking peppermint tea and chatting and toying with the idea of going to bed.

I'm not sure I want to go to the pub, but it seems churlish to refuse, and I allow myself to be swept along with the tide of communal enthusiasm. I receive approximately seven thousand texts about it while I'm in the kitchen, and Willow basically shoves me out of the door. She wants to stay in with Lynnie, who is still very tired, and talk to Tom on Facetime while he's away in London.

I tell myself I will have a nice time. I will have a pint, talk to my friends, and celebrate the arrival of Budbury's latest wonders. I will at least show willing – and besides, Finn will be there and it will be good to feel his arms aroundme. Assuming there's not a cuddle ban as well.

As I walk into the village pub, I'm greeted with a whoosh of warmth and noise and laughter. It's full, as usual, locals perched on tall stools at the bar and the staff dashing around behind it. It's an old place, with an old character, packed with nooks and crannies and a fireplace that roars away in winter. There's a darts game going on in the corner, and the sound of someone playing the fruit machines in the background.

I let my eyes adjust, and glance around looking for my friends. They're not hard to spot, taking up most of one of the side rooms, one of the most raucous gatherings in the pub. There are two empty Champagne bottles on the table, several pint-glasses, and Edie's traditional tot of sherry.

As I walk over, I guess she's maybe not on her first, the dirty stop-out. She's holding forth on the revival of 'lovely traditional names', animatedly saying how she had both a Ruby and a Rose in her family back in the 1930s.

'I've seen them all come and go,' she says, between sips. 'The Lindas and Debbies and Sharons and Tracys and Jackies. And now we've come full circle – so many Charlottes and Emilys, and Edies too! Maybe one day, even my middle name will come back into fashion . . .'

She pauses, and Zoe jumps in: 'Go on then. I'll oblige: what's your middle name?'

'Maud!' replies Edie, clapping her hands together in glee and watching for everybody's reaction.

'Ugggh, no,' says Zoe, pulling a face. 'Edie, I love you, but that is one of the ugliest names ever!'

'Isn't it just!' Edie cackles. 'But if you ever have a baby, Zoe my love, bear it in mind . . .'

'Ha!' answers Zoe firmly. 'That is never going to happen.'

'Never say never,' adds Cal, sitting next to her, looking exotic and edible in his usual cowboy hat get-up.

That provokes a round of 'oohs' and 'aahs' from around the table, and I make the most of the distraction to sidle over towards them. Finn has already spotted me, and gives me a cheeky wink that makes me laugh.

He's out of his work 'uniform' of smart shirt, and instead is modelling a long-sleeved T-shirt in a shade of pale blue that's almost exactly the same colour as his eyes. His long thighs are encased with denim, and his blond hair is freshly washed and silky. He's had it cut, and it's shorter than usual – a bit Daniel Craig in Bond. It's pretty much begging for me to touch it, in fact.

He stands up and walks towards me, and wraps me in his arms. I look up at him, and slip my fingers into his hair.

'Lovely,' I say, grinning. 'Like sprayed-on liquid sunshine. I'm liking the new look. Did you take pictures from *Casino Royale* with you when you went to the barber?'

'Why thank you,' he replies, tugging me closer. 'And of course – I'm getting ready for our Miss Moneypenny-finally-gets-some session.'

'I'm looking forward to that. When will it be?'

He smiles at me, and it's a smile full of promise. In fact it makes Miss Moneypenny melt in all the right places.

'When the time is right,' he says simply. He disengages from me, and we both sit down. Cal goes to the bar, which he's very good at. Must be an Australian thing. He can even carry four pint-glasses at a time, which never ceases to amaze me.

The mood is high and excited, the arrival of Rose and Ruby giving us all a boost. We chat about babies and life and the café and new shows on Netflix, and it's all delightful. I'm tired, but I'm glad I came.

Eventually, we hear the traditional ding-ding-ding for last orders, and Cal leaps to his feet. I'm guessing he'll do what he usually does, and get double for everyone. Never willingly the first out of a pub, that man.

He's standing up, and looking towards the bar, and I see his expression change. I see Zoe's gaze follow his, and a 'yikes' look settle on her face, matched with wide eyes and a chewed lip. I see Cherie and Frank give each other significant looks, and Van staring from the bar to me in concern.

I have the horrible feeling I know what's happening here, but I hope I'm wrong. I hope I'll turn around and see something less scary, like a two-headed man-eating dragon, or the clown from *It*.

I take a deep breath, swivel in my chair, and see Matt lurking at the bar, looking exhausted and a bit sheepish.

Standing by his side, exotic and totally out of place in a countryside pub in England, is Seb.

I realise that everyone is suddenly tense, looking from me to Seb to Finn, not quite knowing how to react. I glance at Finn, and see that he's rigid and upright, his thigh hard against mine. I take his hand, and look into his eyes, and say: 'I'm sorry. I had no idea he was coming.'

Finn shakes his head, as though dismissing it – as though everything is okay – but I can tell it's not.

'Don't worry,' he replies, patting my hand. 'It was bound to happen sometime or another. And truth be told, I'm kind of relieved to get it out of the way. But . . . well, I'm a bit lost for words. He's . . . he's not exactly been hit with the ugly stick, has he?'

I feel so sorry for him, so hurt on his behalf. Because no, Seb hasn't exactly been hit with the ugly stick. All around the pub I can see women and some men taking surreptitious peeks at him. He's impossibly tall, dark and handsome, in a way that feels suddenly unfair. I feel like I should have warned Finn about it, but hey, that's not an easy conversation to have, is it: 'Oh, by the way, I should mention that my ex is a total Adonis.'

'He's nothing compared to you,' I reply reassuringly, as Matt and Seb make their way towards us.

Matt, suddenly realising the awkwardness of the situation, gives Finn a look that is full of apology. It's a look that says: 'Mate, I have well and truly fucked up, and I didn't think this through, and I'm knackered and didn't have my head on straight.'

In return, Finn gives him a brief nod. It's a nod that says: 'It's all right pal, I understand, and it's no big deal.'

Amazing how well I speak Man, isn't it? Or maybe I made that all up, who knows.

Cherie, bless her, breaks the tension by asking Matt how Laura and the babies are, and luckily that takes the focus temporarily away from us. It's a relief – I don't much like being the centre of attention, especially as the filling in a man sandwich. It's strange and weird and feels like I'm about to navigate my way across a minefield.

Seb smiles at me while Matt replies, and it feels too intimate – like we're connected somehow. Finn stands up, and offers his hand.

'Hi,' he says, his voice firm and confident, 'I'm Finn. We've not officially met.'

Seb shakes his hand, and it takes a bit too long. Like neither of them wants to look less manly by stopping first.

'Nice to meet you, Finn,' he responds. 'I've heard a lot about you.'

They stare at each other, neither of them doing anything overtly hostile, but neither of them exactly backing down either. We're back to tense again, and this time it's Cal who breaks the moment. 'Drinks!' he says loudly. 'We all need more drinks! Seb, give me a hand at the bar, would you, mate?'

Seb obliges, and Matt very quickly says: 'God, I'm so sorry. I just didn't think. I should have guessed you'd be here, Finn. I . . . well, after I got kicked out of the ward, I took Lizzie and Nate home, and then I popped round to Hyacinth to tell Seb the news, and give him his boots back. I mentioned the pub, and he looked so . . . lonely, that I invited him along. I've put both my feet in it, haven't I?'

'Don't worry,' replies Finn, before I get the chance to say anything. 'It's all fine. You shouldn't be worrying about us on a night like this. Just enjoy yourself.'

It's the perfect thing to say under the circumstances, and he clearly has Matt fooled. Maybe it's because I know Finn better, or maybe it's because I'm sitting next to him and can feel the tension in his body, but I can tell it's not fine.

Luckily, it's enough for Matt, who moves on to take up a spot by the window with Edie. I see her ask him something, and he grins and gets out his phone, scrolling through the screen. Babies' first photo shoot, I'm guessing.

'Are you all right?' I ask, trying to engage Finn's eyes with mine and failing. Failing because his eyes are fixed on the bar, following Seb and Cal as they get the ales in.

Finn glances back at me, and nods abruptly.

'Of course,' he says. 'It's all fine.'

He's basically repeated what he said to Matt, and I'm not buying it. I'm starting to feel a bit frustrated, with the situation, with myself. With the fact that Finn is clearly bottling up a whole lot of stuff right now.

'Are you about to go all kick-ass on me and cause trouble?' I ask, half-joking. 'Because if you spill those pints, Cal won't be happy.'

He manages a small smile, and shakes his head. There's a look on his face I don't quite recognise, and suddenly it's easier to imagine him in his bad old days. The days of mayhem and berserking.

'I promise I won't,' he answers. 'But this is weird, and I feel even weirder. I know I shouldn't react like this, but I don't seem able to help it. I thought I was a more evolved creature, but it seems like my inner caveman wants to come out to play.'

'Tell him he can't,' I reply quickly. 'Tell him that I'm not a cave woman, and that any attempts to club your rival with a woolly mammoth bone and carry me back to your fire will be met with much anger.'

He nods and agrees, and I can see him make a real effort to relax. Luckily everyone else here is savvy enough to have restarted their various conversations, giving us a bit of space, and by the time Cal and Seb come back to the table in a relay of pint-glasses and wine and bags of crisps, a pleasant buzz of chatter has settled back down over us.

I'm hoping that Seb has the wisdom to go and sit on the other side of the table – ideally the other side of the pub – but of course, he doesn't. Instead, he sits right next to me, so I'm stuck there between the two of them. Arse.

Seb holds his glass up – fizzy water in a pint – and says 'cheers'. Zoe, next along from him, is the only one who joins in.

She sees the look on my face, and obviously decides we need help.

'So,' she says, 'Seb. I believe you were stuck in the back of a van with a woman in labour this morning?'

'I was,' he nods. 'And I have to say, Laura has a hell of a grip. I didn't do much, and I'm glad it all turned out well.'

'You did quite a lot, actually,' I reply, wishing I didn't feel the need to. 'You kept her calm, which was probably the most important thing we could do for her right then. Thank you, because there was no way I could have driven and kept her calm at the same time.'

I see Finn's nostrils flare slightly, but he stays quiet, looks serene. I'm guessing he doesn't feel it, and this is a less than ideal situation – but we all need to take a deep breath and act like bloody grown-ups.

Seb looks pleased with what I've said, and gives me a little salute.

'At your service, querida – at any time,' he says, in an infuriatingly flirtatious way. Looks like he didn't get the memo about being a grown-up.

'How are you enjoying your visit to Budbury?' asks Zoe, her voice several pitches higher than usual as she picks up on the danger signs. 'Must be a change from Barcelona.'

Seb answers her, but his eyes keep flashing back to me. To Finn.

'Very different in some ways,' he says, smiling. 'But also beautiful, and not without its attractions.'

'When will you be going back?' asks Finn, his tone suggesting that perhaps right now might be a splendid idea.

He's staring right at Seb, and this time there's no disguising the fact that there is an alpha male showdown on the cards.

'Not sure,' Seb says, 'it depends on how certain things go.'

He lays a hand on my thigh as he says this, and even I feel like punching him. I have a fleeting and satisfying image of Seb lying splattered on the table, covered in lager dregs and dry-roasted peanuts. I swipe his hand away, and say very clearly: 'Knock it off, Seb.'

He tries to look innocent, raising his eyebrows in a 'Who, me?' kind of way, and I shake my head in a strange combination of disgust and a tiny bit of amusement.

His face breaks out into a grin, and he says: 'I'm sorry – Finn, Auburn, I'm sorry. I try not to be an idiot, but somehow it seems to come naturally to me. Forgive me. This is as strange for me as it is for you, and I've forgotten my manners.'

That partially redeems him – and it's certainly a level of self-awareness and honesty that I wouldn't ever have got from him years ago, when he'd bluff his way through any situation rather than ever admit he was wrong.

'Yes, it must be strange,' replies Finn quietly. 'Being here and seeing your ex-wife with another man.'

I glance at him – I'm starting to feel like I'm at a tennis match here – and see that there is no trace of amusement on his face. Seb's apology doesn't seem to have taken hold, or even registered.

Seb, not being blind, also realises this. The grin falls from his face, and he answers: 'Wife. She's still my wife, not my ex-wife.'

Zoe is also looking from one to the other, on tenterhooks as she waits to see what will happen next in the movie that is my life. Everyone else is being polite enough to ignore our side of the table, apart from Van, who is looking over with a touching big brotherly concern.

That's the moment when I decide that enough is enough. This is all too much, and it's making me desperate for a cigarette. That is never a good sign.

I stand up abruptly, catching the edge of the table and sloshing a bit of booze over its wooden surface.

'Going to the ladies,' I announce, with as much dignity as I can muster. I don't give anybody the chance to reply, and instead stride off in the direction of the loos. I pass the tinkling fruit machines and the loud darts game and the locals on their stools, and make a decision halfway that I'm not going to the ladies. I'm going to leave.

I snake my way through the crowds, and out of the door, not realising until I'm in the fresh air that I'd been holding my breath. I lean back against the wall, and do some in-and-out puffs, and start to calm down. Every sinew in my body is tense and strung out, and my fingers are clenched into tight fists.

I start to stride off in the direction of the cottage, and then spot that Katie's living room light is on. On the spur of the moment, I tap on her window gently, not wanting to disturb anyone if she is in fact asleep.

Within seconds the door is thrown open, and she stands in front of me, in a not exactly demure night gown. In fact it looks like something from a seventies sitcom, fluffy and lacy and very, very small. She looks first a tad disappointed, followed rapidly by embarrassed. I quickly realise what causes these responses, and burst out laughing. The laughter comes as a huge release, and I feel some of the stress flow out of me.

'Expecting a game of Twister?' I ask, grinning at her as she gestures me quickly to come inside. 'Sorry to let you down. Van's still in the pub.'

She makes a shushing gesture as we walk through into the lounge, obviously not wanting me to wake Saul up, and closes the living room door quietly behind me. She grabs a big, faded pink dressing gown and puts it on over her sex doll outfit, which probably comes as a relief to both of us.

I plonk down on the sofa, and she sits across from me on the chair, now firmly belted in to the dressing gown. Tinkerbell, her inappropriately named ginger tomcat, leaps all the way from the windowsill into my lap and curls up into a big fat ball. I stroke him absent-mindedly as she talks.

'Sorry about that,' she says quietly, smiling. 'And yes, I was expecting a game of Twister. How's things?'

'If by "How's things?" you mean, "Why did you turn up on my doorstep late at night?", then the answer is . . . things are getting messy.'

'Messy how? And do you want a cuppa? Or . . . a bottle of bourbon, maybe?'

'Do you have a bottle of bourbon?'

'No. I'm not that interesting. I just thought it sounded good.'

I laugh, and slip off my trainers, and put my feet up. It feels nice to be here, somewhere safe and easy and calm. Katie's house always feels like this – a pleasant but whole-some world of kids' toys and cartoons and plants she manages to keep alive. She's the kind of mum that always has biscuits in, and irons duvet covers.

'No, I'm fine, thanks,' I say. 'No cuppa required. I was just passing on my way home. I'm sure Van will fill you in on all this, but basically we had a bit of a clash of the titans in the pub.'

She looks understandably confused, and I explain what had happened.

'Oh!' she says, covering her surprised mouth with one dainty hand. 'That sounds awful! How did it go?'

'Well, I told them I was going to the ladies and came here instead, so that's how it went . . . bit of a dick move on my part, now I come to think of it. But I couldn't stand being stuck in the middle any more, and didn't want to cause any kind of scene.

'It was horrible, and also embarrassing. Tonight was supposed to be all about Matt and Laura and celebrating the babies. Not about me and my pathetic love life. Anyway, they were both annoying me so much, I knew it wasn't going to lead anywhere good if I stayed.'

She nods, and ponders this, and asks: 'Where do you think it might have led?'

'Hard to say. Bloodshed. Murder. Awkward silences. Finn . . . well, Finn is wonderful. But he's only human, and Seb was winding him up in a way that only Seb can, and it looked like it could turn nasty. So I thought I'd remove the cause of the conflict – me, in other words. They might even have noticed I'm gone by now, if they're not too busy with their invisible penis-measuring contest.'

Katie giggles a bit at this, and tries to hide her amusement, obviously thinking this is a Serious Subject.

'No, it's okay to laugh,' I say, firmly. 'Because it is very silly. Silly and also a bit . . . unsettling. Having them both there was so strange. Of course, they were too busy sizing up the competition to think about how I felt, which is fair enough.'

'And how did you feel? How do you feel? I know you and Finn are just starting out, but you seem so happy. And then Seb is . . . well, Seb is gorgeous, isn't he? I feel disloyal saying that, but he is. And he also seems nice, and like he's working hard on living a better life, and like he genuinely wants you back.'

Damn her. She's gone and unleashed the beast – by putting into words some of what I'd been thinking.

'Aaah, Katie, I don't know. When Seb first got here, I was horrified, and I just wanted him to leave. I still want him to leave – but maybe not for exactly the same reasons.'

'Go on,' she says, making a wind-it-along gesture, 'follow that thought. It might be important.'

I nod, and think, and talk, and possibly the talking and the thinking collide and I only understand some of what I'm thinking when I say it out loud. If that makes sense.

'Well,' I say, 'when he arrived, I wanted him gone because he was the past. He was the past, and the past was bad, and Finn was the future, and I wanted the future to be good. Simple, right? But as you say, he does seem to be working hard – and he is so different than when I first knew him. Not in every way, but he somehow seems to have got rid of the bad parts, and kept hold of the good ones.His sense of humour. His kindness. His way of making me feel like I'm the only woman in the entire world who exists to him.'

'That's an intoxicating mix,' replies Katie understand-ingly. 'Plus the gorgeousness. So . . . do you think you still have feelings for him?'

This, of course, is the question of the moment – and it's not an easy one to answer honestly. Answering it dishonestly, much as I might want to, will be of no benefit to anyone, especially not me.

'I'm not sure,' I say, feeling glum. 'I definitely want him to leave – but I think maybe I want him to leave because I don't feel safe with him here any more. I feel like, if he stays, he'll chip away at me and my resolve, and there is a fraction of a chance that I'll . . . fall for him again. And the logical part of me knows that wouldn't be right. It'd end things with Finn, who is so good for me. And it'd start things with Seb, who isn't good for me, and . . . God, I'm such a mess.'

I puff out a big breath of frustrated air, and hope she has some pearls of wisdom that will clear the whole thing up.

'That's hard,' she says, which is sympathetic but not wise. 'And tricky. And complicated. But . . . okay, then, imagine this. Imagine if Finn wasn't around. Imagine if Tom had given that job at Briarwood to a middle-aged woman with warts and bad breath. Imagine you'd never met him, and Seb had come back into your life. This Seb, the current model – not the old Seb. What would you do then?'

It's an interesting scenario. I try to overlook the logical flaw – that if it wasn't for Finn, I might never have asked for a divorce, and Seb might not have come looking for me – and picture the scene.

If I was single. If I wasn't with Finn. If I was available . . . crikey. It's still complicated, because everything involving me and Seb is.

'I'm not sure it would make any difference,' I reply, after a few moments of trying very hard to work out how I feel. 'I'd still be scared. I'd still be freaked out. Me and Seb . . . well, it was messy. And I'm not at a stage in my life where I want messy.'

She nods, and smiles gently, and says: 'Nobody does. I didn't with Van. But sometimes you have to go through the messy to find the good. I'm not saying that you should be with Seb – only you can make that decision. But being scared of messy probably isn't a good motivation for staying with Finn either.'

She makes it sound so simple when she puts it like that – as though Finn is the straightforward one, and Seb is the chaotic one, and they're both different facets of my personality. Of course, she is unaware of Finn's history – and the glimpse I saw of it in him tonight. That's not Katie's business, and not my story to tell, so I stay quiet

– but I do know that Finn is far from straightforward. He brings his own share of messy as well, as we all do.

I'm saved from continuing the conversation – which is both useful and alarming – by a sharp tap on the window. I look at Katie, and she shrugs.

'If that's Van,' I say, 'expecting you in a negligee, he's going to be totally freaked out when his sister answers the door.'

'At least you're not in a negligee,' she replies as she stands up, taking a sneaky peek through the curtains.

'Nope,' she announces. 'It's not Van. It's for you.'

'Aaaaagh. Which one?' I ask.

'Which one do you want it to be?'

'Edie.'

'Tough luck. It's Finn.'

I let out a groan, and wipe my eyes with my fingers – they seem to have been a bit leaky at some point – and drag myself up from the warm embrace of Katie's couch. I feel about seven hundred years old right now, and would quite like to go and live in a nunnery and learn how to churn butter.

'Okay. I'll talk to him outside, I don't want to wake Saul up. Will you let me back in after?'

'I will,' she says kindly. 'And I'll put the kettle on.'

I nod in thanks, take a deep breath, stand up tall, and walk to the front door. I let myself out, and close it quietly behind me.

It's a beautiful, clear night, the stars bright in the sky, and Finn looks just as beautiful standing there in the moonlight. He has his hands in his pockets, and seems sad. I hate that he's sad. I hate that all of this is happening – but I also know that the only way we'll have a future together is if our foundations are solid. I can't skip this stage and tell Seb to clear out and hope for the best – what little wisdom I've gained as I've blundered my way through life tells me this.

'Hi,' he says quietly. 'You okay?'

'Yeah,' I reply, keeping my voice low. 'I had to leave. I was getting too aroused by all the alpha male big-dog action in there. How did you find me?'

'I had you fitted with a tracking device.'

My eyes pop open, and for a second I believe him. Nobody else would, but last year Tom managed to successfully fit my mother with one via a cleverly designed pendant, so it's not unheard of in Budbury.

'I didn't,' he adds quickly, seeing my response. 'I saw you head here through the window in the pub. Everyone else thought you were having digestive issues.'

'That's good to know. The whole village will be talking about my bowels tomorrow.'

'Ummm . . . no. They probably won't be. They'll probably be talking about you and me and Seb, and what massive tits the two men in that equation made of themselves tonight.'

271

I pull a face, and reply: 'I can't argue with that description. In fact it's doing a disservice to tits. Look . . . I realise that he provoked you, Finn. But that didn't make it any easier to handle. I just . . . I don't like what this is doing to us.'

'Me neither,' he says, nodding. 'That wasn't me back there . . . Well, it was me. A part of me I don't especially like. But it is what it is. I just wanted to apologise. We acted like you weren't even there, like it was all about us.'

That's very true, and very annoying – but I don't expect perfection from Finn, when I'm so far from it myself.

'Well. It's done now. And thank you for apologising. It's okay – maybe one day, I'll even consider it as flattering.'

He thinks about this, and answers: 'I suppose it is, in a way, and some women might even enjoy having men fight over them. But not you – and I don't want to be that man either. I want you to be with me because you choose to be with me, not because I knocked Seb out.'

'You didn't, did you?' I ask, momentarily alarmed. I glance over at the pub, and see no signs of ambulance lights or broken windows.

'No,' he says, laughing. 'But I kind of wanted to, which isn't a good thing. So. I suppose I'd better get going. Unless . . . do you want me to walk you home?'

It sounds so old-fashioned and gentlemanly, I'm almost tempted.

'Thank you, but no. Not tonight. I think maybe we all need to catch our breath and calm down.'

He shrugs and looks disappointed but resigned.

'All right. I understand. My own fault for imposing the sex ban, I suppose. Anyway . . . I'll speak to you tomorrow, then. I'm off to that conference on Tuesday as well, so you'll have plenty of time to . . . catch your breath, like you say. Maybe when I come back, we can see where the land lies.'

I nod, and reach up to caress his face. He rests his cheek in my palm, then gently kisses my fingers.

'Goodnight, Auburn. I love you.'

I lean up and give him a quick kiss on the lips.

'I love you too,' I reply, watching as he walks away, up the moonlit street and towards the hills.

I do love him. I really do. But I'm not quite sure that's enough. I could march over to the pub right now, order Seb to pack his bags and head for the hills, and pretend none of this ever happened.

I could remove Seb from my life – but could I completely remove him from my heart? I'm beginning to suspect that he's been lurking there for a very long time.

Chapter 21

I spend the next couple of days throwing myself into work. Cherie has been busy with Sandra and Willow, putting together the Comfort Food Café care packages, and today is the day I am going to start distributing them.

Finn seems to have gone into some kind of self-imposed exile at Briarwood, and Seb has extensively and fulsomely apologised for his behaviour on the night in the pub. He seems to really mean it, as does Finn, and I do believe them. It doesn't necessarily follow that it wouldn't happen again, but I do believe them.

The whole thing has shaken me up, and also left me feeling trapped – our mama didn't raise us girls to be supporting players in any man's life, and that's kind of how it made me feel. So instead, I'm concentrating on my job, and my friends, and doing the things that matter in my own world. Things I'd be doing regardless of Seb or Finn.

I arrive at the café on a Saturday morning to find it an absolute hive of activity. The weather isn't brilliant this morning, as though it wanted to remind us that this might technically be early summer, but we're still in England after all. There's been a steady drizzle blowing in from the sea in cool gusts and the sky is a flat grey, so the beach is a lot less busy than usual – which in turn means the café is short on paying customers.

What it's not short on is boxes. Big boxes, all in pretty pastel shades, and printed up with the café's logo on the side. The café didn't have anything as fancy as a logo until Lizzie got to work – but her budding marketing genius has resulted in a pretty little design that mimics the sign at the top of the steps, the wrought-iron roses announcing their welcome to the Comfort Food Café.

She's also whipped up flyers to go inside the boxes that basically ask for feedback – for the recipients to go online and leave reviews, to send comments via the Facebook page, to tweet about it. None of this is remotelyimportant to Cherie, who always seems happy enough to let the café business expand or contract organically, but it's quite clever – it allows my merry band of customers to enjoy a box full of goodies without feeling like they're charity cases, and will also help sell the café. Lizzie is a clever little minx.

I'd pointed out that some of these people might not have access to the internet, or be savvy enough to use it – I can't see Mr Pumpwell trending on Twitter or posting on Pinterest – so she's also added a blank section for them to fill in hand-written comments, which they can send back via snail mail, or in person.

At Cherie's prompting, there's also a questionnaire, asking what kinds of events they'd like to see happening in the café and in the village, and what would encourage them or prevent them from coming along. She's suggested a few things – parent and baby mornings; yoga classes for the over-sixties; a tour of Frank's farm; arts and crafts groups, and a get-together for people and pets, which is also open to those who don't have pets but would like to spend some time with them. All good ideas.

By the time I get there, with Lynnie – who suggested the yoga classes, naturally – they're packing the last few items into the ten boxes we're starting with.

I can smell the lemon drizzle cake, and a quick peek inside one also reveals some pots of home-made jam, baskets of fresh scones, bottles of cloudy lemonade, bags of Laura's cookies, and a selection of nuts and candies. Yumlicious.

Lizzie is overseeing all this activity, standing off to one side with a clipboard and pen, her blonde hair bobbing in a ponytail. Laura is still in hospital with the twins, but hopes to be out on Monday – and in the meantime, Lizzie seems to have grown up into a mum herself. She's happily bossing everyone around, and I suspect Nate's life back at the cottage has been pure hell.

Midgebo is fascinated with the whole thing, his big black nose doing overtime as he sniffs around the place, a frustrated look on his doggie face that says he knows there is food around, but the pesky humans won't let him get at it. Bella Swan, our dog, is too dignified for such things, and has curled up in a watchful ball by the bookshelves.

Seb is here too, having become quite the regular at the café, helping to fill the boxes and posing happily when Lizzie wants to take photos. He looks especially exotic next to Edie, who is dressed head to toe in beige – cardigan, skirt, tights, shoes.

Lynnie narrows her eyes at him and mutters something under her breath, then takes herself away to a corner in a huff. I see her lips moving at a distance, and wonder if she's uttering the words to some ancient Druid curse.

'Good morning, Budbury!' I say grandly. 'Are we ready to rock?'

Edie cackles and makes that weird two-fingered salute I associate more with Ozzy Osbourne than a spinster in her nineties – but what do I know? The secret to her long life could be biting the heads off bats in the privacy of her own home.

'Just the ribbons to go,' replies Lizzie, bustling around and handing out strips of brightly coloured fabric. She has very specific ideas about how the ribbons should be tied, and there are a few false starts before the sergeant major is satisfied. Seriously, she's so bossy, I half expect to be told to drop and give her fifty push-ups when I get it wrong.

I have to admit, though, that by the time we're done, all of the boxes look splendid. Seb and Frank are given the job of loading them into my van, which takes them a few trips up and down the hillside, and eventually we're ready to go.

Lynnie stays at the café with Willow and Bella Swan, and Seb announces that he will be coming with me.

'When was that decided?' I ask, hands on hips in the car park, fine rain managing to soak me through within minutes.

'Right now,' he replies, grinning at me. 'You need some help, and I have nothing else to do. I checked with Lizzie and she said it was finc.'

That makes me laugh out loud – this, of course, has nothing to do with Lizzie. And Lizzie is a teenager. But for some reason, she's managed to convince us all that if we get her permission and approval, everything will be all right. She's going to run the world one of these days, and probably a lot more efficiently than the people currently running it.

Seb has kept things light between us since Pub Gate. He's done it on purpose, and he's wise to. We've seen each other at the pharmacy, and we've been for one pub lunch, and we've been for a walk with Bella Swan on the beach.

On each occasion, he's been charming, and funny, and interesting, and generally good, easy company. I can see he's making the effort to do that, and can follow his reasoning – to show me how well we get on. How much we enjoy each other. How simple and easy and pleasurable time spent together can be.

I know he's doing it on purpose, but he's also right. With all the intensity that's been suffocating me recently, I needed some light among the shade. I needed some fun, and bad jokes, and simplicity. I'm not a complete idiot – I'm well aware that things are not as simple as they seem – but all the same, I take it gratefully.

Finn has gone quiet on me, which again I understand. He needs to regroup as well, and he's dealing with things that aren't just about me. He's dealing with his own issues, his own demons. Between the three of us, in fact, there are a lot of demons to go around – we're all so messed up that hell must be entirely empty.

I'm not shallow enough to forget Finn simply because he's retreated a little – you don't stop loving someone when they have problems. You try and help them through their problems instead. But now more than ever I realise that what Finn and I have is new. New and untested and as yet unproven. I don't want to think that Seb being here, and Seb being on a charm offensive, can break it – but if it's actually that fragile, then it probably wouldn't last anyway.

Even thinking that sends a spasm of pain shooting through my chest, as though it might induce a panic attack, or a cardiac event. I don't want to lose him – but at the same time I don't want to keep him if it isn't right between us.

Normal people always face challenges in their relationships. There are arguments and problems and fights about trivia and fights about big stuff and fights about the things in the middle. There might be children in the mix, or long distances keeping them apart, or money worries, or even political or religious differences.

Normal people face these challenges as they go – and sometimes it makes a relationship, sometimes it breaks it. Laura had to find a way to put her past with David behind her before she could move on with Matt. Willow had to find a balance between caring for Lynnie and being with Tom. Zoe had to get over her friend's death, learn how to be a mum to Martha, and open up before she could accept Cal into her life.

Every single one of them has faced big tests. Every single one of them has come through it. Maybe, I tell myself, as I watch Seb slam shut the van doors and walk back around to me, Seb is merely the ultimate test for me and Finn. And hopefully we'll come through it too.

Or maybe, an annoying little voice adds as I climb into the driver's seat and click on my belt, maybe this life – here in Budbury, with Finn – was a test of how I truly feel about Seb.

I scowl at him as he clambers in beside me, and he looks confused.

'What?' he says innocently, holding his hand over his heart. 'What did I do now?'

'Nothing,' I reply, concentrating on starting the van up instead. 'You just exist, and it's annoying.'

I give the van horn a few toots as we drive off, and Cherie and the gang wave as we drive away off up the coastal road. There's usually a lovely view from here, but today it's dull and grey and covered in sulky-looking clouds. I think I may have affected the weather.

'Would you prefer that I don't exist?' he asks, half smiling at me as I drive.

'Sometimes, yes, frankly,' I say. 'Or that maybe you existed in a parallel universe.'

'Right. Well, what about the times you don't wish that? What about the times you're quite happy I exist?'

I ponder that one as I build up some speed, overtaking an ice-cream van that's probably decided to call it a day, and settling onto the dual carriageway.

'I suppose,' I reply, 'that you're not always awful. You're good at cooking tapas. You're good at giving pregnant women massages.'

'Not just pregnant women,' he interjects, his tone flirty. 'All women. In fact, I specialise in over-worked pharmacists with attitude problems. You only have to say the word, and I could massage all your stress away . . .'

'Ha!' I snap back, pulling into fifth gear with way too

much force, 'I don't think so! I think that might unleash a whole new world of stress . . .'

'It could unleash a whole world of other stuff too, couldn't it?'

I ignore him, and concentrate on driving. Of course, that's exactly what I'd be afraid of – no matter how much I tell myself I won't be falling for this man again, and no matter how much I love Finn, there is no way in a million years I'd let him near me with a bottle of almond oil. I'm only human, and he already knows his way around my libido a bit too well.

He seems to realise that the topic is now closed, and we both stay quiet for a while. He's probably planning his next move, and I'm waiting for my heart rate to settle.

Eventually, he changes the subject to safer ground, and starts to ask about the people we will be visiting. I fill him in on the various patients and their lives, careful to blank out any medical details to protect their privacy, and he listens well. This is another aspect of the new and improved Seb that has constantly surprised me.

The old Seb was a bit haphazard when it came to listening. Sometimes, he'd be amazing, and we spent so many nights pondering the meaning of life and soul-searching in that way you only do when you're young and in love. When you've fallen hard, and think this is the only other person on the planet who could possibly understand you.

Other times, especially when he was artificially stimulated, he would literally only let people talk long enough to give him an excuse to start. Every conversation was one way, every chat was a performance, every dinner out was a new instalment in the Seb Show.

Now, though, he's . . . different. He listens, and he asks pertinent questions, and he seems genuinely interested in other people and what's going on with them and ways we might help.

He has some good ideas about Cherie's planned sessions, suggesting neck and shoulder massages for the sleep-deprived mums and the stressed out carers, coming up with a concept for a simple recipe book for nutritious smoothies, setting up a walking group to get them out and about when they're physically capable.

I recognise some of these ideas as ones he's probably used himself, during therapy and recovery, and to keep himself on the straight and narrow. I do admire the way he's turned his life around, the way he lives now.

'Wasn't this all a risk for you?' I ask, interrupting him mid-flow.

'What?' he asks, frowning.

'Coming here. Seeing me. Staying even when you found out I was with Finn. You've . . . well, you've done brilliantly, Seb, getting yourself straight and happy. But all the same, you were taking a risk – one of those danger points that you'll have been warned about in rehab –

stepping into an emotionally threatening environment, leaving your routines behind you.'

He shrugs, and gives it some thought.

'I suppose so,' he replies after a few moments. 'In fact, you're right: it's exactly the kind of situation my doctors would have told me to avoid. But after my dad's death, I realised I was strong enough to handle things, to deal with change. And what is life without a bit of risk, anyway, Auburn? What is life without taking a chance? I have my moments of doubt, sure. I have my . . . what do you call them, wobbles?'

I nod, and grin at his use of the word.

'But just because I wobble doesn't mean I'll fall. And some things – some people – are simply worth the risk.'

I'm guessing he means me, and I blush a little. I didn't ask to be at the centre of this drama, but I'd be lying if I said a tiny part of me wasn't flattered. Moved, even.

'It must be hard though,' I say, ignoring that last line. 'Just being in a pub, or the pharmacy?'

I give him a quick glance before I turn my eyes back to the road, and see him swipe his dark hair away from his forehead.

'The pharmacy,' he replies, sounding darkly amused, 'would have been like a sweet shop not that long ago. I'd have been looking around wondering what I could get away with swiping, wouldn't I? I'd have been desperate to get inside that big cupboard where you keep all the really good drugs . . .'

'Oh, you noticed that, did you?'

'Of course. I'm sober, not dead. And maybe it would have been easier if you had a job as a hairdresser or a traffic warden or a vicar, so I could hang out somewhere temptation-free – but I have to have some trust in myself, or there's no point. There will always be part of me wondering if I could get away with one last high, one last night partying – always. That will never go away. But these days . . . well, I've learned to say no to myself.'

I nod, and realise that I completely understand what he's saying. It's similar with me. Yes, I can now have a few drinks – even quite a lot of drinks – because I'm confident that I won't let it push me over the edge into some insane binge. I can take some paracetamol when I have a headache, knowing it probably won't turn me into a granny-robbing smackhead. But there's always a 'probably' in there, and I have to be aware of when to say no to myself.

Like when offered a massage by my estranged husband, for example. That probably wouldn't turn me into a slavering sex maniac either – but I won't be taking the chance, just in case.

The silence settles again, but it's comfortable enough. Companionable even. He's also much better at being quiet than he used to be – I swear there wasn't an ounce of oxygen he couldn't suck from the room when we were together. He seemed to think of silence as some kind of force of darkness.

Out of the blue, as I leave the main road to follow the winding route up into the hills, he asks: 'How's Finn?'

I blink a few times, and wonder why on earth he's asking that, and what complex pattern of thought led from our last conversation to Finn.

'Erm . . . good. Very good, thanks,' I reply, uncertainly. I'm not sure where this is leading and I'm not sure I want it to lead anywhere.

'He's not been around much. I heard Zoe talking about it to Cal in the café.'

Ah. The village grapevine – it produces an intoxicating vintage.

'He's busy,' I reply, feeling defensive on Finn's behalf. 'And he's got a conference to go to. And . . . well, I suppose he wants to avoid you, doesn't he? After that night in the pub.'

'I really am sorry about that,' he tells me, again. 'I should have handled it differently. I shouldn't have pushed him. It wasn't fair, to either of you. He seems like a decent man.'

'Well, on that particular night, he wasn't at his best – because yes, you pushed him. And because this is hard for him. But he is decent, Seb. Probably the most decent human being I know. He's kind, and he's clever, and he's very, very good for me. We were really happy together . . .'

I trail off here, realising that I've been sucked into talking about things best left untalked about. Certainly with Seb.

'*Were* happy together?' he replies, stressing my accidental use of the past tense.

'Are. We are happy together, okay? Please don't pick away at this, Seb. Just leave it, all right? We both know you've always been able to persuade me that black is white, and talk me into pretty much anything, and I'm asking you now – please don't even try. Not with this. Finn is a good man, and I love him, and no matter how complicated all of this is, I'm holding on to the truth of that. Trying to talk me out of it won't work.'

He looks like he has more to say. I feel like I have more to say. It was a nicespeech, but even I'm not entirely convinced by it. I chew my lip, and prepare for the onslaught.

Instead, he nods, and briefly strokes my thigh, and looks resigned to a situation he doesn't agree with – like he's willing to lose the argument for my sake.

'Okay, Auburn. I'll leave it alone. For you.'

I splutter out a thank you, and have never in my life been more happy to pull up in a driveway, and see a harassed-looking woman holding a screaming, red-faced baby. It's the best thing I've ever witnessed.

We start there, and work our way around most of the people I'm visiting. I have some prescriptions to drop off for some of them, and a few basic health checks to do on others, and of course the boxes to deliver. Most of them are thrilled, and clearly can't wait to delve in and see what's beyond the ribbons.

Seb is an excellent addition, I have to admit, managing to tailor his demeanour to the circumstances. I realise that this is a strange situation, and introduce him to people as my friend, visiting from Spain, always making sure they're okay with him being there even for a brief visit.

Naturally enough, they're all okay with it – especially the young mums, who look like all their Christmases have come at once. Auburn Longville – supplier of drugs, cake, and hunky men.

Our last stop is Mr Pumpwell – I've saved the best for last. If anyone can resist Seb, it's Mr P, I think, as I beep my car horn to tell him we're there.

He makes his way over to us from the donkey paddock, slightly stooped, one hand on his back, trying to pretend that he's not in pain. I can tell from his guarded posture that he is, and make a mental note to get him some more help.

He won't take it from social services or any of the logical places, so I'll have to be creative. I'm thinking maybe that Van would like to visit, possibly bringing Saul with him, under the guise of the little boy wanting to see the animals. And while he was there, he could do a bit of feeding, or maintenance around the place.

Naturally enough I haven't mentioned this to Van, as it's only this minuteoccurred to me – but I'm sure he won't mind.

Mr P holds up one hand in greeting, and pauses while

he takes in Seb, looking him up and down like he's considering cooking him in a pot. I introduce them, and he raises bushy grey eyebrows, and says: 'Well. You'd best come in out of the rain then, if you're from Spain. You might melt.'

We all troop indoors, Seb hefting the box, and Mr P promptly puts the kettle on. It's his default setting.

'How's the pain, Mr P?' I ask, automatically going to get mugs out of the high cupboard to save him from having to stretch. 'Do you want to go into the other room for a chat?'

I'm suggesting this in case he doesn't feel comfortable talking in front of Seb, of course, but I needn't have bothered.

'Been better. Been worse,' he says gruffly.

'But have you been taking your painkillers? I've brought some more – your doctor sent over a repeat prescription for the codeine.'

'I have been taken them, yes, Little Miss Nosy. Mainly to help me sleep through it. I've got a few left, but you might as well leave the new ones. I'll just feed them to Belle if I have any left over. Bloody animal could do with a sedative.'

Seb looks confused, and I explain: 'Belle is Mr P's donkey. I've long suspected she's a Disney villainess who's been cursed to live in donkey form, forever trapped. It's the only possible reason for how horrible she is.'

Mr P snorts at that one, and pours water into the old-fashioned teapot he keeps in a knitted cosy.

'Have you thought about getting some massage on your back, Mr Pumpwell?' Seb asks, as Mr P stirs. 'It can be very helpful.'

It's not a bad idea, but I can't see him going for it.

'Massage?' he asks, in an interested tone. 'I'm not too sureabout that. I don't like anything fancy, all them oils and whale music and the like.'

'No,' says Seb, smiling, 'massage therapy. It can used with physio. It's all very proper, honestly.'

He goes on to talk to Mr P about various treatments that might help with his recovery, and Mr P is a lot more open to the concepts than I thought he would be. I think he's so desperate to feel better, and not to be relying on drugs, that he'd consider just about anything.

Before I know it, Seb has explained that he's a qualified therapist, and offered to come round and see what he can do for him.

'Hang on!' I say, holding my hand up for attention. 'That's a bit of a grey area. Seb won't have insurance over here, and if this is something you want to do, then I can look into getting you a referral for someone local.'

Mr Pumpwell waves this off, and looks at me like I'm a complete idiot.

'Don't be daft, girl,' he replies, firmly. 'I'm not the kind to sue if it hurts. And anyway, Seb here won't be charging me anything, will he, so it won't be a business arrangement – it's just between friends . . .'

'Yes. Exactly,' adds Seb. 'Just between friends.'

I look from one to the other, and realise I've already lost. Bizarrely cast as the sensible one in this scenario, I've clearly been outvoted. I shrug, and reply: 'Well, on your own back be it, you stubborn old goat. Don't come crying to me later. Anyway, here's your lovely box of treats, and here's your lovely box of drugs.'

I pass him the tablets, and he looks at them with a level of loathing as he drinks his tea. He leaves them untouched on the table, and instead asks about the café box.

'I do like a nice scone,' he admits, when I've filled him in on the contents. 'So maybe I'll take a chance on them.'

'You won't regret it,' I say, finishing up my tea. 'And I have another favour to ask – would you mind if my brother comes out to visit, with his . . . his kind of stepson?'

'Kind of stepson?' he says, pulling a face. 'What a complicated world you young people live in!'

'Well. It's his girlfriend's child. He's four, and he loves animals, and I think it'd be really nice for him.'

'This is your brother who works at Frank Farmer's place, is it?' he asks, not fooled for a minute. 'The biggest farm in the area? Are you telling me there aren't enough animals around there to keep the young 'un happy?'

'There's definitely not an evil Disney donkey.'

'True enough. One in a million is our Belle – thank the

Lord! All right, love, if you like . . . but you'll have to warn me when they're coming so I can make sure I've got my teeth in.'

He does have false teeth, Mr Pumpwell, as of course do many people of his generation. He very much enjoys slipping them in and out to surprise me, and I'm sure Saul will be enthralled by the dental comedy routine.

We make our goodbyes, and Seb is thoughtful on the drive back to the village.

'I like him,' he announces, as we wind past Eggardon Hill. It's all grey and misty with rain today.

'He's an interesting character,' I say, nodding.

'It's good, this thing you're doing,' he replies. 'These people you're visiting. It's making a difference to their lives.'

'And to mine,' I say, glancing at him briefly. 'I have to be honest – at least some of my motivation is selfish. It keeps me grounded, and busy, makes me feel useful. Keeps me out of trouble. It's not like I'm a saint.'

He laughs out loud, obviously never having seen me as a saint, and responds: 'I get what you mean. It's the same with me and my voluntary work. It's like we're both trying to . . .make amends for something? Mainly we only ever hurt ourselves, and each other, and maybe our families – but even so. We're trying to be better.'

'We are,' I reply gently. 'We may never get there, but we're trying.'

The mood has suddenly become a bit serious, and I

switch on the radio in an attempt to lighten the atmosphere. Sadly, it's The Smiths, Morrissey wailing on about being killed by a truck. Perfect driving material.

Seb flicks the dial so I can concentrate on the road, and finally finds something more upbeat – Katrina and the Waves, who are apparently 'Walking on Sunshine'.

'So,' he says, after we've both sung along to the chorus, 'what do you want to do now? I thought maybe you'd like to come back to the cottage. We could have some food, watch some TV, relax . . .'

It sounds very cosy. Very friendly. Very tempting. A bit too tempting, in fact, I decide. Things with Seb are settling down into way too easy a setting.

'Sorry,' I reply, making my mind up there and then. 'I'll drop you off at Hyacinth, but then I have plans.'

Chapter 22

Of course, I didn't have any plans. But after I wave goodbye to a sad-looking Seb in the Hyacinth car park, I make some up, very quickly.

First, I make a quick detour to the hospital. Turns out it's official visiting time, so I don't even have to sneak in.

Laura and the babies are doing brilliantly. She seems tired but happy, which I suspect is going to be her natural state for the next year or two, and both Ruby and Rose are gaining small amounts of weight and feeding well.

They still look tiny – they still are tiny; impossibly small and precious. I hold them one after the other, and there's barely any weight in them at all. Yet somehow, each one of them is a perfect miniature human being, with teensy fingernails and little nostrils and wide eyes.

It's so strange, imagining them older. I've not been around many babies, but even I know that they will grow older – they'll be toddlers and schoolkids and teenagers and eventually grown-ups, with all the mess and clutter that grown-up life entails.

'I wonder what they'll do, when they're big,' I say, randomly, as Ruby grabs hold of one of my fingers.

'I have no idea,' replies Laura, half sitting, half lying on her bed, hair askew, trying to feed Rose. 'But I really hope they've stopped pooing in their pants by then. Honestly, I feel like all I do is change nappies at the moment . . . I swear, it's as if they tag team me. I'll change one, and all will be well, and then the other one stinks the place up. It's the same with sleeping and feeding – I had no idea how much harder two babies would be than one . . . it's like having about fifteen of them!'

I laugh, and make sympathetic noises, and fill her in on some of the village gossip. I tell her about the care boxes, and how Lizzie has turned into the village commander-in-chief, and about Edie and Zoe starting a book club that launched with Jilly Cooper's *Riders*, and about Tom and Willow planning a holiday together.

I bat away questions about Seb and Finn, despite her attempts to draw me out, and instead distract her by asking how her parents are. Over the moon seems to be the basic answer. She says this with a slight grimace, as though, much as she loves her mum and dad, having them around all the time is a bit weird. As my dad is dead, and I live with my rollercoaster ride of a mother, I can't comment.

Matt arrives after twenty minutes or so, and I leave them to it. As I leave, I hear her quizzing him about the arrangements he's made at home ready for them being discharged on Monday – has he washed the blankets for the Moses baskets? Has he stocked up on nappies? Has he set up the steriliser unit? Has he bought the fragrance-free wipes, not the ones full of chemicals? I laugh, and suddenly realise where Lizzie gets it from – our sweet and gentle Laura has quite the bossy side to her as well when she feels she needs to!

Next stop on my magical mystery tour is Briarwood. I haven't seen Finn for days, and our conversations have been pleasant but superficial. Our texts have been dominated by emojis rather than words, and I'm starting to feel like a layer of distance is settling over us at exactly the time it shouldn't.

I arrive at the big house just in time to see him emerge from one of the pathways, dressed in a hefty khaki waterproof coat, holding a big stick like a wizard's staff.

'Ahoy, Gandalf the Green!' I say, waving to him. 'What's the haps in Middle Earth?'

He waves the stick at me, and replies: 'Away with you, wench! Begone, evil ginger troll!'

As he draws nearer, we smile at each other, and he reaches out to wipe a droplet of rain off my nose.

'This is a surprise,' he says, gesturing for me to follow him into the building.

'A good one, or a crap one?'

'A good one, of course. I've been out walking.'

'I see that,' I reply, as we make our way through the long

wood-panelled corridor to his rooms. 'You picked a lovely day for it.'

He shrugs off his jacket, and hangs it on the back of the door, where it proceeds to drip onto the carpet.

'Good for the brain,' he says, resting his stick in the corner of the room. 'Getting out and about in bad weather. You're so busy thinking about overhanging branches and turning your ankle on a slippery tree root, you can't think about anything else. Plus, you get to find really cool sticks in the woods.'

'It is a very cool stick,' I agree. 'You can use it to beat hobgoblins with. Or, failing that, young inventors.'

As we talk, he starts to make tea. The English side of him is very much in control, it seems, as he switches on the kettle and assembles mugs and finds a tin of biscuits. I lean against the counter, and feel weirdly awkward. I want to touch him, but I'm not completely sure how he'll react, and that totally sucks.

'Are you all set for your conference?' I ask, as he passes me tea. I have drunk so much tea today I might get tannin poisoning.

'Oh yes,' he replies, nodding wisely. 'I am as prepared as a non-qualified manager of institutional finance processes can possibly be.'

'You are so sexy right now.'

'I know. It's a gift.'

We're saying the right words – making the flirty noises

– but it doesn't feel right. Our hearts aren't in it. This is confirmed when he sits down on the chair, not the sofa, where we'd normally end up snuggled together.

I put my tea down – I really don't want it – and sit opposite him. I let out a sigh, and finally ask: 'Finn, what's going on here? I feel like I'm treading on eggshells around you. Is there something you need to say to me, because if there is, then . . . spit it out. I can take it.'

By this stage, I've convinced myself that he's about to dump me. That he's decided enough is enough, that I'm too messy, too strange, my life too complicated. That I'm simply not worth the effort any more. In some ways, I think I've been expecting that ever since we got together, which is something I'm sure a counsellor would have a real party with.

He gazes away over my shoulder, his face unreadable, before eventually speaking.

'I'm sorry,' he says, sadly. 'I just . . . I want you to make your own choice. I want you to decide where this is going, and what you feel about Seb, and what happens next. I want you to make that choice without me . . . interfering?'

The last word is said as a question, as though he's not quite sure he's got the right one.

'Interfering?' I repeat dumbly, confused but relieved that it's not at least an immediate dumping, like I'd anticipated. 'What do you mean?'

'I mean . . . this is a big deal. I love you, and I want to be with you – but only if that's what you want. I want to respect you, and your decisions, and your needs. And we both saw the other night that it's not guaranteed that I'll play fair, or act properly, or behave in a way that allows you to make that choice. I don't want you to be thinking about me when you do.'

'That makes absolutely no sense,' I say, trying to detangle it in my brain. 'I don't expect you to be perfect, and I'm capable of making my own decisions without your permission.'

'I know you are – I didn't mean to suggest otherwise. But . . . okay, look at it this way – if you weren't worried about hurting me, would you spend more time with him? If you weren't worried about me getting upset, would you even be wanting him to go home? If you take me out of the equation, how would you be feeling?'

I shake my head, and feel a budding sense of anger that I try and control. Losing my temper will help precisely nothing, and only serve to make an already bad situation even worse.

'But I don't want you out of the equation!' I snap back. 'I want you very much in the equation – all over the bloody equation! And why is it a bad thing that I don't want to hurt you? Isn't that the way you're supposed to feel when you love someone? In all honesty, Finn, this sounds like bullshit to me. It sounds a bit like you don't want to be in this mess any more, and you're couching it in terms that sound better.'

I see a spark of responding anger in his blue eyes, and his fingers tighten around his mug. Like me, he's trying hard to calm himself down. Part of me doesn't want him to. Part of me wants to push this and pull it and poke it at until we're both furious. Until he throws that mug in the sink, and we tear each other's clothes off, and have angry sex until we both feel better. That, I realise, is completely screwed up.

'I'm not explaining myself very well,' he replies, putting the mug down on the coffee table. Maybe he's scared he might throw it. 'I suppose what I'm trying to say – badly – is that this shouldn't be a fight. The other night, it felt like a fight. A battle. That you were the prize one of us could win. And that's the bullshit here, isn't it? You're not a prize – you're a human being. A weird, wonderful, drop-dead gorgeous human being, who I desperately want to stay in my life.

'But I won't do it that way. I don't want you seeing him, and feeling bad about it, like you're cheating. And I don't want to feel like I'm somehow holding you back. We said at the start of this that it would be good – that maybe you could finally put Seb behind you. Now, I might be totally getting this wrong, but it doesn't feel entirely like that any more. It feels like possibly there might be some Seb . . . ahead of you. And if that's the case, you owe it to yourself to find out – and not shut the idea down because of me.'

Wow. My eyes go wide, and I am literally at a loss for words. Maybe this will all make sense later, like in a million years. Maybe I'm just being especially thick, and don't have the emotional subtlety to completely get it. Maybe – and this is entirely possible – it actually does make sense, but I don't like the sense it makes, so my brain refuses to process it.

I stand up. He stands up. There is a freeze-frame moment where all we do is stare at each other, both at a loss as to how to make this better.

In the end, I decide I can't. That the only thing I can do if I stay, or I respond, or try to persuade him differently, is make it worse.

'Have a good conference,' I say miserably, and turn to leave.

Chapter 23

I make an executive decision to spend the rest of the weekend blissfully man-free. Unless you count my brother, which I don't.

On Sunday, Willow and I take Lynnie to a craft fair in Wiltshire, which is full of her spiritual brothers and sisters – yoga-lean, lentil-eating, grey panthers buying the supplies to make their dream-catchers and altars to Gaia.

The sun is shining again, and it's a lovely day. Willow can tell there's something wrong, but I manage to fake my way through the trip with style, elegance, and a lot of loud singing in the car. I very deliberately block thoughts of both Finn and Seb out of my mind, because my mind is getting hopelesslyoverwhelmed – the poor thing needs a duvet day.

We stop off at a country pub for our dinner on the way home, and Lynnie is on good form. She's talking to us both as though we're friends, not her daughters, and again referring to Willow as Joanna – but she's thrilled with the bits and bobs we picked up at the fair, and even if her reality isn't quite the same as ours right now, it's one she seems happy in. Sometimes that's the best you can hope for.

By the time I get into the pharmacy on Monday morning, I'm ready to face the week. Ideally a week not filled with romantic riddles, but with some energy and determination if nothing else.

I bump into Katie outside, and she's looking a little less energetic herself.

'You okay?' I ask, as I deal with the locks and lead us both inside.

'I suppose,' she replies, which by Katie's standards is admitting the world is falling in. 'Yes. I'm being weird, that's all.'

'In that case, it's your lucky day – weird is my specialist subject. What's up?'

We walk together through to the kitchen, automatically going about the morning rituals of taking off jackets and hanging them up and getting the coffee ready.

'Nothing's up. It's just that Jason – that's Saul's dad, you remember? – well, Jason and Jo, his wife, have invited Saul to go and visit them to meet his new little brother, Dougal.'

'Dougal?' I say, blinking. 'They called their son Dougal?'

A stern look from Katie tells me that maybe I've fixated on the wrong thing here, and I quickly add: 'Right. Okay. You saw them at Easter, didn't you?'

'We did. But now the baby's here. And it's Saul's brother, after all, so it's only natural that they'd want them to meet each other.'

'Natural, but . . . awkward?' I supply, as she pours the boiling water.

'Awkward. Yes. For me, not Saul – which is what counts. So anyway – it's not a big deal. It's nothing bad. In fact it's good. But it's made me feel a bit off my game today.'

'I can see that,' I reply, as she continues to pour water into a full mug, until it starts running down the sides and onto the drainer. She glances down, makes a disgusted 'ooh!' sound, and immediately starts cleaning it up.

'Look,' I say, leaving her to it – which is a selfless act because Katie loves cleaning – 'I'm not an expert on relationships. Or in fact anything. But I think it's under-standable that this is difficult for you, and you should let yourself be freaked out for a while. Things are changing, and that's always unsettling, especially when it involves your kid. I do, though, have every faith in you Katie – you'll get through it like you always do, and one day you'll look back and wonder what all the fuss was about.'

I wonder if I'm over-simplifying, but the pep talk seems to help. She perks up a bit, and nods, and says: 'I'm sure you're right. Things that seem like huge deals at the time look minuscule with a bit of time and space.'

'That's right,' I reply, winking. 'I saw Brian Cox say that on the telly once.'

'I quite fancy him,' she says, leaning back on the counter and smiling. 'Don't tell Van.'

'Don't worry, I will,' I respond, winking again.

'Have you got something wrong with your eye?' she asks. 'And anyway – enough about me. What's going on in your life? I can count on your mess to make me feel better about mine.'

Auburn Longville – at your service. I think about it for a moment, then shrug.

'I think I'm taking a break from it,' I say simply, walking through to the pharmacy with my coffee.

'Taking a break?' she repeats, trailing behind me. 'What do you mean? Has Seb gone?'

'Not as far as I'm aware. He's probably bought a house in the village by now and hung up a sign advertising his massage clinic. And Finn is setting off for London, for a conference. Me? I'm taking a break. I need to stop thinking about them, and us, and what might happen, or my brain will explode.'

'That,' she replies, as the first customer of the day pings the bell as they walk through the door, 'isa very neat trick. I'm impressed.'

I give her a small bow, accepting her praise, and we both put on smiley faces for Audrey Mason, who is undoubtedly here to tell us about her bowel movements.

Mondays are usually relatively busy in the pharmacy, especially as the day wears on. People tend to hold out on seeing the GP over the weekend, and then there's a mad rush on Monday morning – resulting in an avalanche of prescriptions to be filled. And by avalanche, I mean anywhere up to ten.

Nevertheless, it's enough to keep us occupied, and that's what I need right now. We have a steady stream of customers right to lunchtime, when we take turns in nipping to the café for a sandwich and a break.

It's while Katie's gone that I get the phone call. I'm tempted to ignore it, as I'm very busy reading a fascinating article about developments in blood sugar monitoring for self-managing diabetics. A quick glance at the screen, though, shows that it's my favourite grumpy old man, so I tear myself away from my research.

'Mr P!' I say cheerily, hoping he's okay. 'What can I do for you on this fine day?'

I hear him rustling about, untangling the curly cord on his landline. He doesn't have a mobile, despite my best efforts to convince him it's a sensible measure in case Belle attacks him in the paddock. His landline is like something from a museum – one of those ancient ones with a rotary dial.

'Is that you, Auburn?' he says, shouting a bit. He always seems to assume that that's what you do when you've called a mobile number.

'It is, and I'm not deaf!'

'Oh! Right. Sorry. Anyhow, sorry to bother you . . .'

'You're not bothering me, Mr P. What's the problem?'

He pauses, and I hear more rustling, and then he replies: 'Well, I'm sure I'm just being daft here, love, but didn't you bring me some new pills when you came round the other day?'

'I did, Mr P,' I say, sitting up straight, suddenly alert. The door pings as Katie returns, and I give her a wave, pointing unnecessarily at the phone to tell her I'm on a call. 'Can't you find them?'

People lose their pills all the time. They misplace them, they put them somewhere so safe they forget where they are, they drop them down the sides of sofas and put them in the bin by mistake, they leave them in the car or change handbags and forget about it. On one occasion, I even had a man in because his dog had eaten his Viagra. True story.

When you do my job, you learn to recognise these genuine cases, and you learn to recognise when someone is trying it on because they want more drugs. Admittedly this doesn't happen as often here in Budbury as it did in London, and I'm 100 per cent certain it's not the case with Mr P.

Most times, you can refer them back to the GP, and it can be resolved. There's always the risk that they've left potentially dangerous substances lying on the bus or what-ever, but there's only so much you can do – human beings are what they are. We lose things. It's an essential part of being alive.

With Mr Pumpwell, I'm not worried about him displaying drug-seeking behaviour, and I'm not worried that he's left strong and possibly addictive painkillers in a place where a child might find them. But I am worried that he's becoming confused and misplacing things, and that he is in pain without them. He may be elderly, but he's usually sharp as a tack. Given the state of my mum, though, I'm maybe a bit more alert to potential mental decline than most people.

'I can't love, no,' he replies, still speaking a bit loudly. 'I've looked everywhere. I even went out to check the feed bins in case I'd had one of those, what do you call them, senior moments?'

I laugh out loud at that one. The fact that he's aware of senior moments means he probably isn't having one.

'Well, I did bring them, you've not imagined it. And when we left, they were on the kitchen table. First things first, Mr P – are you in pain right now? Do you need some more? Because I can speak to the GP about what's happened, and sort something out for you.'

'No, girl, it's not that – I do have a couple left from the last packet. I just don't like losing things. If you're not careful, first it's a packet of bloody tablets, next it's your marbles. As it happens, I'm feeling much better this morning, after your young gentleman friend visited. Magic fingers, that one. Never thought I'd feel comfy with it, but he was very professional.'

It takes me a moment to catch up with what he's describing. I've been doing such a good job of banning the words 'Seb' and 'Finn' from my mind that it doesn't immediately register. Seb, of course, had promised to go and visit Mr P when we delivered the Comfort Food care boxes. And the super-strength codeine.

I freeze momentarily, as nasty thoughts flood in and take over my think-tank. Mr P had a full packet of pills on his kitchen table. As far as he remembers, they were still there later. Seb visits, and the pills have miraculously disappeared.

I don't want to think what I'm thinking. I don't want to admit that it's the first place my mind goes. I don't want to imagine Seb that way. I don't want to feel the suspicions that I can't quite hold back.

He seems so different now. He seems so clean, and controlled, and set on rewriting his future. But Seb, as I know better than most, is also incredibly clever, and incredibly persuasive, and incredibly good at fooling people. So many times, in our past together, I'd hope for the best, because he seemed so genuine – and so many times, he disappointed me. I let myself believe that things could be different, was lulled into a false sense of security and optimism, only to have the rug pulled from beneath my feet. I'm right back there now, and it deflates me.

'You still there, Auburn?' Mr Pumpwell yells, so loud that even Katie looks up from her work. I hold the phone away from my ear, wondering if my drums have been perforated, and reply: 'Still here, Mr P. Look, why don't you keep looking, and in the meantime, I'll speak to the GP. I'll tell him it's not urgent, but we don't want you to run out of pills – they're good to have around just in case you need to poison the donkey.'

He snorts out a quick laugh, and shouts back: 'Righty-ho! Speak to you later, love.'

Once he's gone, I put my phone down and sit in silence for a few moments, turning it all over in my mind. The more I turn it, the more I can't escape the conclusion that Seb has relapsed. I recall how sad he was that afternoon, because of our conversation in the car. And because I left him alone that night, and refused to play along with what he probably hoped was turning into a scene of happy families.

I remember the way he looked when I dropped him off at Hyacinth, waving forlornly at me as I beeped the horn and drove away – all the way to Finn, who had his own man-bomb to drop on me.

Seb is a social creature. Much as he may seem to have changed, that aspect has stayed the same. Since he's arrived in Budbury he's spent time here in the pharmacy, in the café, in the pub. He's befriended people who were initially wary of him. He's won people over, wormed his way into their lives – because he can't stand being alone.

I've always known this about him, and it's not a big deal – a lot of people are like that. With Seb, in the past, it's been damaging – contributed to his party posse tendencies and the fact that he surrounded himself with fake friends and a fake community.

He'd even started to win me over, if I'm totally honest – but maybe leaving him alone, after a difficult afternoon of emotional battery, was too much for him. Maybe it pushed him too far. I recall part of our talk that day, in the van – and the words he used to describe himself. The way he acknowledged his potential 'wobbles', and admitted that there would always be part of him wondering if he could get away with one last high.

Was this it? Was this the wobble that finally knocked him over – being in Mr P's kitchen, those pills left out there like candy, calling to him? You'd have to have been an addict of some form or another to understand the temptation that never, ever quite goes away. The fine line between resisting and giving in.

I am filled with certainty that this is what has happened. That Seb has given in. I feel angry, and humiliated, and disappointed, and above all sad – sad that it's come to this. Sad for me, because I'd started to trust him and now he's let me down. Sad for him because of how hard he's worked.

'Are you all right?' asks Katie, sounding concerned. 'You've gone really pale. And I unwrapped a whistle pop for you five minutes ago and you didn't even hear it.'

Usually I react like a bloodhound at the crinkle of a lolly wrapper – but I've been too tied up in my thoughts, my conclusions, to even notice.

'Um . . . I'm all right. Yes. Just thinking. You know I can't think and do anything else at the same time, Katie.'

She smiles and nods, but I can tell she's not convinced. I drag myself through the rest of the day as best I can, all the time the subject of Seb hovering in the back of my mind. I call Mr P again, to make sure he's not found the tablets, and then I check my van and my handbag, in case I did one of those weird things you're sure you didn't do but might have – like picked them back up again.

I'm desperate for him to have located them, or for me to find them lurking in my glovebox. Neither is the case, and I feel increasingly glum as the afternoon wears on.

By closing time, Katie is clearly very worried. As we clear away, check the computer for any prescriptions sent through for the next day, and double lock the cupboard – the one with the 'really good drugs' inside, as Seb pointed out – she gently probes me to find out what the problem is.

Eventually, she gives up on that, but says: 'My mum's picked up Saul from school. I'm at a loose end, and I'm sure he's driving her nuts by now. Do you want us to go around to the cottage and sit with Lynnie for a bit? Give you a little break?'

Lynnie's care schedule is a complex thing, with me and

Van and Willow all doing our best to combine our work lives and our personal lives and our domestic lives. Tonight, Willow is going round to visit Laura with Edie, Van was planning a night out with Sam, and I'm on home duty. It's not a chore – she's our mother and we love her – but it is complicated and sometimes difficult.

I ponder what she's offered, and eventually reply: 'Katie, that would be brilliant. I do need a bit of time to . . . do some stuff. Are you sure, though? I don't want to put you out.'

'Don't be daft. It's no trouble. It's actually a bit of a rest for me too, to be honest – Saul and your mum entertain each other so much, I usually end up drinking coffee and keeping an eye on them, just in case they decide to do something mad, like try and break the speed record for sliding down hills on cardboard, or doing yoga in tree branches, or dressing Bella Swan up as a circus sea lion and trying to get her to balance a ball on her nose. She really doesn't like it when they do that . . .'

These are all real-life examples of what Saul and Lynnie can get up to together. They both have a flair for the dramatic.

'Okay. I know they're in safe hands. And thanks.'

She makes no-worries noises, and we part ways outside the pharmacy. It's a beautiful evening, warm and with only a gentle breeze, and she insists that she wants to walk to the Café to collect Saul and then across Frank's fields to the cottage to relieve Willow. I toy with the idea of walking to my destination as well, but decide I might need the safety cocoon of my van at some point.

I text Willow to tell her about the change in plan, and reluctantly set off. I don't want to do this – but I also know that I need to.

By the time I arrive at the Rockery, the sun is hovering lower in the sky, and even the birdsong sounds sleepy. The gardens here are beautiful, thanks to Matt, who is a master gardener. I wonder absently if he'll have any time for that now the babies are here.

I'm on the verge of popping in to say hello, when I realise that I'm not in the right frame of mind – plus I'm sure Laura is up to her eyeballs in poo anyway, and could do without unexpected visitors randomly knocking on the door.

I take a while deciding this, perched on the bonnet of the van, my face turned up to the fading sunshine like a light-seeking flower – I take a while because I'm procrastinating. I bite my lip, lock my van, and tell myself that enough is enough.

That doesn't stop me walking slowly towards Hyacinth, though, stopping every now and then to gaze at a patch of petunias, or a fragrant tangle of honeysuckle. In fact I stop and start all the way there, eventually standing in front of the cottage's wooden door with its quaint name sign, feeling as grim as the garden looks gorgeous.

I clang the brass knocker, and wait for a few moments. Maybe he's not in, I tell myself. Maybe he's at the café. Maybe he's in the shower. Maybe he's in a drug-induced coma . . .

I knock again, and this time I hear his voice yelling hello, and the sound of feet thudding down the stairs. He pulls the door open, and I see that the shower option had been the correct one. His hair is damp, and shedding droplets over the tan skin of his bare shoulders. His black jeans have obviously been tugged on quickly, the studs as yet unfastened. His feet are bare, and he looks . . . happy to see me.

'Auburn!' he says, gesturing for me to come inside. 'What a nice surprise! Or . . . had we arranged something, and I'd forgotten?'

He looks slightly confused, and I walk past him into the living room. The place is tidy enough – nowhere could survive Hurricane Seb without some collateral damage. I gaze around, unsure what I'm looking for. Unsure how to broach the subject. If I'm right, I need to know. If I'm not, I could do a lot of harm if I blunder into this the wrong way.

'No, I just needed to talk to you,' I reply, too tense to sit even when he gestures at the sofa.

'That sounds serious,' he says, frowning. 'Is something wrong? Is your mum okay? Laura and the babies?'

'They're fine,' I respond quickly. 'It's Mr Pumpwell I came to talk about.'

'I saw him yesterday and he was okay when I left him – in fact he seemed in good spirits. Is there something wrong with him?'

Seb has, over the years, proved to me that he is a fantastic actor – especially back in the days when all I wanted to do was believe the best about him. So now, despite his apparently genuine combination of confusion and concern, I can't let it sway me. The man could win an Oscar.

'Nothing wrong, no,' I say, meeting his eyes firmly. 'But he has been on the phone to me today. It seems that his prescription has gone missing. The pills were there on the kitchen table yesterday, but now they're not.'

I leave the words there, dangling between us, like a toxic cord connecting us to each other. I want to tear my eyes away, to look out of the window at the honey-suckle. To look at the fruit in the big wooden bowl on the table. To look at anything but Seb, and the way his face changes as realisation dawns.

He's not an idiot, and he quickly makes the connection. His expression goes from worry about Mr P to disbelief to an awe-inspiring level of sadness.

He shakes his head wearily, and smiles in a way that speaks of pain and misery more than joy.

'And you think I took them,' he says eventually. It's not a question – it's a statement.

'I . . . I'm not saying you did, Seb. But it crossed my mind.'

He nods, and grabs up a T-shirt from the back of the chair. He's voluntarily putting clothing on his body, which tells me how upset he is. I think he's buying time, hiding his face, thinking about how to respond.

He runs his hands through his wet hair, and replies: 'Of course it did. Drugs go missing, let's blame the drug addict. It makes perfect sense. I wouldn't expect anything more. Hope, maybe, but not expect.'

This is torturous, but I won't let him guilt me into leaving without some answers.

'Seb, I'm not accusing – I'm asking. I'm asking you, right here and now – did you take them? If you did, I won't judge. I understand what it's like. If you didn't, I will make the biggest apology the world has ever seen, and will own up to the fact that I'm a complete twat. But I need to know.'

'Why do you need to know?' he snaps, some anger finally seeping into his tone. 'What is it to do with you anyway, Auburn? You've made it perfectly clear that you and I are over. You've made it perfectly clear that you're in love with your almighty Finn, the man with no demons. You've made it perfectly clear that there's nothing left between us. So tell me, why do you need to know?'

He's lashing out, and it feels unfair, but I can accept that. He's hurting, so he's attacking. Tried and tested Seb technique, that, and one that doesn't have the same effect on me it used to, all those years ago. Back then, when I was so tangled up in it all I couldn't see beyond the web we'd woven around each other, I'd have risen to the bait. I'd have snapped back and argued, or apologised, or placated, or somehow backed down.

'You're not answering my question,' I reply calmly, insistently.

'And I'm not going to. The fact that you even came here to accuse – sorry, to "ask"! – says it all. Don't worry. I'll be packed and out of your hair before you can say "rehab". Now, I'm going to ask you to leave.'

'Seb, there's no point reacting like this – just talk to me, damn it! Tell me I'm wrong! Tell me I'm an idiot, for goodness' sake! That's all I need to hear!'

'Is it, though?' he asks, stalking away from me, so much energy and emotion fizzing through him that he looks like he needs to run or jump or scream or all three at the same time. 'Is that all you need to hear? If I tell you you're wrong, tell you you're an idiot, will it be enough? Will you believe me? Or will you still be wondering? Will you always be wondering?'

I try and place a calming hand on his arm, but he shakes me off abruptly, as if disturbed by the contact.

I feel tears spring into my eyes, and a weakness and regret and sense of exhaustion sweep over me. Here I am, again – arguing with this man. This wonderful, stubborn, funny, deceitful man. My husband.

He sees how upset I am, and takes in a deep breath. I

can almost feel the tangible effort he's making to rein in his reaction, the way he's trying to steady himself.

'Look,' he adds, gazing over my shoulder, off through the window to the fields out back. 'I get it. I do. This is exactly the kind of stunt I'd have pulled when we were together. And this is exactly the kind of way I'd have reacted – angry, defensive, making you feel like you were going mad to suspect me even when all your instincts told you you were right. That was the way I behaved with you back then, and believe me I regret it. It's my own fault that this is the way you see me. But I can't change the past, and apparently you won't let me change the future – so there is nothing to be gained from this, for either of us.

'We both need to protect ourselves, I see that now. And maybe too much has happened for there to ever be trust again. So please – please just go, Auburn. No blame, no recriminations, no more games. Just go.'

I stare at him for a few moments, not knowing what to do. What to say. I want to comfort him. I want to console him. I want to apologise and tell him I'm sorry the thought even crossed my mind; that I'm a fool.

Instead, I remind myself that he still hasn't answered my question. That he's my husband in name only. That leaving is entirely probably the very best thing I can do.

He's turned away from me, standing tall and distant, his shoulders tense and hard. I want to reach out and touch him so badly.

I walk out of the door, and into a fresh summer's evening that now feels tainted. I walk past Black Rose, and see the hazy outline of Laura inside, strolling around with two babies in her arms. I walk back to my van, and sit and sob for what feels like forever. I'm crying for him, and for me, and for Finn. For all that was, all that wasn't, and all that could be but probably won't.

Sometimes, life just sucks.

Chapter 24

I arrive home to the cottage to find that Lynnie is, thank the lord, tired out from her escapades with Saul. They've re-dressed our garden scarecrow in a paisley dressing gown, a feather boa, and a red beret placed at a jaunty angle. They've done some weeding. They've baked chocolate chip cookies. Now they're busily drawing up plans for a new deluxe tree-house.

There are sheets of paper and pencils and rulers scattered over the kitchen table, and when I inspect their fanciful designs, Lynnie announces that she's going to ask 'that nice young man who lives in the motor home' to construct one for them.

'That's Van, silly billy!' says Saul in a no-nonsense tone. 'He's your actual son, and you're his mum – you must have forgotten again!'

Saul, of course, is only four – and he treads where angels fear to tiptoe. Lynnie gazes into the distance for a while, then grins broadly.

'You're so right! I am a silly billy!' she replies, piling the papers up into a neat stack. Saul complains a bit when Katie tells him it's time to leave, but eventually gives in and starts helping Lynnie pack away the pencils 'in rainbow order'.

Katie takes in my swollen eyes and unhappy expression, and immediately asks if I want a cookie.

'That bad?' I say, shaking my head. I feel that crappy that not even a cookie will help.

'Not at all,' she lies, gathering up her coat and Saul's Iron Man backpack. 'But you know where I am if you need me.'

She pats my arm, and the two of them set off for their adventure – a walk across the fields and back home, where Tinkerbell will be awaiting them in all his ginger glory.

Once I've made sure Lynnie is well and settled – watching a re-run of a weird show she likes called *Dog with a Blog* – I take a shower and mooch around the house. I feel a bit like a zombie, I'm so drained, and a cursory glance in the bathroom mirror tells me I don't look much better. I'm glad it's all steamed up and I can pretend I didn't see it.

I pull together some cheese on toast for the two of us, and a couple of mugs of peppermint tea, and we settle in to watch TV while we wait for Willow to get back. I must have crossed paths with her as I left the Rockery and she arrived.

When she does come back, she has lots of lovely photos

of the babies. The babies with Laura, and Matt, and her, and Edie, who she took with her, and with Lizzie and Nate, and one very funny one where Midgebo is licking one of their tiny heads, evidently caught in the nano-second before Laura shooed him off.

The pictures cheer us all up – you'd have to be heartless not to love them – and Willow joins us for some tea. I can see she's giving me sideways glances, and that she knows something's wrong, but I don't enlighten her. There's no point dragging everyone down with me.

'Are you okay?' she whispers, while Mum chortles away at an episode of *Fawlty Towers* – we were all Disneyed out. 'Laura said she thought she saw you at the Rockery.'

'I'm fine, Basil!' I reply, in a passable Sybil impression, but don't think I'm fooling her. Mum, who had seemed totally distracted, pipes up: 'It's his fault. That one from Spain.'

I can't tell whether she's talking about Seb or Manuel, so I shrug and leave it at that. Not long after, I make my excuses, claim tiredness, and head for my room. It is, in fact, 8.58p.m. – so in two minutes' time it will be a perfectly acceptable bedtime for a working lady such as myself.

I'm too numb to even get changed, so I fall on top of the duvet wearing my jogging pants and T-shirt with a picture of a Teletubby on it. I have no idea which Teletubby – the green one – and I have no idea why I own this particular T-shirt. It made its way into my wardrobe at some point, though, and is now one of my favourites. I have paired that stylish outfit with some bang ontrend candy-striped fluffy bed socks, and am now rocking the runway by lying flat out and staring at the ceiling. Budbury's Next Top Model.

I absently wonder what Finn is up to right now. He sent a lacklustre text, informing me he's in London, ready for his conference to start tomorrow. I wonder if he's lying on his bed thinking about me. I wonder if I should jump in the van and drive there through the night. Then I wonder if I have the energy to even get under the blankets.

My phone starts to ring next to me, and I fling out one arm to find it. Naturally, I knock it off the bed, and it skitters off across the floor, still ringing. Muttering various inventive swear words, I retrieve the evil device, and a glance at the screen shows me that it's Mr Pumpwell.

I answer as quickly as my fingers will let me, and say hello, settling myself back down onto the mattress.

'Is that you, Auburn?' he shouts, as usual. You have to laugh. When I confirm that it is indeed me, he continues: 'Good. Sorry to bother you so late in the day.'

I'm about to point out that it's only nine o'clock, but I realise that (a) I'm already in bed, and (b) he works on the land and this is practically midnight for him.

'No bother, Mr P,' I say reassuringly. 'I spoke to the GP this afternoon – he's sending out a new prescription for me to fill, and I'll drop it off tomorrow.'

'Well, that's the thing, see . . . ' he yells, then hesitates.

'What's the thing?' I ask, trying to stifle a yawn.

'The thing is, I only went and found them, didn't I?'

I sit up again, suddenly more alert than I was five seconds ago.

'The pills?' I ask, possibly stupidly.

'Of course the bloody pills – what else would I be talking about?' he responds, with his usual charm and charisma.

'You found them.'

'That's what I said – can you not hear me properly?'

He raises his voice another few decibels with that, and I quickly explain that yes, I can hear him fine, thank you very much.

'What happened?' I enquire, wondering if Seb somehow snuck them back. Knowing that if the next words out of Mr P's mouth involve an impromptu visit from his favourite massage therapist that evening, then I'll know exactly what happened.

'Me being a useless old fool is what happened,' he says, sounding exasperated – though it's hard to tell whether he's out of patience with me, or him, or the passage of time.

'And did Seb come around again?'

'What? Seb? Why would you think that, woman? What's up with you tonight? No, no . . . I found them in that bloody box – the one with all the café stuff in it. I only came across them because I was fishing out the last scone

– you were right on that one, love, they were delicious. Now, don't ask me why I put the pill packet in there, because I haven't the foggiest. I don't even remember doing it, but obviously I must have. There's no bugger else around to hide them for me. I also found my tea bags in the fridge the other day, but that's another story . . .'

He witters on for a small while, about getting older and being more forgetful and losing his mind, until I realise that he's genuinely worried.

'Don't be daft, Mr P – you're sharp as they come. I found my van keys in the soap dish on Friday, and Katie lost her phone for hours the other week, before she remembered she'd put it in the airing cupboard with her towels. We all forget stuff every now and then, and it's nothing to worry about. If it carries on happening, we can talk some more, but please don't upset yourself about it. I'm only glad you found your painkillers.'

'Yes, love – me too. Though I'm still feeling pretty decent after that massage, I have to say. Anyway. I'll leave you to it –I justwanted to let you know. If I left it till morning, I might have forgotten!'

He ends the conversation abruptly, as he usually does, and I am left lying on my bed, in a Teletubbies T-shirt, feeling about as awful as I've ever felt.

If only I'd waited. If only I'd given it more time. If only I didn't have the history I have with Seb, and hadn't automatically jumped to the conclusions I did.

I didn't accuse him, no – but I asked. And I asked in such a way that obviously left him with little doubt about what I thought had happened.

I was unfair, and I was wrong. I forgot the basic Budbury principle that everyone deserves a second chance. And now I need to apologise.

I only hope I'm not too late.

Chapter 25

The lights are still on in Hyacinth, which is probably a good sign. It's dark outside now, the sky a deep inky blue streaked with almost neon pink cloud. It's quite psychedelic in its own way, and on another night, I might be tempted to take out my phone for some photos. Not this night, though.

I'm standing on the doorstep, holding a cake in a tin. It's a white chocolate and raspberry torte that Willow had brought home from the café, made by Cherie that afternoon. It feels pretty lame now I'm lurking here in the dark – 'Hi, I'm sorry I accused you of being a thief, a liar, and a druggie, but hey, these things happen – fancy a slice of cake?'

It seemed like a good idea at the time, and at least it gives me something to do with my hands while I wait for him to answer the door.

When he does open it, he stares at me for a few seconds, surprised, his eyes going from me to the cake tin and back again. He says nothing, but raises his eyebrows in query.

'I'm an idiot. I'm sorry. I brought you a cake . . . ' I say, holding it forward.

He stands there, arms crossed over his chest, and for a moment I don't think he's going to let me in. Can't say that I'd blame him.

'What kind of cake?' he eventually asks, sternly.

'The world's most delicious cake, to go with the world's most genuine apology. I'm so sorry, Seb. I really am. I was way too quick to jump to the wrong conclusions, to assume the worst about you. Please say you'll forgive me.'

He gestures me inside, and replies: 'I'll think about it.'

I glance around, and see that the place has been tidied up. The fruit has been emptied from the big wooden bowl, the scattered clothes have been removed, and the Spanish-language paperback he'd been reading has gone. All that's left in the room is me, him, and his packed suitcase.

'Are you leaving?' I ask, laying the cake tin on the table.

'Maybe,' he says, sounding way more casual than he must feel. There are lines on his face that I swear weren't there this afternoon, and he sounds exhausted. 'Why are you here, Auburn?'

'Like I said: I'm here to apologise. Mr Pumpwell found his tablets, and I was a jackass about it.'

He nods, looks marginally satisfied, then asks: 'And if he hadn't found them? Would you still be apologising?'

I can't think of anything to say to that other than 'No,

probably not', which won't help the situation. He knows that anyway – he's just making a point.

I feel bad about all of this – terrible – but in my defence there were reasons for me reacting the way I did. I'm not an inherently judgemental person – I would never have come to the same conclusion if, for example, Matt had been there when the tablets went missing. I didn't leap from A to B without a behavioural road map.

'Seb, I said I'm sorry, and I truly am – but it wasn't the world's most crazy idea, was it? I'm sorry if it hurts to hear that, and I'm probably not very good at this apology business, but it's true. You turn up here, out of the blue, after years and years, saying you've changed. But you can't expect me to automatically go along with that. I was wrong about the pills, and I regret it all – but I had my reasons . . .'

He lets out a sigh, and runs his hands over his face like he's washing it, and tries on a sad smile.

'I know. I have to accept that, I suppose, Auburn. It just . . . well, what's that thing you used to say, knocked me for seven?'

'Six. But I know what you mean.'

He looks around at the clean room, at the suitcase, and then at me. His eyes linger on my face, and I feel a slow blush spread over my cheeks. For some reason, it suddenly feels quite warm in here.

'I don't know what I'm doing any more, Auburn . . . I

came here to see if there was any spark left between us. To see if my wife was still the woman I loved. I found that my wife isn't the woman I loved – she's an even better version of her. And I found that on my side at least, the spark hadn't died.'

His eyes are fixed on mine, as though he's trying to see into my mind.

'I hoped . . . God, I don't know what I hoped,' he continues, sounding exasperated with himself. 'That you'd feel the same, maybe? That you'd realise there was still something there . . . something that time and history and Finn couldn't quite extinguish. So now it's my turn to ask a question, Auburn. Tell me – was I wrong? Because I'm not so sure I was . . .'

I'm leaning against the back of the door, and he is walking towards me, taking smooth and easy steps, reminding me of some exotic black cat. Angel of Darkness on the prowl. He's getting closer, and he's staring at my lips, and I'm feeling both trapped and excited.

Was he wrong? Is there a spark after all this time? Do I still have feelings for this man, and if I do, what are they? Right now, he's stalking towards me, closing the distance in a way that should have me running scared. Pushing him away. Screaming for help. Telling him no – that there is nothing left. No spark. That he is wrong, and always has been. That everything that once existed between us is dead and buried and will never be resurrected.

I don't do any of those things. I don't say any of those things. I'm not sure I even feel any of those things. Instead, I stand there, helplessly, feeling the tug of physical attraction that I've been trying to deny ever since he arrived. The tug of our history, and what we once meant to each other. The tug of those vows we made, all those years ago. The tug of our story, which never seems to end – just takes twists and turns.

He's so close I can see the glittering specks of gold in his eyes, and feel the warmth of his breath on my skin, and the heat of his body against mine. He pauses, reaches out. Gently strokes my face in a way that feels both excitingly exotic and achingly familiar.

He leans in. He kisses me. And God damn it all, I let him.

Chapter 26

Nothing says 'happiness' quite like cake for breakfast. Rule No 1 of the Auburn-verse.

I am sitting in the café, and I feel on top of the world. The place isn't technically open yet, but I happen to know the people who run it, so I get special treatment. And anyway, I need to load up now – I have a long journey ahead of me later today.

Willow is going about her morning routine, filling salt and pepper shakers and stocking bowls of sugar cubes and replenishing the cold drinks in the chiller cabinet. Cherie is getting freshly baked bread out of the oven, and the smell is divine.

Lynnie is at home with Van, working on their plans for a tree-house, and all is quite simply well with the world.

I am sitting at a small table alone, unless you count my big, whopping bowl of coffee and walnut gateau and freshly poured cream. I do count it. In fact I might marry it one day, it's so delicious.

I'm tired after last night, but in a good way – the kind of tired that tells you you're alive and kicking. I am filled with a new zest for life, for cake, and for the rest of the day.

'You look happy!' yells Cherie, as she starts slicing the bread up for the lunchtime sandwich selection. 'Like the cat that got all the cream in the cream shop!'

I grin, and lick my spoon – I have indeed got all the cream. I'm even very luxuriously reading a newspaper, which I have spread out on the table. I'm limiting myself to the TV reviews and travel section, though, as the rest is too depressing for the mood I'm in right now.

I sip my coffee – a decadent mocha that goes perfectly with the cake – and sigh. The sunlight is streaming through the long windows, and I'm toying with the idea of a walk on the beach before I head over to the pharmacy. It feels like the right thing to do – to walk, and enjoy nature, and offer up a little prayer of thanks to whoever might be listening for all my blessings.

I stretch out, and listen to the hum of activity around me: the sounds of Willow moving around, the gentle humming from Cherie as she works, the waves on the bay, the occasional cry of a seabird. It's quiet, but not quiet, and it all adds to my sense of wellbeing.

Just as I feel I'm reaching a peak of zen-like mindfulness that might qualify me to start my own YouTube channel, the doors to the café are flung forcefully open. They bang hard against the wall and clatter backwards and forwards for a moment.

The loud thud destroys the harmony, and all three of us – me, Willow, Cherie – stop what we're doing and stare across the room with slightly offended looks on our faces. The girls were chillaxing together, and this has startled us.

I'm even more startled when I see Finn standing in the doorway, framed in the sunshine, squinting his eyes against the light inside. He's wearing a suit and tie, but looks like a tramp doing a *GQ* photoshoot – all creased and ruffled and in a state of disarray I never associate with him.

We all freeze for a moment, Willow and Cherie looking at me, me looking at Finn, the seagull perched on one of the tables looking at all of us.

He spots me, and strides over, letting the door fall shut behind him. Cherie and Willow very noisily and ostentatiously go back to what they were doing, and Cherie quickly flicks on the radio to give us the Comfort Food Café version of a privacy screen.

Up close, he looks even more dishevelled. His hair is in tufts, and his eyes are red-rimmed, and he looks like he's not slept for years.

'Finn!' I say, standing up and staring at him. 'What are you doing here? Do you want some cake?'

He glances at the table, and shakes his head.

'No,' he replies firmly. 'No cake. I need to talk to you. Right now. It's important.'

He sounds serious, and determined, and I try and hide the fact that I gulp a little. I eyeball Willow, who has paused in her domestics and is looking right at us with a curiosity that she can't possibly hide. I pull a face at her, and she suddenly becomes engrossed in slicing up butter pats.

Finn is oblivious to Willow, or the butter pats, or it seems anything but me.

'Okay . . . ' I reply, grabbing up my things, and taking one last, long sorrowful look at my newfound love, coffee and walnut gateau. Farewell, sweet friend – we'll always have tomorrow.

'Let's go for a walk down on the beach,' I suggest, heading to the doors, hoping he follows. This place is nosy enough without the two of us performing live for everyone.

He's silent on the way down the hill, stomping on the steps, his face set and lined. Whatever it is he's got to say to me, it's definitely not going to be small talk. It's going to be Big Talk, and my tummy flutters with nerves. I can feel his tension, and it's contagious, seeping through to me and making me feel jittery.

The beach is empty apart from dog walkers at this time of day – later on, in this sunshine, there'll be families and walkers and fossil hunters galore. The ice cream van will be here, and the car park will be full, and the café will be brimming with customers. Now, this early? It's almost serene.

Finn, however, is definitely not feeling the serenity. He

walks ahead of me for a few minutes, the smooth-soled leather brogues he wears with his suit sinking into the sand with every step.

Eventually, he finds a place that seems to satisfy him – or maybe he simply works up enough energy to say what it is he wants to say. He whirls around to face me, and my stomach is churning now, throwing up acid and nausea in a nasty rhythmic dance.

'Auburn,' he announces, in that kind of tone that signals a speech is on the way, 'I love you.'

Well. That's probably not what I was expecting, and I'm about to open my mouth and reply when he holds one hand up and stops me.

'No. Don't. Let me talk. I've been driving since five this morning and I might not be at my most lucid – so let me get this out, all right?'

I nod, and make a zipped-up gesture on my lips.

He pauses, and stares up into the sun with slitted eyes, then turns them back on me.

'I love you,' he continues, 'and I want to be with you. I want to fight for you. I want to do whatever it takes to make this work. I realise that what we have is new, and that Seb will always have a place in your heart, but I'm ready to do whatever it takes to make this work. All those sensible things I said about leaving you alone to make your decision were wrong. I was wrong - I was being a coward. I wasn't willing to take the chance on really, really fighting for this. I was scared of it – but now I see that fighting isn't always bad. It isn't always a sign of me being angry, or aggressive, or going back to the way I was.

'It's also a sign of passion and commitment and determination. And I am all of those things, Auburn – all of those things and more when it comes to you! So, I've decided I'm not going to give you space. I'm not going to let it all happen around me. I've decided I'm very much in the picture, and I am going to stay there, until you tell me otherwise. And even then, I won't give up so easily – because you're worth it.'

This is quite a speech, and he trails off a little towards the end, gazing at me as though he's run out of steam.

'Did you rehearse all of that in the car?' I ask.

He manages a small grin, and replies: 'I did, yeah. That's why I couldn't let you talk, you might have ruined my flow.'

'It's annoying when other people don't play along with your meticulously prepared one-sided scripts, isn't it? So . . . when did you come to all of these decisions, Finn?'

He slips his hands in his pockets, and meets my eyes. I notice that his tie is partly undone, the knot unfurling along with his usual composure.

'Last night. This morning. I got to the hotel, and I couldn't sleep. At all. I was awake all night thinking about you, and missing you, and knowing that I'd messed up. That I needed to fix it. To start with I was going to call you, and see you when I got back, but . . . well. I was up and dressed for business by 4a.m. I had an action-packed day of seminars and workshops planned. And . . . I couldn't face it. I just couldn't. So I got in the car, and drove.'

'And here you are.'

'Yes. Here I am. And now I've said my piece, and you've not even responded, and you seem strange, and I'm starting to think maybe I'm too late. That I left it too long. That you've made your choice, and it wasn't me.'

He sounds so sad, so deflated. My heart aches for him, and I realise that my strangeness, my lack of immediate response, is bordering on the cruel – but I'm so surprised by it all that I'm momentarily lost for words.

'I did make a choice, you're right,' I say, reaching out to touch his arm. 'Last night . . . last night, Seb kissed me. I'm not going to lie about it, or even apologise – because I think it needed to happen. A lot of that stuff you'd said, about me needing to figure it out, about me needing to decide where he stood in my life, was spot on. I did need to.

'So last night, he kissed me.'

He's gritting his teeth by this stage, and his hands are clenched, and he looks as though he might be considering walking away.

'He kissed me,' I continue, 'and I felt nothing. Absolutely, 100 per cent, totally positively *nothing* – other than relief. Relief that I'd finally found out. Relief that it was over.

Relief that I knew, without any shadow of a doubt, who I wanted to be with. You, Finn. I want to be with you. I was planning to drive to London today, to tell you face to face.'

I see him take this in, and process it in his usual Finn way, and I see the slow spread of realisation and joy cross his handsome, exhausted face.

'And Seb?' he asks, finally.

'Seb has gone. We had a difficult conversation, and he left last night. He's flying back to Barcelona today. We . . . well, we might stay in touch. I'm not going to lie about that either. But he's signing the divorce papers, and he's gone. Budbury is officially Seb free – as am I. I can't begin to tell you how good that feels, Finn – it's like a weight lifted from my spirit. I'm finally free – free from him, free from the past. Free to be happy – with you.'

I have more to say. More that I want to say, and more that I need to say – but I don't get the chance. I'm suddenly in Finn's arms, lifted from the ground, spun in circles, kissed so hard and so well I lose my breath.

I'm free. I'm happy. I'm safe. I'm exactly where I need to be.

Epilogue

One Year Later

Have you ever seen a Viking zombie up close? I'm guessing not. Most people haven't, due to, you know, one part of that equation being fictional and the other part being historical.

Well, I tell you – it's a pretty terrifying sight. And right now, the garden of the Comfort Food Café is swarming with them.

Everywhere I look, I see ghastly torn flesh, claws, tattered clothing, drinking horns, and hair. Lots and lots and lots of hair, of every possible colour, length and style. A lot of it is gnarled and tangled, covered in mud, splashed with blood and hanging loose in knots. Not big on styling products, your average zombie Viking, it seems.

There's a wooden bar set up in the style of a Viking longboat, the staff behind it outfitted in undead uniforms and dispensing cider and ale in horn-shaped paper cups. There's a catering table laid out with bowls in the shape of upturned brains, and a massive tureen of candied eyeballs floating in red jelly. There's even a small portable photo booth, crammed with every accessory a Viking zombie could ever want, staffed by a man dressed as Asterix.

The band – all appropriately costumed, of course – are playing a hard rock version of 'Monster Mash', and the zombie Viking horde is loving it.

I'm sitting with Willow on the edge of the wooden pergola that's now decorated with round shields and blunt longswords, watching the spectacle in front of us.

She's kept her hair pink, but grown it long. Her eyes are adorned with lenses that make them look completely black, which is beyond weird, and her clothes are pure apocalypse – torn lace, slashed satin, tangled ribbons. It's all in various shades of white – with bloodstains of course – and she looks like a bride who was bitten at the altar.

I'm more Viking than zombie, with a full-on warrior princess style get-up, complete with massive kick-ass boots and a shawl. She's braided my hair for me, so it runs in red plaits down the side of my face, and we added some blood spatter to make it both more Viking and more zombie at the same time. It wasn't the most traditional of scenes in the cottage this morning, it has to be said – especially as our mum and Van are just as dramatically attired.

'So,' says Willow, laughing at Cal throwing Zoe around like a zombie doll, 'we did it, sis. We're both now officially old married women.'

'Speak for yourself,' I reply, nudging her so hard she almost falls over. 'I'm a Viking warrior princess, looking forward to conquering new territories.'

'I suppose we are, in a way – conquering new territories anyway. I still can't quite believe it . . .'

It has, I must admit, been a pretty surreal day. A pretty surreal year, in fact. The double wedding idea was Cherie's, once we were both engaged – but the theme came from us. From that long ago conversation, sitting in the café with Laura, what feels like a lifetime away. Especially to Laura, I suspect.

She's here, Laura, bless her, curly hair swept up onto her head and sprayed white. Ruby and Rose are both wearing skeleton onesies – turns out there's a shocking lack of baby zombie Viking outfits on the market – snoozing in the double buggy that now seems to be an extension of Laura's arms.

The teenagers are all on fine form, every single one of them decked up in stripy prison clothes and covered in fake gore – they ignored the Viking bit, and went full-on Orange is the New Walking Dead instead.

Everyone else has thrown themselves into the concept as well – Cherie and Frank are wearing huge helmets with horns sprouting out of the sides; Becca and Sam are in fur-lined cloaks, as is Little Edie, stomping around now in toddler Doc Martens.

Katie somehow manages to look petite and lovely in a floor-length medieval gown she's spattered with red paint, and Saul is there as zombie Iron Man, in a fancy dress outfit with added claw marks.

Edie May is sitting with our mum, both their faces painted sludge-grey, their hair covered in twigs and cobwebs. They've set up a craft table to keep the kids happy, making Viking brooches and painting cardboard shields and, in Lynnie's case, telling stories about Norse gods and goddesses so vividly you'd think she was one of them.

Tom, I can see, is with a gang of the Briarwood residents, at the centre of some kind of drinking game that involves massive horns full of mead. Tom's hair is, as ever, cropped short – but his outfit is a perfect match for Willow's; a traditional top hat and tails set that is covered in tears and bite marks.

Mr Pumpwell is here, and he's even submitted to a bit of green face paint. He's sitting with some of the young mums and the other families I've been visiting, looking slightly awkward to be in so much company, but still there. Bit by bit, Cherie has managed to edge them more into her orbit – or maybe extended hers out to them, who can say? Either way, it's lovely to see them all.

'It's been a brilliant day, hasn't it?' I say, feeling a sudden rush of affection for all of these idiots – from babes in arms to people in their nineties, they've all embraced the Budbury way and gone full-on fancy dress at the drop of a Viking hat.

'It has,' she replies, stretching out her long legs in their tattered white fishnets. 'We're very lucky – which is not something I thought I'd ever say.'

This time two years ago, she was struggling alone, looking after Lynnie, working, torn in pieces by all the demands she was juggling. Our family was split up, cast far and wide, and it would be fair to say that neither of us ever expected to fall in love and end up married. We were too busy, too messed up, too closed off.

It's amazing how much has changed in such a short amount of time. The problems haven't gone away – Lynnie isn't going to get miraculously better, for a start. Finn still has issues with his parents, neither of whom is here today because they couldn't even set aside their differences for their son's wedding.

But for the time being, Lynnie is holding steady – and Finn does have his Granddad Christian here from Denmark. He's tall and silver-haired and blue-eyed and tells improbable stories about wood elves and forest spirits whenever you give him the chance.

He's sitting with Finn right now, eating black cherry trifle from an upturned brain bowl. Finn seems to sense me looking, and meets my gaze across the bouncing horns and helmets and horror hairstyles.

He's grown his hair for the wedding, and it hangs long and lustrous and thick and golden to his shoulders, matched by a silky blond beard. His top is partly open, and his long legs are wrapped in leggings and criss-crossed leather bindings. He looks like the cover of a Viking romance novel, and I sigh out loud.

He grins, raises his paper drinking horn in my direction, and mouths the words: 'I love you.'

I smile, and say it back, and hold Willow's hand, twining my fingers into hers as we watch the Comfort Food Café do what it does best – spread a little bit of magic dust over everyone who visits. Even Seb got a sprinkling, and is doing well back in Spain. He's stayed in touch, and is working on a plan to open a café of his own on the Spanish coast – his version of this place. I've suggested he calls it the Casa del Comfort, but he said that sounded a bit like a brothel, so I'll leave it up to him.

I really do feel, though, that there should be more Comfort Food Cafés in the universe – because the more I think about it, the more I come to the conclusion that there actually is something magical about this place.

Part of that magic comes from its location, perched like it is on the edge of the world. The glorious bay below us, spread out in sunshine like a blanket of yellow and green and blue, the clifftops stretching out into the distance.

Part of the magic comes from the food, offering comfort to all.

But mainly, that magic comes from its people. The wonderful, bonkers, kind-hearted people – always looking out for each other. Always there with an encouraging word, a daft joke, an inspiring story. Always together, no matter what.

Quite simply, it is a place where dreams can come true.

Dreams come in many shapes and sizes these days, of course. If your dream is to marry a footballer or own a Ferrari or have a yacht or appear on *Love Island*, then they probably wouldn't come true here.

But if your dream involves love, and friendship, and community, and being accepted for what and who you are, and the very best cake in the whole wide world? Then head for the Comfort Food Café – because it's all here waiting for you.

A Note from Debbie

The comment I get most about the *Comfort Food Café* books is that people wish it was real. That they could pop in for a slice of coffee cake, and get a hug from Cherie, and meet all the regulars.

I completely understand that, because I wish it was real too. To me, after writing six books set there, it practically does feel real – I can imagine every table in the café, see every street in the village, picture the beautiful bay as the seasons change, imagine scratching Midgebo's velvety ears. The women whose stories I have told – Laura, Becca, Zoe, Willow, Katie and Auburn – are like close friends.

This book is my last Café story, which means I am saying a bittersweet goodbye to all of that. I know a lot of readers will be sad, but I wanted to end on a high, while I still loved what I was writing, and while I still had fresh ideas and genuine enthusiasm.

I think we've all been in a position where we can tell, as readers, when an author has lost his or her love for a series, and is writing them for career or financial reasons.

There's nothing wrong with that – in the real world, we all have bills to pay – but it always feels like a bit of a disappointment, doesn't it? So, I decided that for me, the Budbury tales would draw to a close with Auburn.

But while this is the last book, in my mind the characters' lives go on. I was trying to imagine how their worlds would evolve, and thought I'd share a few of those ideas with you – but you might have your own. You might imagine different futures for them, and that is absolutely wonderful – in fact, come on over to my Facebook page (www.facebook.com/debbiejohnsonauthor), and let me know!

Laura was the first of my Budbury ladies, and remains very much a favourite. I see nothing but joy for her and Matt – because she deserves it. I think the two of them stay together forever, raise their beautiful baby girls, and grow old surrounded by the people (and dogs!) they love. The image of Matt and Laura, grey-haired and retired, sitting in front of a log fire holding hands is one I adore – and you have to wish them long lives and happiness and many grandchildren.

Lizzie, I suspect, will go on to wonderful things. She's had a boyfriend, Josh, since she moved to Budbury, but in the way of first loves, that probably won't work out. Lizzie's natural entrepreneurship and talent for marketing and photography will give her a great platform for life – she could quite easily end up running the whole world, and probably doing a great job of it. Nate, I think, might follow in the footsteps of Matt and become a vet.

Becca, Laura's little sister, is a more complicated lady. I think she's happy with Sam, and adores Little Edie, and knows that life in Budbury has changed her world forever – but I'm not sure if she stays. I can see that little family possibly moving back to Sam's native Ireland.

Zoe is my favourite Budbury lady. I have a weakness for very snappy, sarcastic characters with a heart of gold – and Zoe is exactly that. For her and Martha, moving to the village accidentally rescued them from an abyss of grief and self-destruction – and Cal coming into their lives made it perfect.

I don't think Zoe ever has children of her own. I think sharing Martha is enough for her, and that her difficult childhood left her forever slightly cynical about family life, despite her happy ending. I think Zoe will always have a solitary edge to her, preferring to lose herself in a good book than to do anything else. I think her and Cal watch Martha thrive at Oxford, and go on to great things. I think at some point, the two of them spend a few years together in Cal's home in Australia, and that while she's there, Zoe finally gets around to writing a book of her own – possibly some kind of gritty thriller set in the Outback!

Willow is one of the loveliest of the bunch, and she is someone who I desperately want to have a happy ending – so I'm giving her one, because I invented her and I can!

We see her married to Tom at the end of this book, and the two of them are perfect for each other. I think that once Lynnie is no longer with them – tragic but inevitable – Willow and Tom will spread their wings together.

Willow's never really travelled, or lived anywhere but Budbury, because of her duties as a daughter – but I think she will. I think her and Tom will go on a magical world adventure, from Alaskan wilderness trekking to dancing the tango in Buenos Aires. They may even take in a few Comic Cons along the way. The two of them will eventually come back to Budbury – it's where Willow's heart will always lie, and Tom's lies with Willow's – but not until they've seen all the wonders of the world. I like to think that the two of them become parents at some point, and that Willow keeps her pink hair!

Katie and Van and Saul definitely stay together as a family unit – and they definitely expand it. Katie is only young, and she's such a good mum, I can see them having another two children at least – and can also imagine those children growing up together, playing with their cousins and friends, running wild and free in the beautiful countryside. I can see Van being a doting dad, and building them treehouses, and being completely wrapped around the finger of any daughters that come his way.

As for Auburn, who I've just married off – well, I love Auburn. She's more flawed than most, but is so self-aware that you have to forgive her. She's also very funny, and has a slightly off-centre way of viewing the world. She's been through a lot, and has earned her happiness – though I'm not sure that anything with Auburn will ever be plain sailing. She's a complicated woman, and although Finn totally gets her and adores her, I can imagine them also having some rare but entirely spectacular rows.

I think she will stay in Budbury for a while, but then possibly the two of them will leave together – I can see a situation where Finn inherits his granddad's home in the Danish countryside, and they move there, at least for a while.

Although these are the main characters from each of the books, one of the things that makes Budbury so special is its rich sense of community – and the rich variety of people who live there. I also think that the sheer age ranges also make it relatable – we have tiny babies through to a woman in her nineties, and everything in between.

Edie May is, I know, a favourite of many of you – me too! I love her wisecracks, and her wisdom, and her naughty sense of humour. I love the sadness of her history, and the place she holds in the hearts of everyone in the village. I have to be honest, and confess that I have considered killing Edie off in pretty much every single book – but the more I thought about it, the more I realised that I'd only be doing it for shock value, or a plot twist. And Edie is worth much more than that.

So, we have Edie in her nineties, and Frank in his eighties, and Cherie in her seventies. It is inevitable, of course, that they won't live forever – but I'm not going to depress myself by thinking about their ends! Instead, I like to imagine the richness of the years they have left.

Edie, a retired librarian and still sharp as a tack, will spend some of her later years setting up a small Budbury museum, funded by Tom. You might remember that he found a load of photos and documents in Briarwood when he was renovating it, and Edie was helping him to catalogue them. I think that expands, and eventually the Edie May Museum of Budbury will immortalise the wonderful woman she was.

Frank will remain active in the management of his farm, but bit by bit he will delegate the hard work and the day-to-day running of it to Cal and Van. Frank's son lives on the other side of the world and is a surgeon – he has no interest in being a farmer. So, I think that eventually, when that sad day comes and Frank and Cherie are no more, that he will do something grand and community-minded with it – he'll leave it to Cal and Van, to run for the benefit of the village.

Cherie Moon was actually the first character I dreamed up for the Comfort Food Café – in fact she was probably what started the whole thing. I loved the idea of this older woman, rich in life experience, kind and wise but still a bit of a rebel rock chick at heart, sneaking off for the odd 'herbal' cigarette and listening to The Who on vinyl.

As you get older yourself, your concept of what is old, and how older people should behave, changes – and for me Cherie is the ultimate example of growing old gracefully, remaining true to herself. Her future is pretty much as her present, I think – until the day she dies she will be involved in the café, in the village, whipping up comfort food for customers, and finding ways to be benignly interfering as she goes! She expands the Café outreach programme that started in this book, and is instrumental in making so many people's lives better and less lonely – which is exactly what the Comfort Food Café is all about.

As I said, you might have your own ideas about what happens to everyone – and that's fine. This is your world as much as it is mine.

Writing a series of books like this is a team effort. I might be the one who sits around in her pyjamas, tapping away on the laptop and chain-drinking coffee, but a lot of people are involved along the way from that initial idea through to it being published. People like agents, and cover designers, and PR and marketing gurus, and booksellers.

I have to say thank you to the team at HarperImpulse and HarperCollins, who helped me take this simple idea – the Comfort Food Café – and transform it into a world that has been shared with hundreds of thousands of people. I'd especially like to thank Charlotte Ledger, my editor and friend, who fell for Budbury like a ton of bricks with the first ever book and has stayed in love with it ever since

– her enthusiasm and energy has always been a vital ingredient in the Comfort Food Café recipe book!

I also have to thank friends and family for listening to me bleat on, and to author friends who provide a listening ear and occasionally a beer or seven – in particular Milly Johnson, Catherine Isaac, Carmel Harrington and Jane Linfoot. You're all good 'uns, and I'd be lonely without you.

Mainly, though, I have to thank you – the readers. I can't tell you how fabulous it feels to see your reviews, or your emails, or your Facebook messages, and to know that the Comfort Food Café has touched your lives in such a positive way. That you, too, wish it were real.

Thanks for coming on the Budbury magical mystery tour with me – and please stay in touch! My next book is out early in 2020, and I'd love it if you came on that magical mystery tour as well. The best places to find me are at www.facebook.com/debbiejohnsonauthor or @ debbiemjohnson on Twitter. It might be goodbye to Budbury – but not to you!

Find out how it all began in the first book of the
Comfort Food Café series,
Summer at the Comfort Food Café

Chapter 1

COOK WANTED – MUST BE COMFORTING

We are looking for a summer-season cook for our busy seaside café. The job will also involve taking orders and waiting on tables. The successful applicant will be naturally friendly, be able to boil an egg, enjoy a chat and have a well-developed sense of empathy with other human beings. Good sense of humour absolutely vital. The only experience required is experience of life, along with decent cooking skills. Pay is pitiful, but the position comes with six weeks' free use of a luxury holiday cottage in a family-friendly setting near the Jurassic Coast, with use of a swimming pool, games room and playground. Children, dogs, cats, guinea pigs and stray maiden aunts all welcome. No application form needed – if you're interested, send us your heart and soul in letter form, telling us why you think you're right for the job. Post your essays to Cherie Moon, The Comfort Food Café, Willington Hill, near Budbury, Dorset.

Chapter 2

Dear Cherie,

I'm writing to you about the job you advertised for a cook at the Comfort Food Café in Dorset.

This is about my sixth attempt at composing this letter, and all the rest have ended up as soggy, crumpled balls lying on the floor around the bin – my aim seems to be as off as my writing skills. I've promised myself that this time, no matter how long it gets, or how many mistakes I might make, this will be the final version. From the heart, like you asked for, even if it takes me the rest of the day. If nothing else it's pretty good therapy.

This is probably not the most professional or brilliant way to make a first impression, and you're most likely thinking about filing this under 'N for nutter' – or possibly 'B for bin'. I can only apologise – my hand's a bit cramped now and I have a blister coming up on my ring finger. I haven't written this much since my A levels, so please forgive me if it gets a bit messy.

To be honest, everything in my life is a bit messy. It got that way just over two years ago, when my husband, David, died. He was the same age as me – I'm thirty-five now – and he was the love of my life. I can't give you a romantic story about how we met at a wedding or got set up on a blind date by friends, or how our eyes met across a crowded nightclub – mainly because our eyes actually met across a crowded playground when we were seven years old.

He'd joined our school a few years in and appeared like a space alien at the start of term one in September. He was really good at football, was impossible to catch in a game of tag and liked drawing cartoons about his dogs, Jimbo and Jambo. We sat next to each other on the Turquoise Table in Miss Hennessey's class, and that was that – my fate was sealed.

That story sounds completely crazy now, I know. I look at my own kids and think there's no way anyone they mix with at their age could turn out to be the love of their life. That's what my parents thought – and his. I lost track of the number of times we were told we were too young. I think they thought it was sweet when we were seven, saying we were boyfriend and girlfriend – innocent and cute. By the time we were sixteen and we'd stayed together all through high school, they didn't think it was quite so cute any more.

I get it, I really do. They wanted us to see a bit of the world. See other people. Although they were all too polite to say it, they wanted us to split up. My parents would always phrase it nicely, saying things like 'I've nothing against David – he's a lovely lad – but don't you want to travel? Go to university? Have a few adventures before you settle down? Follow your own dreams? And anyway, if it's meant to be, you'll come back to each other in a few years' time.'

He got the same speeches from his family, too. We used to laugh about it and compare notes on the different ways they all tried to express the same thing: You're Too Young and You're Making a Mistake. We weren't angry – we knew it was because they loved us, wanted the best for us. But what they didn't get – what they never really understood – was that we were already following our dreams. We were already having the biggest adventure of our lives. We loved each other beyond belief from the age of seven, and we never, ever stopped. What we had was rare and precious and so much more valuable than anything we could have done apart.

We got married when we were twenty, and no matter how happy I was, people still commented on it. I even found my mum crying in the loo at the reception – she thought I was wasting my life. I'd got decent enough grades in my exams – including a grade A in home economics, I should probably point out, as it's the first relevant thing I've said. So did David. He got a job as a trainee at the local bank, and I initially worked in what I'd like to claim was some fancy five-star restaurant, but was actually a McDonald's on a retail park on the outskirts of Manchester.

I know it sounds boring, but it wasn't. It was brilliant. We bought a little two-up two-down in a decent part of the city, and even at that stage we were thinking about schools – because we knew we wanted kids, and soon. Lizzie came along not too long after, and she's fourteen now. She has his blonde hair and my green eyes, and at the moment is equal parts smiley and surly. I can't blame her. It's been tough losing her dad. I've done my best to stay strong for her, but I suspect my best hasn't been up to much. She's fourteen. Do you remember being a four-teen-year-old girl? It wasn't ever easy, was it? Even without dead dads and zombified mums.

Nate is twelve and he's a heartbreaker. Quite literally, when I look at him, it feels like my heart is breaking. He got David's blonde hair too, and also his sparkly blue eyes. You know, those Paul Newman eyes? And David's smile. And that one dimple on the left-hand side of his mouth.

He looks so much like his dad that people used to call him David's 'mini me'! Sometimes I hug him so tight he complains that I'm breaking his ribs. I laugh and let him go, even though I want to carry on squeezing and keep this tiny, perfect little human being safe for the rest of his life. We all know that's not possible now and sometimes I think that's the biggest casualty of David dying – none of us feel safe any more, which really isn't fair when you're twelve, is it?

But I have to remind myself that we had so much. We loved so much, and laughed so much, and shared so much. All of it was perfect, even the arguments. Especially the arguments – or the aftermath at least. Sometimes I wonder if that was the problem – we had too much that was too good, too young. Even after thirteen years of marriage he could still give me that cheeky little grin of his that made my heart beat a bit faster, and I could never, ever stay angry with him. It was the uni-dimple. It just made it impossible.

One of David's favourite things was holidays. He worked hard at the bank, got promoted and enjoyed his job – but it was his family life that really mattered to him. We saved up and every year we'd have a brilliant holiday together. He loved researching them and planning them almost as much as going on them.

To start with, they were 'baby' holidays – the most important thing was finding somewhere we'd be safe with the little ones. So we stayed in the UK or did short flights to places like Majorca or Spain.

As the kids got older, we got more adventurous – or he did at least! We started by expanding our horizons and going on camping holidays on the continent. Tents in Tuscany, driving to the South of France with the car loaded up, a mobile home in Holland. The last two before he died were the most exciting ever – a yachting trip around Turkey, where the kids learned to sail and I learned to sunbathe, and three weeks in Florida doing the theme parks but then driving all the way down to the Keys and going native for a week.

Every holiday, for every year, was also given its own photo album when we got home.

It wasn't enough for him to keep the pictures online, he got them all printed out and each album had the year it related to and the place we'd visited written on the spine on a sticker.

They're all there now, on the bookshelf in the living room. Lined up in order – a photographic journey through time and space. Lizzie as a baby; Lizzie as a toddler and me pregnant; Nate joining the party. They grow up in those photo albums, right before our eyes – missing teeth and changing tastes and different haircuts, getting taller each year.

I suppose we age as well – I definitely put a bit of weight on as the years go by; David loses a bit of hair, gets more laughter lines. We never lose our smiles, though

– that's one thing that never changes.

The only year we didn't have a holiday was when the kids were too old to share a room any more, and we had to buy a bigger house. We were skint, so we stayed at home – and even then, David set up a massive tent in our new garden and bought a load of sand from a builder's yard to make our very own beach! Even that one has its own album, although on quite a few of the photos we're wearing our swimming costumes in the rain!

If I'm entirely honest, the main reason I'm applying for this job – and doing a very bad job of it, I know – is because of all those holidays, and the memories that David managed to build for our children. For me. The memories that are all we have left of him now.

The last holiday David planned was over two years ago. We were going to Australia, flying in to Sydney and touring up to Queensland. The kids were buzzing about seeing koalas and kangaroos, and I was slightly concerned about them getting eaten by sharks or bitten by a killer spider. David was in his element.

He never got to go on that holiday. It was the first properly sunny day after winter – February 12th, to be exact – and he decided to do some house maintenance, the way you do once the sun comes out again.

While he was clearing some leaves out of the guttering, he slipped off the ladder and banged his head on the concrete patio. He seemed all right at first – we laughed about it, joked about his hard head. We thought we'd been lucky.

We were wrong. We didn't know it at the time, but he had bleeding around his brain – his brain was swelling and bit by bit a disaster was going on inside his skull.

By the time he started to complain of a headache, he'd probably been feeling bad for hours. Taking Paracetamol for his 'bump' and trying to get on with his weekend. Eventually he collapsed in front of all three of us – fell right off his chair at the dinner table. At first the kids just laughed – he was a bit of a buffoon, David. He was always doing daft things to amuse them – it was like living with Norman Wisdom sometimes, the amount of slapstick that went on in our house!

But he wasn't joking. And even though the ambulance got there so fast and the hospital was so good, it was too late. He was gone. He was put on a life-support machine and his parents and my parents came and his brother came, all to say goodbye. The kids? That was a hard decision. Nate was just ten and Lizzie was only twelve – but I thought they deserved it, the chance to say their farewells. I still don't know if it was the right decision or not – it was impossible to weigh up whether the trauma of seeing him like that, hooked up to machines, would be worse than knowing they never got to see him off to heaven. Was it the right thing to do? I suppose I'll have to wait and see how messed up they are over the next few years before I get my answer.

I can't go into any detail about how I felt, Cherie, having to make those kinds of decisions. I just can't. I'll never, ever get this letter written if I do that – it's too big and too raw, and even now, after all this time, I still have moments where the pain paralyses me – where I struggle to even get out of bed and put one foot in front of the other. They are only moments, though, and they are becoming further and further apart – I suppose that means my own brain injury is healing, which makes me feel strangely guilty.

I hate the fact that he died doing such a mundane thing. Cleaning the gutters. He was funny and kind and quietly brave – he was the type of man who would have thrown himself under a bus to save a child, or would have jumped into a raging sea to rescue a Labrador. Losing him because of leaves in the gutters seems so… pointless. He was an organ donor, though, which is some small comfort – the thought of all the lives he saved or changed for the better through that does help. I take consolation from someone walking around with that big, beautiful heart of his beating inside them.

So… by now, you're either hooked and wondering how this story ends, or you're considering calling the police to get a restraining order in case this crazy woman turns up at your café and tries to comfort random people.

The answer is, of course, that the story hasn't ended – the story is still playing out, albeit at a very slow pace. We had a holiday the year after he died, and it was a disaster – a trip to Crete to stay in a hotel that turned out to be full of eighteen to thirty-year-olds, all on a mission to give themselves liver failure and complete their set of STD top trumps. It was loud, it was foul, and we all hated it – mainly, of course, because he wasn't there. It was awful.

Now, I'm looking ahead and I see that there needs to be a change. David left us with enough life insurance to pay off the mortgage and the car loans, and to live on for a little while. We have no debt at all, which I know puts us at a big advantage over lots of families who are struggling to make ends meet.

But there's nothing coming in – no income. Which means no holiday – not because of my lack of planning skills, but because we can't afford it. Not if we want to eat as well. Don't get me wrong, our heads are above water, but there isn't much spare after paying the bills and doing the shopping and coping with what feels like the mountain of expense a teenage girl piles up!

If we ration we'll be fine for another year. Rationing means no holiday – and I just can't face it. I think we need a holiday – one that we actually enjoy, this time. We've all started to feel just a little bit better now. Almost against our will, there is more laughter, more easy chat, more smiling.

The kids' lives have moved on, certainly a lot more than mine! They're both in high school now, both starting to grow into young adults, both changing. I'd like to add another photo album to that shelf before they're too cool to be bothered with their poor old mum.

I also know that I need to get my act together. I need to get a job – and not just for the money. I need to get out there, back into the world. Because the kids *are* that little bit older and more independent now. They don't need me as much. They're out a lot – or Lizzie is at least, and Nate is showing signs of following suit. That's only right – it's good. It's what I want for them, to have normal lives. But me sitting at home in a rocking chair, counting cobwebs and watching *The Good Wife* on repeat isn't going to do any of us any good.

Getting a job will help me to meet new people. Get away from my own problems. Make my world bigger. I have my sister, my parents and his family too – but sometimes, if I'm honest, that feels like more of a responsibility than a help. They're all so worried about me all the time, I feel like I'm under a microscope. I think they're waiting for me to crack.

I think they're scared that long term, I can't live without him. Maybe they're right, I don't know – but I have to try. I don't want to forget David – that would be impossible even if I did – but I do need to start living my life After David. AD, if you like.

I started looking at jobs a few months ago and came to the depressing conclusion that I'm officially useless. I have the aforementioned Home Economics A level, which is the pinnacle of my academic achievement (I also have a C in Health and Social Care and a B in General Studies, which are really of no use to anybody). I worked at McDonald's for a year before I had the kids and I got a food hygiene certificate when I did volunteer work at the school kitchen. Not hugely impressive, I know – it's not like Marco Pierre White is hammering on the door with a job offer.

But I do cook – I cook a lot. Family dinners, occasional forays into something more exotic like Thai or Japanese. I do a mean roast and can make my own meatballs. I can bake and I can whip up marinades, and I can do a full English fry-up with my eyes closed.

I wouldn't get very far on *Masterchef*, but I can cook – proper home-made stuff – the kind of food that isn't just good for your body but good for your soul as well. At least I like to think so. I'm amazed, in fact, that the kids aren't the size of that giant marshmallow man in *Ghostbusters* by now – one of the ways I've tried to console them (and if I'm honest, myself as well) over the last few years is through feeding them. It keeps me busy, it makes me feel like I'm doing something positive, and it's a way to show I love them now they're too old for public displays of affection.

They just scarf it down, of course, they're kids – but perhaps, at somewhere like the Comfort Food Café, I could actually be of some use. It would be really, really nice to feel useful again – and to spend the summer in Dorset, and fill up another one of those albums.

So. There we go. I think that's everything. Probably more than everything. I'm not sure this is what you meant when you said send your heart and soul in letter form, but that serves you right for being so vague! I bet you got some really strange replies – this one being possibly the strangest of all.

I won't hold it against you, Cherie, if I never hear from you. But if you want to talk to me, or find out anything more, then let me know. Whatever happens, good luck to you.

All the best,
Laura Walker

WEEK 1

In which I travel to Dorset, sing a lot of Meatloaf songs, accidentally inhale what might possibly be marijuana, wrap my bra around a strange man's head and become completely betwattled...

Discover
Debbie Johnson's
bestselling romantic comedies

'A sheer delight'
— *Sunday Express*

Stay in touch with
Debbie
JOHNSON

Chat with Debbie and get to know the other fans
of the Comfort Food Café series:

f /Debbie Johnson Author

🐦 /@debbiemjohnson

You can also pop over to Debbie's website and sign up to
her newsletter for all the latest gossip from the café,
book news and exclusive competitions.

www.debbiejohnsonauthor.com